WORLD FAMOUS GREAT SPEECHES

REFERENCE BOOK FOR AUTHORS, WRITERS, PROFESSORS, SPEAKERS, JOURNALISTS AND STUDENTS

Dr. Gagan Jain, *D.Litt.*

MG BOOKS
NEW DELHI (INDIA)

WORLD FAMOUS
GREAT
SPEECHES

REFERENCE BOOK FOR AUTHORS, WRITERS, PROFESSORS, SPEAKERS, JOURNALISTS AND STUDENTS

Published by

MG BOOKS

An Imprint of

MAANU GRAPHICS

MAANU GRAPHICS

(PUBLISHERS OF GENERAL BOOKS)

5FF, Ganpati Bhawan, 21 Ansari Road,
Darya Ganj, New Delhi-110002
Ph: 65285220, 64138266
E-mail : maanugraphics@yahoo.com
mgbooks.maanu@yahoo.com

Printed at : Satyam Enterprises, Delhi

CONTENTS

ABRAHAM LINCOLN

INTRODUCTION

U.S. Republican statesman and 16th President (1861-65); in 1846 he was elected to a single term in Congress when he spoke against the extension of slavery and in 1860 was elected President. When the Civil war began in 1861, he defined the issues in terms of national integrity, not anti-slavery. He in fact declared freedom for all slaves on areas of rebellion. He was re-elected President in 1864. Lincoln's victory in that election thus changed the racial future of the United States. It also agitated Southern-sympathizer and Negrophobe John Wilkes Booth, who began to conspire first to abduct Lincoln and later to kill him. On Apr. 14, 1865, five days after Robert E. Lee's surrender to Grant at Appomattox Court House, Lincoln attended a performance of Our American Cousin at Ford's Theatre in Washington. One Mr. Booth entered the presidential box and shot Lincoln. The next morning at 7:22 Lincoln died.

FIRST INAUGURAL ADDRESS
MONDAY, MARCH 4, 1861
WASHINGTON, D.C.

Fellow-Citizens of the United States:

IN compliance with a custom as old as the Government

itself, I appear before you to address you briefly and to take in your presence the oath prescribed by the Constitution of the United States to be taken by the President "before he enters on the execution of this office."

I do not consider it necessary at present for me to discuss those matters of administration about which there is no special anxiety or excitement.

Apprehension seems to exist among the people of the Southern States that by the accession of a Republican Administration their property and their peace and personal security are to be endangered. There has never been any reasonable cause for such apprehension. Indeed, the most ample evidence to the contrary has all the while existed and been open to their inspection. It is found in nearly all the published speeches of him who now addresses you. I do but quote from one of those speeches when I declare that—

I have no purpose, directly or indirectly, to interfere with the institution of slavery in the States where it exists. I believe I have no lawful right to do so, and I have no inclination to do so.

Those who nominated and elected me did so with full knowledge that I had made this and many similar declarations and had never recanted them; and more than this, they placed in the platform for my acceptance, and as a law to themselves and to me, the clear and emphatic resolution which I now read:

Resolved, That the maintenance inviolate of the rights of the States, and especially the right of each State to order and control its own domestic institutions according to its own judgment exclusively, is essential to that balance of power on which the perfection and endurance of our political fabric depend; and we denounce the lawless invasion by armed force of the soil of any State or Territory, no matter what pretext, as among the gravest of crimes.

I now reiterate these sentiments, and in doing so I only press upon the public attention the most conclusive evidence of which the case is susceptible that the property, peace, and security of no section are to be in any wise endangered by the now incoming Administration. I add, too, that all the protection which, consistently with the Constitution and the laws, can be given will be cheerfully given to all the States when lawfully demanded, for whatever cause — as cheerfully to one section as to another.

There is much controversy about the delivering up of fugitives from service or labor. The clause I now read is as plainly written in the Constitution as any other of its provisions:

No person held to service or labor in one State, under the laws thereof, escaping into another, shall in consequence of any law or regulation therein be discharged from such service or labor, but shall be delivered up on claim of the party to whom such service or labor may be due.

It is scarcely questioned that this provision was intended by those who made it for the reclaiming of what we call fugitive slaves; and the intention of the lawgiver is the law. All members of Congress swear their support to the whole Constitution — to this provision as much as to any other. To the proposition, then, that slaves whose cases come within the terms of this clause "shall be delivered up" their oaths are unanimous. Now, if they would make the effort in good temper, could they not with nearly equal unanimity frame and pass a law by means of which to keep good that unanimous oath? 7 There is some difference of opinion whether this clause should be enforced by national or by State authority, but surely that difference is not a very material one. If the slave is to be surrendered, it can be of but little consequence to him or to others by which authority it is done. And should anyone in any case be content that his oath shall go unkept on a merely unsubstantial controversy as to how it shall be kept?

Again: In any law upon this subject ought not all the safeguards of liberty known in civilized and humane jurisprudence to be introduced, so that a free man be not in any case surrendered as a slave? And might it not be well at the same time to provide by law for the enforcement of that clause in the Constitution which guarantees that "the citizens of each State shall be entitled to all privileges and immunities of citizens in the several States"?

I take the official oath to-day with no mental reservations and with no purpose to construe the Constitution or laws by any hypercritical rules; and while I do not choose now to specify particular acts of Congress as proper to be enforced, I do suggest that it will be much safer for all, both in official and private stations, to conform to and abide by all those acts which stand unrepealed than to violate any of them trusting to find impunity in having them held to be unconstitutional.

It is seventy-two years since the first inauguration of a President under our National Constitution. During that period fifteen different and greatly distinguished citizens have in succession administered the executive branch of the Government. They have conducted it through many perils, and generally with great success. Yet, with all this scope of precedent, I now enter upon the same task for the brief constitutional term of four years under great and peculiar difficulty. A disruption of the Federal Union, heretofore only menaced, is now formidably attempted.

I hold that in contemplation of universal law and of the Constitution the Union of these States is perpetual. Perpetuity is implied, if not expressed, in the fundamental law of all national governments. It is safe to assert that no government proper ever had a provision in its organic law for its own termination. Continue to execute all the express provisions of our National Constitution, and the Union will endure forever, it being impossible to destroy it except by some action not provided for in the instrument itself.

Again: If the United States be not a government proper, but an association of States in the nature of contract merely, can it, as a contract, be peaceably unmade by less than all the parties who made it? One party to a contract may violate it — break it, so to speak — but does it not require all to lawfully rescind it?

Descending from these general principles, we find the proposition that in legal contemplation the Union is perpetual confirmed by the history of the Union itself. The Union is much older than the Constitution. It was formed, in fact, by the Articles of Association in 1774. It was matured and continued by the Declaration of Independence in 1776. It was further matured, and the faith of all the then thirteen States expressly plighted and engaged that it should be perpetual, by the Articles of Confederation in 1778. And finally, in 1787, one of the declared objects for ordaining and establishing the Constitution was "to form a more perfect Union."

But if destruction of the Union by one or by a part only of the States be lawfully possible, the Union is less perfect than before the Constitution, having lost the vital element of perpetuity.

It follows from these views that no State upon its own mere motion can lawfully get out of the Union; that resolves and ordinances to that effect are legally void, and that acts of violence within any State or States against the authority of the United States are insurrectionary or revolutionary, according to circumstances.

I therefore consider that in view of the Constitution and the laws the Union is unbroken, and to the extent of my ability, I shall take care, as the Constitution itself expressly enjoins upon me, that the laws of the Union be faithfully executed in all the States. Doing this I deem to be only a simple duty on my part, and I shall perform it so far as practicable unless my rightful masters, the American people, shall withhold the requisite means or in some authoritative manner direct the contrary. I trust this will not be regarded as a menace, but only as the declared purpose of the Union that it will constitutionally defend and maintain itself.

In doing this there needs to be no bloodshed or violence, and there shall be none unless it be forced upon the national authority. The power confided to me will be used to hold, occupy, and possess the property and places belonging to the Government and to collect the duties and imposts; but beyond what may be necessary for these objects, there will be no invasion, no using of force against or among the people anywhere. Where hostility to the United States in any interior locality shall be so great and universal as to prevent competent resident citizens from holding the Federal offices, there will be no attempt to force obnoxious strangers among the people for that object. While the strict legal right may exist in the Government to enforce the exercise of these offices, the attempt to do so would be so irritating and so nearly impracticable withal that I deem it better to forego for the time the uses of such offices.

The mails, unless repelled, will continue to be furnished in all parts of the Union. So far as possible the people everywhere shall have that sense of perfect security which is most favorable to calm thought and reflection. The course here indicated will be followed unless current events and experience shall show a modification or change to be proper, and in every case and exigency my best discretion will be exercised, according to circumstances actually existing and with a view and a hope of a peaceful solution of the national troubles and the restoration of fraternal sympathies and affections.

That there are persons in one section or another who seek to destroy the Union at all events and are glad of any pretext to do it I will neither affirm nor deny; but if there be such, I need address no word to them. To those, however, who really love the Union may I not speak?

Before entering upon so grave a matter as the destruction of our national fabric, with all its benefits, its memories, and its hopes, would it not be wise to ascertain precisely why we do it? Will you hazard so desperate a step while there is any possibility that any portion of the ills you fly from have no real existence? Will you, while the certain ills you fly to are greater than all the real ones you fly from, will you risk the commission of so fearful a mistake?

All profess to be content in the Union if all constitutional rights can be maintained. Is it true, then, that any right plainly written in the Constitution has been denied? I think not. Happily, the human mind is so constituted that no party can reach to the audacity of doing this. Think, if you can, of a single instance in which a plainly written provision of the Constitution has ever been denied. If by the mere force of numbers a majority should deprive a minority of any clearly written constitutional right, it might in a moral point of view justify revolution; certainly would if such right were a vital one. But such is not our case. All the vital rights of minorities and of individuals are so plainly assured to them by affirmations and negations, guaranties and prohibitions, in the Constitution that controversies never arise concerning them. But no organic law can ever be framed with a provision specifically applicable to every question which may occur in practical administration. No foresight can anticipate nor any document of reasonable length contain express provisions for all possible questions. Shall fugitives from labor be surrendered by national or by State authority? The Constitution does not expressly say. May Congress prohibit slavery in the Territories? The Constitution does not expressly say. Must Congress protect slavery in the Territories? The Constitution does not expressly say.

From questions of this class spring all our constitutional controversies, and we divide upon them into majorities and minorities. If the minority will not acquiesce, the majority must, or the Government must cease. There is no other alternative, for continuing the Government is acquiescence on one side or the other. If a minority in such case will secede rather than acquiesce, they make a precedent which in turn will divide and ruin them, for a minority of their own will secede from them whenever a majority refuses to be controlled by such minority. For instance, why may not any portion of a new confederacy a year or two hence arbitrarily secede again, precisely as portions of the present Union now claim to secede from it? All who cherish disunion sentiments are now being educated to the exact temper of doing this.

Is there such perfect identity of interests among the States to compose a new union as to produce harmony only and prevent renewed secession?

Plainly the central idea of secession is the essence of anarchy. A majority held in restraint by constitutional checks and limitations, and always changing easily with deliberate changes of popular opinions and sentiments, is the only true sovereign of a free people. Whoever rejects it does of necessity fly to anarchy or to despotism. Unanimity is impossible. The rule of a minority, as a permanent arrangement, is wholly inadmissible; so that, rejecting the majority principle, anarchy or despotism in some form is all that is left.

I do not forget the position assumed by some that constitutional questions are to be decided by the Supreme Court, nor do I deny that such decisions must be binding in any case upon the parties to a suit as to the object of that suit, while they are also entitled to very high respect and consideration in all parallel cases by all other departments of the Government. And while it is obviously possible that such decision may be erroneous in any given case, still the evil effect following it, being limited to that particular case, with the chance that it may be overruled and never become a precedent for other cases, can better be borne than could the evils of a different practice. At the same time, the candid citizen must confess that if the policy of the Government upon vital questions affecting the whole people is to be irrevocably fixed by decisions of the Supreme Court, the instant they are made in ordinary litigation between parties in personal actions the people will have ceased to be their own rulers, having to that extent practically resigned their Government into the hands of that eminent tribunal. Nor is there in this view any assault upon the court or the judges. It is a duty from which they may not shrink to decide cases properly brought before them, and it is no fault of theirs if others seek to turn their decisions to political purposes.

One section of our country believes slavery is right and ought to be extended, while the other believes it is wrong and ought not to be extended. This is the only substantial dispute. The fugitive-slave clause of the Constitution and the law for the suppression of the foreign slave trade are each as well enforced, perhaps, as any law can ever be in a community where the moral sense of the people imperfectly supports the law itself. The great body of the people abide by the dry legal obligation in both cases, and a few break over in each. This, I think, can not be perfectly cured, and it would be worse in both cases after the separation of the sections than before. The foreign slave trade, now imperfectly suppressed, would be ultimately revived without restriction in one section, while fugitive slaves, now only partially surrendered, would not be surrendered at all by the other.

Physically speaking, we can not separate. We can not remove our respective sections from each other nor build an impassable wall between them. A husband and wife may be divorced and go out of the presence and beyond the reach of each other, but the different parts of our country can not do this. They can not but remain face to face, and intercourse, either amicable or hostile, must continue between them. Is it possible, then, to make that intercourse more advantageous or more satisfactory after separation than before? Can aliens make treaties easier than friends can make laws? Can treaties be more faithfully enforced between aliens than laws can among friends? Suppose you go to war, you can not fight always; and when, after much loss on both sides and no gain on either, you cease fighting, the identical old questions, as to terms of intercourse, are again upon you.

This country, with its institutions, belongs to the people who inhabit it. Whenever they shall grow weary of the existing Government, they can exercise their constitutional right of amending it or their revolutionary right to dismember or overthrow it. I can not be ignorant of the fact that many worthy and patriotic citizens are desirous of having the National Constitution amended. While I make no recommendation of amendments, I fully recognize the rightful authority of the people over the whole subject, to be exercised in either of the modes prescribed in the instrument itself; and I should, under existing circumstances, favor rather than oppose a fair opportunity being afforded the people to act upon it. I will venture to add that to me the convention mode seems preferable, in that it allows amendments to originate with the people themselves, instead of only permitting them to take or reject propositions originated by others, not especially chosen for the purpose, and which might not be precisely such as they would wish to either accept or refuse. I understand a proposed amendment to the Constitution — which amendment, however, I have not seen — has passed Congress, to the effect that the Federal Government shall never interfere with the domestic institutions of the States, including that of persons held to service. To avoid misconstruction of what I have said, I depart from my purpose not to speak of particular amendments so far as to say that, holding such a provision to now be implied constitutional law, I have no objection to its being made express and irrevocable.

The Chief Magistrate derives all his authority from the people, and they have referred none upon him to fix terms for the separation of the States. The people themselves can do this if also they choose, but the Executive as such has nothing to do with it. His duty is to administer the present Government as it came to his hands and to transmit it unimpaired by him to his successor.

Why should there not be a patient confidence in the ultimate justice of the people? Is there any better or equal hope in the world? In our present differences, is either party without faith of being in the right? If the Almighty Ruler of Nations, with His eternal truth and justice, be on your side of the North, or on yours of the South, that truth and that justice will surely prevail by the judgment of this great tribunal of the American people.

By the frame of the Government under which we live this same people have wisely given their public servants but little power for mischief, and have with equal wisdom provided for the return of that little to their own hands at very short intervals. While the people retain their virtue and vigilance no Administration by any extreme of wickedness or folly can very seriously injure the Government in the short space of four years.

My countrymen, one and all, think calmly and well upon this whole subject. Nothing valuable can be lost by taking time. If there be an object to hurry any of you in hot haste to a step which you would never take deliberately, that object will be frustrated by taking time; but no good object can be frustrated by it. Such of you as are now dissatisfied still have the old Constitution unimpaired, and, on the sensitive point, the laws of your own framing under it; while the new Administration will have no immediate power, if it would, to change either. If it were admitted that you who are dissatisfied hold the right side in the dispute, there still is no single good reason for precipitate action. Intelligence, patriotism, Christianity, and a firm reliance on Him who has never yet forsaken this favored land are still competent to adjust in the best way all our present difficulty.

In your hands, my dissatisfied fellow-countrymen, and not in mine, is the momentous issue of civil war. The Government will not assail you. You can have no conflict without being yourselves the aggressors. You have no oath registered in heaven to destroy the Government, while I shall have the most solemn one to "preserve, protect, and defend it."

I am loath to close. We are not enemies, but friends. We must not be enemies. Though passion may have strained it must not break our bonds of affection. The mystic chords of memory, stretching from every battlefield and patriot grave to every living heart and hearthstone all over this broad land, will yet swell the chorus of the Union, when again touched, as surely they will be, by the better angels of our nature.

THE GETTYSBURG ADDRESS
NOVEMBER 19, 1863

FOUR score and seven years ago our fathers brought forth on this continent, a new nation, conceived in liberty, and dedicated to the proposition that all men are created equal.

Now we are engaged in a great civil war, testing whether that nation, or any nation so conceived and so dedicated, can long endure. We are met on a great battlefield of that war. We have come to dedicate a portion of that field, as a final resting place for those who here gave their lives that that nation might live. It is altogether fitting and proper that we should do this.

But in a larger sense, we cannot dedicate - we cannot consecrate - we cannot hallow - this ground. The brave men, living and dead, who struggled here, have consecrated it, far above our poor power to add or detract. The world will little note, nor long remember, what we say here, but it can never forget what they did here. It is for us the living, rather, to be dedicated here to the unfinished work which they who fought here have thus far so nobly advanced. It is rather for us to be here dedicated to the great task remaining before us - that from these honored dead we take increased devotion to that cause for which they gave the last full measure of devotion - that we here highly resolve that these dead shall not have died in vain - that this nation, under God, shall have a new birth of freedom - and that government of the people, by the people, for the people, shall not perish from the earth.

SECOND INAUGURAL ADDRESS
SATURDAY, MARCH 4, 1865

Fellow-Countrymen:

AT this second appearing to take the oath of the Presidential office there is less occasion for an extended address than there was at the first. Then a statement somewhat in detail of a course to be pursued seemed fitting and proper. Now, at the expiration of four years, during which public declarations have been constantly called forth on every point and phase of the great contest which still absorbs the attention and engrosses the energies of the nation, little that is new could be presented. The progress of our arms, upon which all else chiefly depends, is as well known to the public as to myself, and it is, I trust, reasonably satisfactory and encouraging to all. With high hope for the future, no prediction in regard to it is ventured. *1* On the occasion corresponding to this four years ago all thoughts were anxiously directed to an impending civil war. All dreaded it; all sought to avert it. While the inaugural address was being delivered from this place, devoted altogether to *saving* the Union without war, urgent agents were in the city seeking to *destroy* it without war—seeking to dissolve the Union and divide effects by negotiation. Both parties deprecated war, but one of them would *make* war rather than let the nation survive, and the other would *accept* war rather than let it perish, and the war came. *2* One-eighth of the whole population were colored slaves, not distributed generally over the Union, but localized in the southern part of it. These slaves constituted a peculiar and powerful interest. All knew that this interest was somehow the cause of the war. To strengthen, perpetuate, and extend this interest was the object for which the insurgents would rend the Union even by war, while the Government claimed no right to do more than to restrict the territorial enlargement of it. Neither party expected for the war the magnitude or the duration which it has already attained. Neither anticipated that the *cause* of the conflict might cease with or even before the conflict itself should cease. Each looked for an easier triumph, and a result less fundamental and astounding. Both read the same Bible and pray to the same God, and each invokes His aid against the other. It may seem strange that any men should dare to ask a just God's assistance in wringing their bread from the sweat of other men's faces, but let us judge not, that we be not judged. The prayers of both could not be answered. That of neither has been answered fully. The Almighty has His own purposes. "Woe unto the world because of offenses; for it must needs be that offenses come, but woe to that man by whom the offense cometh." If we shall suppose that American slavery is one of those offenses which, in the providence of God, must needs come, but which, having continued through His appointed time, He now wills to remove, and that He gives to both North and South this terrible war as the woe due to those by whom the offense came, shall we discern therein any departure from those divine attributes which the believers in a living God always ascribe to Him?

Fondly do we hope, fervently do we pray, that this mighty scourge of war may speedily pass away. Yet, if God wills that it continue until all the wealth piled by the bondsman's two hundred and fifty years of unrequited toil shall be sunk, and until every drop of blood drawn with the lash shall be paid by another drawn with the sword, as was said three thousand years ago, so still it must be said "the judgments of the Lord are true and righteous altogether." *3* With malice toward none, with charity for all, with firmness in the right as God gives us to see the right, let us strive on to finish the work we are in, to bind up the nation's wounds, to care for him who shall have borne the battle and for his widow and his orphan, to do all which may achieve and cherish a just and lasting peace among ourselves and with all nations.

ADOLF HITLER

INTRODUCTION

ON April 20th, 1889 a child was born in the small town of Branau, Austria. The name of the child was Adolf Hitler. He was the son a Customs official Alois Hitler, and his third wife Klara.

Responsible for launching World War II under the leadership of National Socialist (Nazi) Party. Reich Chancellor In 1933 and Fuhrer in 1934, he climbed to power by ruthless execution of opponents. He was an arch enemy of England, USA, France and later on Russia. His defeat In World War 11 made him commit suicide. We give below excerpts from his speech delivered by him at Wilhelmshaven on 1st April 1939. It shows the working of his destructive mind and desire for revenge against political enemies.

ADOLPH HITLER'S SPEECH TO GERMANS IN 1935

German Fellow Citizens:

HE who wants to have the deepest impression of the decay and resurrection of Germany most vividly must go and see the development of a city like Wilhelmshaven, which today reverberates with life and activity and which still a short time ago was a dead spot nearly without means of existence and without prospects of a future—it pays to re-visualize this past.

When this city experienced its first upward move it coincided with the rise of the German Reich after its unification. Thus Germany was in a state of peace.

During the same time as the so-called peace-loving and Puritan nations led a great number of wars, Germany then had only one aim: to maintain peace, to work in peace, to rise the prosperity of its inhabitants and thereby to contribute to human culture and civilization.

Even though Germany through the decades was the safest guarantor of peace, and even though she occupied herself with peaceful means, she was unable to prevent other nations from following this rise with envy and hatred and finally to answer with a war.

We know from numerous findings and publications that in England the conception is that it would be necessary to bring down Germany militarily because its destruction would insure every British citizen a greater abundance of life's possessions.

Certainly at that time Germany made mistakes. Its most serious mistake was to see this encirclement and not to stave it off in time.

The only fault we can blame the regime of that time for is that the Reich had full knowledge of this devilish plan of a raid and yet it did not have the power of decision to ward it off in time and could only let this encirclement ripen until the beginning of the catastrophe.

The result was the World War. In this war the German people, although they had by no means the best armaments, fought heroically. No people can claim the glory for itself to have forced us down—much less that nation whose statesmen today speak the greatest words.

Germany at that time remained undefeated and unconquered on land, at sea and in the air—however, it was a weak Germany.

But there was the power of the lie of some nations and the poison of propaganda which did not balk at misinterpretation and untruth. Thus Germany faced the world in absolute defenselessness because it was unprepared.

When Wilson's Fourteen Points were published, not only many German fellow-citizens but above all the "leading" men saw in these Fourteen Points not only the possibilities of ending the World War but also the pacification of the world at large. A peace or reconciliation and understanding was promised—a peace that was to know neither victor nor vanquished, a peace of equal justice for all, a peace of equal distribution of colonial domains and equal recognition of colonial desires, a peace that was to be finally crowned by a league of all free nations. It was to be a guarantor of equal rights that would make it seem superfluous in the future for peoples to bear the armaments that previously, so it was said, were so heavily burdensome.

Therefore, disarmament—disarmament of all the nations.

Germany was to go ahead as a good example. Everybody was obliged to follow this disarmament. Also the age of secret diplomacy was to be ended. All problems henceforth were to be discussed openly and freely.

First of all, however, the right of self-determination of nations was to have been finally settled and raised to its proper importance.

Germany believed in these assurances. With faith in these declarations it had dropped its weapons. And then a breach of a pledge began such as world history had never seen before. When our nation had dropped its weapons, a period of supersession, blackmailing, plundering and slavery began. Not another word about peace without victor or vanquished, but an endless sentence of condemnation for the-vanquished. Not another word about justice on your side and injustice and illegality on the other. Robbery upon robbery, oppression upon oppression were the consequences. No one in this democratic world bothered himself any more about the sufferings of our people. Hundreds of thousands fell in the war, not from enemy weapons, but from the hunger blockades. And after the war ended, this blockade was continued for months in order to oppress our people still more. Many Germans made prisoners after an endless time, had to remain in captivity. The German colonies were stolen from us, Germans' foreign holdings were simply seized and our merchant marine was taken away.

Added to that was a financial plundering such as the world had never before seen. The monetary penalties which were imposed on the German people reached astronomical figures.

On these an English statesman said that they could only be fulfilled when the German standard of living was reduced to the lowest possible level and Germans worked fourteen hours daily.

What German spirit, German alertness, and German labour through decades and decades had accumulated and saved was lost in a few years. Millions of Germans were either torn away from the Reich or were prevented from returning to the Reich. The League of Nations was not an instrument of a just policy of understanding among nations, but it is and was a guarantee of the meanest dictation men ever invented.

So was a great people raped and led toward a misery that you all know. A great people through a broken pledge was cheated of its rights and its existence rendered practically impossible. A French statesman coined the following expression: "There are 20,000,000 Germans too many in the world."

Germans ended their lives out of despair, others slid into lethargy and an inevitable destiny and still others were of the opinion that everything must be destroyed; still others set their teeth and clinched their fists in unconscious rage. Still others believed that the past should be restored—restored just as it was.

Every one had an idea of some sort. And I, as an unknown soldier of the World War, drew my conclusions. It was a very short and simple programme. It ran—Removal of the internal enemies of the nation, termination of the divisions within Germany, the gathering up of the entire national strength of our people into a new community, and the breaking of the peace treaty—in one way or the other.

For as long as this dictate of Versailles weighed upon the German people it was actually damned to go to the ground. If, however, other statesmen now declare that right must rule on this earth, then they should be told that their crime is no right, that their dictate is neither right nor law but above this dictate stand the eternal rights of peoples to live. The German people were not created by rovidence in order to follow obediently a law which suits the English or the French, but rather in order to champion their right to live. That is why we are here! I was determined to take up this battle of advocating the German right to live. I took it up first within the nation.

In place of a great number of parties, social ranks, and societies, a single community now has taken its place the German national community! To bring it to realization and to deepen it more and more is our task. I had to hurt many in this time. However, I believe that the good fortune in which the entire nation is participating today must richly compensate every single one for what he had to give up dearly on his own part.

You all have sacrificed your parties, societies, and associations, but you have obtained in return a great strong Reich. And the Reich today, thank God, is strong enough to take your rights under its protection. We are no longer dependent on the good graces or disgraces of other states or their statesmen.

When, more than six years ago, I obtained power, I took over a wretched inheritance. The Reich seemed to possess no more possibilities of existence for its citizens. I undertook the work at that time with the one single capital which I possessed. It was the capital of your strength to work. Your strength to work, my fellow citizens, I now have begun to put to use. I had no foreign exchange. I had no gold reserve. I had only one thing—my faith and your work! Thus we began the gigantic work of rebuilding based upon the confidence of the nation, instilled *with* the belief and the confidence in its eternal values.

Now we have found a new economic system, a system which is this: Capital is the power of labour and coverage of money lies in our production.

We have founded a system based on the most sincere foundation there is, namely: Form your life yourself! Work for your existence! Help yourself and God will help you!

Within a few years we have wrenched Germany from despair. But the work did not help us. If today an English statesman says one can and must solve all problems through frank deliberations, I should like to tell this statesman just this: an opportunity was open for fifteen years before our time.

And one must say: "They did not apply virtuous methods!"

For three hundred years England acted without virtue in order now in maturity to speak of virtue. Thus it would appear that during this British period without virtue 46,000,000 Englishmen have subdued nearly one-quarter of the world while 80,000,000 Germans, because of their virtue, must live in a rate of 140 to one square kilometer.

For fifteen years Germany patiently bore its lot and fate. I also sought in the beginning to solve every problem through talks. I made an offer in the case of each problem and each time it was turned down!

When, today, a British statesman demands that every problem which lies in the midst of Germany's life-interest should first be discussed with England, then I too, could demand just as well that every British problem first is to be discussed with us.

Just as we Germans have little to do in Palestine, just as little business has England mixing in our German sector of existence. And if they now declare that it involves general questions of law and justice I could approve of this opinion only if it was considered as binding to both of us.

Anyway, we have not slaughtered thousands in Central Europe, but instead we have regulated our problems with law and order.

When the Allies, without regard of purpose, right, tradition, or even reasonableness, changed the map of Europe, we had not the power to prevent it. If, however, they expect the Germany of today to sit patiently until the very last day when this same result would again be repeated—while they create satellite states and set them against Germany—then they are mistaking the Germany of today for the Germany of before the war. He who declares himself ready to pull the chestnuts the war. He who declares himself ready to pull the chestnuts out of the fire for these powers must realize he bums his fingers.

Really, we feel not hatred against the Czech people. We have lived together for years. The English statesmen do not know this. They have no idea that Hradschin castle was not built by an Englishman but by a German and that the St. Vitus Cathedral likewise was not erected by Englishmen but German hands did it. Even the French were not active there. They do not know already at a time when England still was very small, a German Kaiser was paid homage on this hill (Hardcany castle)—that one thousand years before me the first German King stood there and accepted the homage of this people.

Despite this, however, we would have had nothing against an Independent Czech State if, first, it had not suppressed Germans, and, second, if it had not been intended as the instrument of future attack on Germany. When, however, a former French Air Minister writes in a newspaper that on the basis of their prominent position it is the task of these Czechs to strike at the heart of German industry with air attacks during war, then one understands that this is not without interest to us and that we draw certain conclusions from it.

It would have been up to England to defend this air base. Upon us fell the task of preventing such an attack at all events. I sought to accomplish this by a natural and simple way.

When I first saw that every effort of that kind was destined to be wrecked and that elements hostile to Germany again would win the upper hand, and as I further saw that this state had long since tost its inner vitality—indeed that it was already broken to pieces—I again carried through the old German Reich. And I joined together again what had to be united by history and geographical positions, and according to all rules of reason. Not to oppress the Czech people! It will enjoy more freedom than the suppressed people of the virtuous nations.

I have, so I believe, thereby rendered peace a great service, because I have rendered innocuous in time an instrument which was destined to become effective in war against Germany. If they now say that this is the signal that Germany now wants to attack the entire world, I do not believe that this is meant seriously: such could only be the expression of a bad conscience. Perhaps it is rage over the failure of some far flung plan; perhaps it is an attempt to create tactical preconditions for a new policy of encirclement.

Be that as it may: it is my conviction that thereby I have rendered peace a great service and out of conviction

I decided three week ago to name the coming party rally the "Party Convention of Peace."

For Germany has no intention of attacking other people. What we, however, do not want to renounce is the reviewing of our economic relations. We have a right thereto and I do not accept any condition from a European or non-European statesman.

The German Reich is not only a great producer but also a gigantic consumer, just as we as a producer will be an irreplaceable trade partner, so as a producer will be an irreplaceable trade partner, so as a consumer we are capable of honourably and fairly paying for what we consume.

We are not thinking about making war on other peoples. However, our precondition is that they leave us in peace. In any case the German Reich is not ready everlastingly to accept intimidation or even a policy of encirclement.

I once made an agreement with England—namely: the Naval Treaty. It is based on the earnest desire which we all possess never to go to war against England. But this wish can only be a mutual one.

If this wish no longer exists in England, then the practical preconditions for this agreement therewith are removed and Germany also would accept this very calmly. We are self-assured because we are strong, and we are strong because we are united and because in addition we are looking forward. And in this city, my fellow citizens, I can address the one exhortation to you: Look into the world and to all its happenings with open eyes. Do not deceive yourself about the most important precondition in life—namely, the necessity to be strong.

We have experienced this for fifteen years. Therefore I have made Germany strong again and erected an armed force, an army on land, at sea and in the air.

I believe that the time is not far distant in which the philosophical community between Fascist Italy and National Socialist Germany will prove essentially different than the one between democratic Great Britain and the Bolshevist Russia of Stalin. However if there really should be no ideological differences, then I can only say: How correct, indeed, is my position towards Marxism and communism and democracy! Why the two phenomena if they possess the same contents?

My fellow citizens, I believe that all states will be facing the same problem which we have faced. State after state will either fall under the Jewish-Bolshevist pest or it will defend itself.

We have done it and have now erected a National German People's State. This People's State wants to live in peace and friendship with any other state but it will never again let itself be forced down by another state.

I do not know whether the world would become Fascist! But I am deeply convinced that this world in the end will defend itself against the most severe Bolshevistic threat that exists. Therefore I believe that a final understanding between nations will come sooner or later. Only when this Jewish wedge among people is removed can the establishment of cooperation among nations be built on lasting understanding.

Today we must rely upon our own strength! And we can be satisfied with the results of this trust in ourselves—inwardly and outwardly.

Twenty years ago the party was founded—at that time a tiny organisation. Consider the road from the time until today! Consider the wonders which have occurred about us. Believe, therefore, because of this wonderful road, also in the course of the German people in its coming great future!

Germany—Sieg Heil! Sieg Heil! Sieg Heil!

ATAL BIHARI VAJPAYEE

INTRODUCTION

Shri Vajpayee was Prime Minister of India from May 16-31, 1996 and a second time from March 19, 1998 to May 13, 2004. With his swearing-in as Prime Minister, he has been the only Prime Minister since Jawaharlal Nehru to occupy the office of the Prime Minister of India through three successive mandates. Shri Vajpayee has also been the first Prime Minister since Smt. Indira Gandhi to lead his party to victory in successive elections.

Born on December 25, 1924 at Gwalior, Madhya Pradesh to Shri Krishna Bihari Vajpayee and Smt. Krishna Devi, Shri Vajpayee brings with him a long parliamentary experience spanning over four decades. He has been a Member of Parliament since 1957. He was elected to the 5th, 6th and 7th Lok Sabha and again to the 10th, 11th 12th and 13th Lok Sabha and to Rajya Sabha in 1962 and 1986.

AT THE BANQUET ORGANIZED AT LAHORE BY PAKISTAN PRIME MINISTER NAWAZ SHARIEF, DURING THE FORMER'S FEB 18-20 VISIT TO PAKISTAN.

Mr Prime Minister, friends, sisters and brothers:

AS we break bread together; a new century and a new millennium knocks on our doors. Fifty years of our independence have gone by. On one side there is pride and on the other regret.

Pride because both the countries have been successful in retaining their independence; but regret because even after 50 years we have not liberated ourselves from the curse of poverty and unemployment.

I am grateful to you, Mr Prime Minister, for hosting this banquet in such a historic location. It was in this magnificent fort that Shahjahan was born; it is here than Akbar lived for over a decade.

My delegation and I are overwhelmed by the warmth of your welcome, and the gracious hospitality extended to us. Mr Prime Minister, you have upheld the nobility of this fort and the tradition of the historic city of Lahore. On this occasion, I am reminded of the lines of the 11th century poet Mas'ud bin S'ad bin Salman.

'Shud dar gham 'Lohur rawanam Yarab! Yarab! Ki dar arzu-e anam Yarab!' (My soul goes out in longing for Lohur, O God! How I long for it)

Excellency, this is the first visit by an Indian prime minister to Pakistan in 10 years. I am delighted to be here. When I inspected the guard of honour and saw the beautiful panorama of the setting sun, I was overwhelmed by mixed feelings. It gave me joy that I was returning here after 21 years with the message of friendship. My regret is that we have spent so much time in mutual bitterness. It is unworthy of two nations the size of India and Pakistan to have wasted so much time in mutual ill-will.

Earlier when I came to Pakistan, I was alone. This time we have representatives from every section of Indian society.

The bus service between Lahore and Delhi is not a means only to ease travel from one country to another. The running of the bus between the two countries symbolises the desire of the people to improve relations and come together. Indeed, if this was only a bus made of metal, it would not have caused such excitement and expectations, not only in our two nations but all over the world.

It is our duty, Mr Prime Minister, to pursue the desires and wishes of our peoples; to develop, trust, confidence, amity and to create a solid structure for co-operation.

We have been encouraged that our interaction in recent months has focussed on issues which directly benefit the lives of our peoples. Our two countries have engaged within the composite dialogue process to work out mechanisms to ensure that humanitarian concerns are addressed quickly; that possibilities of economic and commercial co-operation such as sale of power are identified and pursued; that confidence-building measures are discussed and agreed upon. But this marks only a beginning. We will, together, give directions to our officials to accelerate what we have jointly set in motion.

We have also discussed those areas of relationship on which we do not see eye to eye. That is only inevitable. As we seek to resolve issues, we have to be conscious that there is nothing which cannot be solved through goodwill and direct dialogue. That is the only path.

I am convinced that there is nothing in our bilateral relations that can ever be resolved through violence. The solution of complex outstanding issues can only be sought in an atmosphere free from prejudice and by adopting the path of balance, moderation and realism. To those that preach, practice or foment violence, I have only one message: understand the simple truth of the path of peace and amity. That is why, as part of the composite dialogue process, we welcome sustained discussions on all outstanding issues, including Jammu and Kashmir. As we approach a new millennium, the future beckons us. It calls upon us, indeed demands of us, to think of the welfare of our children and their children, and of the generations that are yet to come.

I have brought but one message from India. There can be no greater legacy that we can leave behind than to do away with mistrust, to abjure and eliminate conflict, to erect an edifice of durable peace amity, harmony and co-operation. I am confident that through our combined efforts we will succeed in doing so, no matter how hard we have to work in achieving it.

Permit me to extend to you, Mr Prime Minister and to Begum Sahiba a most cordial invitation to visit India. Let me assure you that you will find in India a very warm welcome. We look forward to receiving both of you soon in India.

I express my best wishes for your progress and prosperity, for the establishment of durable peace and co-operation between India and Pakistan.

BILL CLINTON

INTRODUCTION

President Clinton was born William Jefferson Blythe IV on August 19, 1946, in Hope, Arkansas, three months after his father died in a traffic accident.

When he was four years old, his mother wed Roger Clinton, of Hot Springs, Arkansas.

"I HAVE SINNED"
SEPTEMBER 11, 1998

THANK you very much, ladies and gentlemen. Welcome to the White House and to this day to which Hillary and the vice president and I look forward so much every year.

This is always an important day for our country, for the reasons that the vice president said. It is an unusual and, I think, unusually important day today. I may not be quite as easy with my words today as I have been in years past, and I was up rather late last night thinking about and praying about what I ought to say today. And rather unusual for me, I actually tried to write it down. So if you will forgive me, I will do my best to say what it is I want to say to you - and I may have to take my glasses out to read my own writing.

First, I want to say to all of you that, as you might imagine, I have been on quite a journey these last few weeks to get to the end of this, to the rock bottom truth of where I am and where we all are.

I agree with those who have said that in my first statement after I testified I was not contrite enough. I don't think there is a fancy way to say that I have sinned.

It is important to me that everybody who has been hurt know that the sorrow I feel is genuine: first and most important, my family; also my friends, my staff, my Cabinet, Monica Lewinsky and her family, and the American people. I have asked all for their forgiveness.

But I believe that to be forgiven, more than sorrow is required - at least two more things. First, genuine repentance - a determination to change and to repair breaches of my own making. I have repented. Second, what my bible calls a "broken spirit"; an understanding that I must have God's help to be the person that I want to be; a willingness to give the very forgiveness I seek; a renunciation of the pride and the anger which cloud judgment, lead people to excuse and compare and to blame and complain.

Now, what does all this mean for me and for us? First, I will instruct my lawyers to mount a vigorous defense, using all available appropriate arguments. But legal language must not obscure the fact that I have done wrong. Second, I will continue on the path of repentance, seeking pastoral support and that of other caring people so that they can hold me accountable for my own commitment.

Third, I will intensify my efforts to lead our country and the world toward peace and freedom, prosperity and harmony, in the hope that with a broken spirit and a still strong heart I can be used for greater good, for we have many blessings and many challenges and so much work to do.

In this, I ask for your prayers and for your help in healing our nation. And though I cannot move beyond or forget this -

indeed, I must always keep it as a caution light in my life - it is very important that our nation move forward.

I am very grateful for the many, many people - clergy and ordinary citizens alike - who have written me with wise counsel. I am profoundly grateful for the support of so many Americans who somehow through it all seem to still know that I care about them a great deal, that I care about their problems and their dreams. I am grateful for those who have stood by me and who say that in this case and many others, the bounds of privacy have been excessively and unwisely invaded. That may be. Nevertheless, in this case, it may be a blessing, because I still sinned. And if my repentance is genuine and sustained, and if I can maintain both a broken spirit and a strong heart, then good can come of this for our country as well as for me and my family.

The children of this country can learn in a profound way that integrity is important and selfishness is wrong, but God can change us and make us strong at the broken places. I want to embody those lessons for the children of this country - for that little boy in Florida who came up to me and said that he wanted to grow up and be President and to be just like me. I want the parents of all the children in America to be able to say that to their children.

A couple of days ago when I was in Florida a Jewish friend of mine gave me this liturgy book called "Gates of Repentance." And there was this incredible passage from the Yom Kippur liturgy. I would like to read it to you:

"Now is the time for turning. The leaves are beginning to turn from green to red to orange. The birds are beginning to turn and are heading once more toward the south. The animals are beginning to turn to storing their food for the winter. For leaves, birds and animals, turning comes instinctively. But for us, turning does not come so easily. It takes an act of will for us to make a turn. It means breaking old habits. It means admitting that we have been wrong, and this is never easy. It means losing face. It means starting all over again. And this is always painful. It means saying I am sorry. It means recognizing that we have the ability to change. These things are terribly hard to do. But unless we turn, we will be trapped forever in yesterday's ways. Lord help us to turn, from callousness to sensitivity, from hostility to love, from pettiness to purpose, from envy to contentment, from carelessness to discipline, from fear to faith. Turn us around, O Lord, and bring us back toward you. Revive our lives as at the beginning, and turn us toward each other, Lord, for in isolation there is no life."

I thank my friend for that. I thank you for being here. I ask you to share my prayer that God will search me and know my heart, try me and know my anxious thoughts, see if there is any hurtfulness in me, and lead me toward the life everlasting. I ask that God give me a clean heart, let me walk by faith and not sight.

I ask once again to be able to love my neighbor - all my neighbors - as my self, to be an instrument of God's peace; to let the words of my mouth and the meditations of my heart and, in the end, the work of my hands, be pleasing. This is what I wanted to say to you today.

Thank you. God bless you.

DWIGHT D. EISENHOWER

INTRODUCTION

Born in Texas in 1890, brought up in Abilene, Kansas, Eisenhower was the third of seven sons. Stationed in Texas as a second lieutenant, he met Mamie Geneva Doud, whom he married in 1916.

In his early Army career, he excelled in staff assignments, serving under Generals John J. Pershing, Douglas MacArthur, and Walter Krueger. After Pearl Harbor, General George C. Marshall called him to Washington for a war plans assignment. He commanded the Allied Forces landing in North Africa in November 1942; on D-Day, 1944, he was Supreme Commander of the troops invading France. After the war, he became President of Columbia University, then took leave to assume supreme command over the new NATO forces being assembled in 1951. Republican emissaries to his headquarters near Paris persuaded him to run for President in 1952. He was president of U.S.A. from 1953 to 1961.

FIRST INAUGURAL ADDRESS
TUESDAY, JANUARY 20, 1953

MY friends, before I begin the expression of those thoughts that I deem appropriate to this moment, would you permit me the privilege of uttering a little private prayer of my own. And

I ask that you bow your heads:

Almighty God, as we stand here at this moment my future associates in the executive branch of government join me in beseeching that Thou will make full and complete our dedication to the service of the people in this throng, and their fellow citizens everywhere.

Give us, we pray, the power to discern clearly right from wrong, and allow all our words and actions to be governed thereby, and by the laws of this land. Especially we pray that our concern shall be for all the people regardless of station, race, or calling.

May cooperation be permitted and be the mutual aim of those who, under the concepts of our Constitution, hold to differing political faiths; so that all may work for the good of our beloved country and Thy glory. Amen.

My fellow citizens:

The world and we have passed the midway point of a century of continuing challenge. We sense with all our faculties that forces of good and evil are massed and armed and opposed as rarely before in history.

This fact defines the meaning of this day. We are summoned by this honored and historic ceremony to witness more than the act of one citizen swearing his oath of service, in the presence of God. We are called as a people to give testimony in the sight of the world to our faith that the future shall belong to the free.

Since this century's beginning, a time of tempest has seemed to come upon the continents of the earth. Masses of Asia have awakened to strike off shackles of the past. Great nations of Europe have fought their bloodiest wars. Thrones have toppled and their vast empires have disappeared. New nations have been born.

For our own country, it has been a time of recurring trial. We have grown in power and in responsibility. We have passed through the anxieties of depression and of war to a summit unmatched in man's history. Seeking to secure peace in the world, we have had to fight through the forests of the Argonne, to the shores of Iwo Jima, and to the cold mountains of Korea.

In the swift rush of great events, we find ourselves groping to know the full sense and meaning of these times in which we live. In our quest of understanding, we beseech God's guidance. We summon all our knowledge of the past and we scan all signs of the future. We bring all our wit and all our will to meet the question:

How far have we come in man's long pilgrimage from darkness toward light? Are we nearing the light—a day of freedom and of peace for all mankind? Or are the shadows of another night closing in upon us?

Great as are the preoccupations absorbing us at home, concerned as we are with matters that deeply affect our livelihood today and our vision of the future, each of these domestic problems is dwarfed by, and often even created by, this question that involves all humankind.

This trial comes at a moment when man's power to achieve good or to inflict evil surpasses the brightest hopes and the sharpest fears of all ages. We can turn rivers in their courses, level mountains to the plains. Oceans and land and sky are avenues for our colossal commerce. Disease diminishes and life lengthens.

Yet the promise of this life is imperiled by the very genius that has made it possible. Nations amass wealth. Labor sweats to create—and turns out devices to level not only mountains but also cities. Science seems ready to confer upon us, as its final gift, the power to erase human life from this planet.

At such a time in history, we who are free must proclaim anew our faith. This faith is the abiding creed of our fathers. It is our faith in the deathless dignity of man, governed by eternal moral and natural laws.

This faith defines our full view of life. It establishes, beyond debate, those gifts of the Creator that are man's inalienable rights, and that make all men equal in His sight.

In the light of this equality, we know that the virtues most cherished by free people—love of truth, pride of work, devotion to country—all are treasures equally precious in the lives of the most humble and of the most exalted. The men who mine coal and fire furnaces and balance ledgers and turn lathes and pick cotton and heal the sick and plant corn—all serve as proudly, and as profitably, for America as the statesmen who draft treaties and the legislators who enact laws.

This faith rules our whole way of life. It decrees that we, the people, elect leaders not to rule but to serve. It asserts that we have the right to choice of our own work and to the reward of our own toil. It inspires the initiative that makes our productivity the wonder of the world. And it warns that any man who seeks to deny equality among all his brothers betrays the spirit of the free and invites the mockery of the tyrant.

It is because we, all of us, hold to these principles that the political changes accomplished this day do not imply turbulence, upheaval or disorder. Rather this change expresses a purpose of strengthening our dedication and devotion to the precepts of our founding documents, a conscious renewal of faith in our country and in the watchfulness of a Divine Providence.

The enemies of this faith know no god but force, no devotion but its use. They tutor men in treason. They feed upon the hunger of others. Whatever defies them, they torture, especially the truth.

Here, then, is joined no argument between slightly differing philosophies. This conflict strikes directly at the faith of our fathers and the lives of our sons. No principle or treasure that we hold, from the spiritual knowledge of our free schools and churches to the creative magic of free labor and capital, nothing lies safely beyond the reach of this struggle.

Freedom is pitted against slavery; lightness against the dark.

The faith we hold belongs not to us alone but to the free of all the world. This common bond binds the grower of rice in Burma and the planter of wheat in Iowa, the shepherd in southern Italy and the mountaineer in the Andes. It confers a common dignity upon the French soldier who dies in Indo-China, the British soldier killed in Malaya, the American life given in Korea.

We know, beyond this, that we are linked to all free peoples not merely by a noble idea but by a simple need. No free people can for long cling to any privilege or enjoy any safety in economic solitude. For all our own material might, even we need markets in the world for the surpluses of our farms and our factories. Equally, we need for these same farms and factories vital materials and products of distant lands. This basic law of interdependence, so manifest in the commerce of peace, applies with thousand-fold intensity in the event of war.

So we are persuaded by necessity and by belief that the strength of all free peoples lies in unity; their danger, in discord.

To produce this unity, to meet the challenge of our time, destiny has laid upon our country the responsibility of the free world's leadership.

So it is proper that we assure our friends once again that, in the discharge of this responsibility, we Americans know and we observe the difference between world leadership and imperialism; between firmness and truculence; between a thoughtfully calculated goal and spasmodic reaction to the stimulus of emergencies.

We wish our friends the world over to know this above all: we face the threat—not with dread and confusion—but with confidence and conviction.

We feel this moral strength because we know that we are not helpless prisoners of history. We are free men. We shall remain free, never to be proven guilty of the one capital offense against freedom, a lack of stanch faith.

In pleading our just cause before the bar of history and in pressing our labor for world peace, we shall be guided by certain fixed principles.

These principles are:

Abhorring war as a chosen way to balk the purposes of those who threaten us, we hold it to be the first task of statesmanship to develop the strength that will deter the forces of aggression and promote the conditions of peace. For, as it must be the supreme purpose of all free men, so it must be the dedication of their leaders, to save humanity from preying upon itself.

In the light of this principle, we stand ready to engage with any and all others in joint effort to remove the causes of mutual fear and distrust among nations, so as to make possible drastic reduction of armaments. The sole requisites for undertaking such effort are that—in their purpose—they be aimed logically and honestly toward secure peace for all; and that—in their result—they provide methods by which every participating nation will prove good faith in carrying out its pledge.

Realizing that common sense and common decency alike dictate the futility of appeasement, we shall never try to placate an aggressor by the false and wicked bargain of trading honor for security. Americans, indeed all free men, remember that in the final choice a soldier's pack is not so heavy a burden as a prisoner's chains.

Knowing that only a United States that is strong and immensely productive can help defend freedom in our world, we view our Nation's strength and security as a trust upon which rests the hope of free men everywhere. It is the firm duty of each of our free citizens and of every free citizen everywhere to place the cause of his country before the comfort, the convenience of himself.

Honoring the identity and the special heritage of each nation in the world, we shall never use our strength to try to impress upon another people our own cherished political and economic institutions.

Assessing realistically the needs and capacities of proven friends of freedom, we shall strive to help them to achieve their own security and well-being. Likewise, we shall count upon them to assume, within the limits of their resources, their full and just burdens in the common defense of freedom.

Recognizing economic health as an indispensable basis of military strength and the free world's peace, we shall strive to foster everywhere, and to practice ourselves, policies that encourage productivity and profitable trade. For the impoverishment of any single people in the world means danger to the well-being of all other peoples.

Appreciating that economic need, military security and political wisdom combine to suggest regional groupings of free peoples, we hope, within the framework of the United Nations, to help strengthen such special bonds the world over. The nature of these ties must vary with the different problems of different areas.

In the Western Hemisphere, we enthusiastically join with all our neighbors in the work of perfecting a community of fraternal trust and common purpose.

In Europe, we ask that enlightened and inspired leaders of

the Western nations strive with renewed vigor to make the unity of their peoples a reality. Only as free Europe unitedly marshals its strength can it effectively safeguard, even with our help, its spiritual and cultural heritage.

Conceiving the defense of freedom, like freedom itself, to be one and indivisible, we hold all continents and peoples in equal regard and honor. We reject any insinuation that one race or another, one people or another, is in any sense inferior or expendable.

Respecting the United Nations as the living sign of all people's hope for peace, we shall strive to make it not merely an eloquent symbol but an effective force. And in our quest for an honorable peace, we shall neither compromise, nor tire, nor ever cease.

By these rules of conduct, we hope to be known to all peoples.

By their observance, an earth of peace may become not a vision but a fact.

This hope—this supreme aspiration—must rule the way we live.

We must be ready to dare all for our country. For history does not long entrust the care of freedom to the weak or the timid. We must acquire proficiency in defense and display stamina in purpose.

We must be willing, individually and as a Nation, to accept whatever sacrifices may be required of us. A people that values its privileges above its principles soon loses both.

These basic precepts are not lofty abstractions, far removed from matters of daily living. They are laws of spiritual strength that generate and define our material strength. Patriotism means equipped forces and a prepared citizenry. Moral stamina means more energy and more productivity, on the farm and in the factory. Love of liberty means the guarding of every resource that makes freedom possible—from the sanctity of our families and the wealth of our soil to the genius of our scientists.

And so each citizen plays an indispensable role. The productivity of our heads, our hands, and our hearts is the source of all the strength we can command, for both the enrichment of our lives and the winning of the peace.

No person, no home, no community can be beyond the reach of this call. We are summoned to act in wisdom and in conscience, to work with industry, to teach with persuasion, to preach with conviction, to weigh our every deed with care and with compassion. For this truth must be clear before us: whatever America hopes to bring to pass in the world must first come to pass in the heart of America.

The peace we seek, then, is nothing less than the practice and fulfillment of our whole faith among ourselves and in our dealings with others. This signifies more than the stilling of guns, easing the sorrow of war. More than escape from death, it is a way of life. More than a haven for the weary, it is a hope for the brave.

This is the hope that beckons us onward in this century of trial. This is the work that awaits us all, to be done with bravery, with charity, and with prayer to Almighty God.

SECOND INAUGURAL ADDRESS
MONDAY, JANUARY 21, 1957

THE PRICE OF PEACE

MR. Chairman, Mr. Vice President, Mr. Chief Justice, Mr. Speaker, members of my family and friends, my countrymen, and the friends of my country, wherever they may be, we meet again, as upon a like moment four years ago, and again you have witnessed my solemn oath of service to you.

I, too, am a witness, today testifying in your name to the principles and purposes to which we, as a people, are pledged.

Before all else, we seek, upon our common labor as a nation, the blessings of Almighty God. And the hopes in our hearts fashion the deepest prayers of our whole people.

May we pursue the right—without self-righteousness.

May we know unity—without conformity.

May we grow in strength—without pride in self.

May we, in our dealings with all peoples of the earth, ever speak truth and serve justice.

And so shall America—in the sight of all men of good will—prove true to the honorable purposes that bind and rule us as a people in all this time of trial through which we pass.

We live in a land of plenty, but rarely has this earth known such peril as today.

In our nation work and wealth abound. Our population grows. Commerce crowds our rivers and rails, our skies, harbors, and highways. Our soil is fertile, our agriculture productive. The air rings with the song of our industry—rolling mills and blast furnaces, dynamos, dams, and assembly lines—the chorus of America the bountiful. This is our home—yet this is not the whole of our world. For our world is where our full destiny lies—with men, of all people, and all nations, who are or would be free. And for them—and so for us—this is no time of ease or of rest.

In too much of the earth there is want, discord, danger. New forces and new nations stir and strive across the earth, with power to bring, by their fate, great good or great evil to the free world's future. From the deserts of North Africa to the islands of the South Pacific one third of all mankind has entered upon an historic struggle for a new freedom; freedom from grinding poverty. Across all continents, nearly a billion people seek, sometimes almost in desperation, for the skills and knowledge and assistance by which they may satisfy from their own resources, the material wants common to all mankind.

No nation, however old or great, escapes this tempest of change and turmoil. Some, impoverished by the recent World War, seek to restore their means of livelihood. In the heart of Europe, Germany still stands tragically divided. So is the whole continent divided. And so, too, is all the world.

The divisive force is International Communism and the power that it controls.

The designs of that power, dark in purpose, are clear in practice. It strives to seal forever the fate of those it has enslaved. It strives to break the ties that unite the free. And it strives to capture—to exploit for its own greater power—all forces of change in the world, especially the needs of the hungry and the hopes of the oppressed.

Yet the world of International Communism has itself been shaken by a fierce and mighty force: the readiness of men who love freedom to pledge their lives to that love. Through the night of their bondage, the unconquerable will of heroes has struck with the swift, sharp thrust of lightning. Budapest is no longer merely the name of a city; henceforth it is a new and shining symbol of man's yearning to be free.

Thus across all the globe there harshly blow the winds of change. And, we—though fortunate be our lot—know that we can never turn our backs to them.

We look upon this shaken earth, and we declare our firm and fixed purpose—the building of a peace with justice in a world where moral law prevails.

The building of such a peace is a bold and solemn purpose. To proclaim it is easy. To serve it will be hard. And to attain it, we must be aware of its full meaning—and ready to pay its full price.

We know clearly what we seek, and why.

We seek peace, knowing that peace is the climate of freedom. And now, as in no other age, we seek it because we have been warned, by the power of modern weapons, that peace may be the only climate possible for human life itself.

Yet this peace we seek cannot be born of fear alone: it must be rooted in the lives of nations. There must be justice, sensed and shared by all peoples, for, without justice the world can know only a tense and unstable truce. There must be law, steadily invoked and respected by all nations, for without law, the world promises only such meager justice as the pity of the strong upon the weak. But the law of which we speak, comprehending the values of freedom, affirms the equality of all nations, great and small.

Splendid as can be the blessings of such a peace, high will be its cost: in toil patiently sustained, in help honorably given, in sacrifice calmly borne.

We are called to meet the price of this peace.

To counter the threat of those who seek to rule by force, we must pay the costs of our own needed military strength, and help to build the security of others.

We must use our skills and knowledge and, at times, our substance, to help others rise from misery, however far the scene of suffering may be from our shores. For wherever in the world a people knows desperate want, there must appear at least the spark of hope, the hope of progress—or there will surely rise at last the flames of conflict.

We recognize and accept our own deep involvement in the destiny of men everywhere. We are accordingly pledged to honor, and to strive to fortify, the authority of the United Nations. For in that body rests the best hope of our age for the assertion of that law by which all nations may live in dignity.

And, beyond this general resolve, we are called to act a responsible role in the world's great concerns or conflicts—whether they touch upon the affairs of a vast region, the fate of an island in the Pacific, or the use of a canal in the Middle East. Only in respecting the hopes and cultures of others will we practice the equality of all nations. Only as we show willingness and wisdom in giving counsel—in receiving counsel—and in sharing burdens, will we wisely perform the work of peace.

For one truth must rule all we think and all we do. No people can live to itself alone. The unity of all who dwell in freedom is their only sure defense. The economic need of all nations—in mutual dependence—makes isolation an impossibility; not even America's prosperity could long survive if other nations did not also prosper. No nation can longer be a fortress, lone and strong and safe. And any people, seeking such shelter for themselves, can now build only their own prison.

Our pledge to these principles is constant, because we believe in their rightness.

We do not fear this world of change. America is no stranger to much of its spirit. Everywhere we see the seeds of the same growth that America itself has known. The American experiment has, for generations, fired the passion and the courage of millions elsewhere seeking freedom, equality, and opportunity. And the American story of material progress has helped excite the longing of all needy peoples for some satisfaction of their human wants. These hopes that we have helped to inspire, we can help to fulfill.

In this confidence, we speak plainly to all peoples.

We cherish our friendship with all nations that are or would be free. We respect, no less, their independence. And when, in time of want or peril, they ask our help, they may honorably receive it; for we no more seek to buy their sovereignty than we would sell our own. Sovereignty is never bartered among freemen.

We honor the aspirations of those nations which, now captive, long for freedom. We seek neither their military alliance nor any artificial imitation of our society. And they can know the warmth of the welcome that awaits them when, as must be, they join again the ranks of freedom.

We honor, no less in this divided world than in a less tormented time, the people of Russia. We do not dread, rather do we welcome, their progress in education and industry. We wish them success in their demands for more intellectual freedom, greater security before their own laws, fuller enjoyment of the rewards of their own toil. For as such things come to pass, the more certain will be the coming of that day when our peoples may freely meet in friendship.

So we voice our hope and our belief that we can help to heal this divided world. Thus may the nations cease to live in trembling before the menace of force. Thus may the weight of fear and the weight of arms be taken from the burdened shoulders of mankind.

This, nothing less, is the labor to which we are called and our strength dedicated.

And so the prayer of our people carries far beyond our own frontiers, to the wide world of our duty and our destiny.

May the light of freedom, coming to all darkened lands, flame brightly—until at last the darkness is no more.

May the turbulence of our age yield to a true time of peace, when men and nations shall share a life that honors the dignity of each, the brotherhood of all.

EDWARD VIII

INTRODUCTION

Edward VIII (1894-1972) was King of England for only one year, 1936, abdicating the throne to marry the "woman I love," the twice-divorced Wallis Simpson. He was Duke of Windsor after his abdication.

ABDICATES THE THRONE OF ENGLAND
DECEMBER 11, 1936

AT long last I am able to say a few words of my own. I have never wanted to withhold anything, but until now it has not been constitutionally possible for me to speak.

A few hours ago I discharged my last duty as King and Emperor, and now that I have been succeeded by my brother, the Duke of York, my first words must be to declare my allegiance to him. This I do with all my heart.

You all know the reasons which have impelled me to renounce the throne. But I want you to understand that in making up my mind I did not forget the country or the empire, which, as Prince of Wales and lately as King, I have for twenty-five years tried to serve.

But you must believe me when I tell you that I have found it impossible to carry the heavy burden of responsibility and to discharge my duties as King as I would wish to do without the help and support of the woman I love.

And I want you to know that the decision I have made has been mine and mine alone. This was a thing I had to judge entirely for myself. The other person most nearly concerned has tried up to the last to persuade me to take a different course.

I have made this, the most serious decision of my life, only upon the single thought of what would, in the end, be best for all.

This decision has been made less difficult to me by the sure knowledge that my brother, with his long training in the public affairs of this country and with his fine qualities, will be able to take my place forthwith without interruption or injury to the life and progress of the empire. And he has one matchless blessing, enjoyed by so many of you, and not bestowed on me — a happy home with his wife and children.

During these hard days I have been comforted by her majesty my mother and by my family. The ministers of the crown, and in particular, Mr. Baldwin, the Prime Minister, have always treated me with full consideration. There has never been any constitutional difference between me and them, and between me and Parliament. Bred in the constitutional tradition by my father, I should never have allowed any such issue to arise.

Ever since I was Prince of Wales, and later on when I occupied the throne, I have been treated with the greatest kindness by all classes of the people wherever I have lived or journeyed throughout the empire. For that I am very grateful.

I now quit altogether public affairs and I lay down my burden. It may be some time before I return to my native land, but I shall always follow the fortunes of the British race and empire with profound interest, and if at any time in the future I can be found of service to his majesty in a private station, I shall not fail.

And now, we all have a new King. I wish him and you, his people, happiness and prosperity with all my heart. God bless you all! God save the King!

FRANKLIN DELANO ROOSEVELT

INTRODUCTION

Born in 1882 at Hyde Park, New York—now a national historic site—he attended Harvard University and Columbia Law School. On St. Patrick's Day, 1905, he married Eleanor Roosevelt.

He was elected President in November 1932, to the first of four terms. In 1936 he was re-elected by a top-heavy margin.

When the Japanese attacked Pearl Harbor on December 7, 1941, Roosevelt directed organization of the Nation's manpower and resources for global war. As the war drew to a close, Roosevelt's health deteriorated, and on April 12, 1945, while at Warm Springs, Georgia, he died of a cerebral hemorrhage.

FIRST INAUGURAL ADDRESS
SATURDAY, MARCH 4, 1933

I AM certain that my fellow Americans expect that on my induction into the Presidency I will address them with a candor and a decision which the present situation of our Nation impels. This is preeminently the time to speak the truth, the whole truth, frankly and boldly. Nor need we shrink from honestly facing conditions in our country today. This great Nation will endure as it has endured, will revive and will prosper. So, first of all, let me assert my firm belief that the only thing we have to fear is fear itself—nameless, unreasoning, unjustified terror which paralyzes needed efforts to convert retreat into advance. In every dark hour of our national life a leadership of frankness and vigor has met with that understanding and support of the people themselves which is essential to victory. I am convinced that you will again give that support to leadership in these critical days.

In such a spirit on my part and on yours we face our common difficulties. They concern, thank God, only material things. Values have shrunken to fantastic levels; taxes have risen; our ability to pay has fallen; government of all kinds is faced by serious curtailment of income; the means of exchange are frozen in the currents of trade; the withered leaves of industrial enterprise lie on every side; farmers find no markets for their produce; the savings of many years in thousands of families are gone.

More important, a host of unemployed citizens face the grim problem of existence, and an equally great number toil with little return. Only a foolish optimist can deny the dark realities of the moment.

Yet our distress comes from no failure of substance. We are stricken by no plague of locusts. Compared with the perils which our forefathers conquered because they believed and were not afraid, we have still much to be thankful for. Nature still offers her bounty and human efforts have multiplied it. Plenty is at our doorstep, but a generous use of it languishes in the very sight of the supply. Primarily this is because the rulers of the exchange of mankind's goods have failed, through their own stubbornness and their own incompetence, have admitted their failure, and abdicated. Practices of the unscrupulous money changers stand indicted in the court of public opinion, rejected by the hearts and minds of men.

True they have tried, but their efforts have been cast in the pattern of an outworn tradition. Faced by failure of credit they have proposed only the lending of more money. Stripped of the lure of profit by which to induce our people to follow their false leadership, they have resorted to exhortations, pleading tearfully for restored confidence. They know only the rules of a generation of self-seekers. They have no vision, and when there is no vision the people perish.

The money changers have fled from their high seats in the temple of our civilization. We may now restore that temple to the ancient truths. The measure of the restoration lies in the extent to which we apply social values more noble than mere monetary profit.

Happiness lies not in the mere possession of money; it lies in the joy of achievement, in the thrill of creative effort. The joy and moral stimulation of work no longer must be forgotten in the mad chase of evanescent profits. These dark days will be worth all they cost us if they teach us that our true destiny is not to be ministered unto but to minister to ourselves and to our fellow men.

Recognition of the falsity of material wealth as the standard of success goes hand in hand with the abandonment of the false belief that public office and high political position are to be valued only by the standards of pride of place and personal profit; and there must be an end to a conduct in banking and in business which too often has given to a sacred trust the likeness of callous and selfish wrongdoing. Small wonder that confidence languishes, for it thrives only on honesty, on honor, on the sacredness of obligations, on faithful protection, on unselfish performance; without them it cannot live.

Restoration calls, however, not for changes in ethics alone. This Nation asks for action, and action now.

Our greatest primary task is to put people to work. This is no unsolvable problem if we face it wisely and courageously. It can be accomplished in part by direct recruiting by the Government itself, treating the task as we would treat the emergency of a war, but at the same time, through this employment, accomplishing greatly needed projects to stimulate and reorganize the use of our natural resources.

Hand in hand with this we must frankly recognize the overbalance of population in our industrial centers and, by engaging on a national scale in a redistribution, endeavor to provide a better use of the land for those best fitted for the land. The task can be helped by definite efforts to raise the values of agricultural products and with this the power to purchase the output of our cities. It can be helped by preventing realistically the tragedy of the growing loss through foreclosure of our small homes and our farms. It can be helped by insistence that the Federal, State, and local governments act forthwith on the demand that their cost be drastically reduced. It can be helped by the unifying of relief activities which today are often scattered, uneconomical, and unequal. It can be helped by national planning for and supervision of all forms of transportation and of communications and other utilities which have a definitely public character. There are many ways in which it can be helped, but it can never be helped merely by talking about it. We must act and act quickly.

Finally, in our progress toward a resumption of work we require two safeguards against a return of the evils of the old order; there must be a strict supervision of all banking and credits and investments; there must be an end to speculation with other people's money, and there must be provision for an adequate but sound currency.

There are the lines of attack. I shall presently urge upon a new Congress in special session detailed measures for their fulfillment, and I shall seek the immediate assistance of the several States.

Through this program of action we address ourselves to putting our own national house in order and making income balance outgo. Our international trade relations, though vastly important, are in point of time and necessity secondary to the establishment of a sound national economy. I favor as a practical policy the putting of first things first. I shall spare no effort to restore world trade by international economic readjustment, but the emergency at home cannot wait on that accomplishment.

The basic thought that guides these specific means of national recovery is not narrowly nationalistic. It is the insistence, as a first consideration, upon the interdependence of the various elements in all parts of the United States—a recognition of the old and permanently important manifestation of the American spirit of the pioneer. It is the way to recovery. It is the immediate way. It is the strongest assurance that the recovery will endure.

In the field of world policy I would dedicate this Nation to the policy of the good neighbor—the neighbor who resolutely respects himself and, because he does so, respects the rights of others—the neighbor who respects his obligations and respects the sanctity of his agreements in and with a world of neighbors.

If I read the temper of our people correctly, we now realize as we have never realized before our interdependence on each other; that we can not merely take but we must give as well; that if we are to go forward, we must move as a trained and loyal army willing to sacrifice for the good of a common discipline, because without such discipline no progress is made, no leadership becomes effective. We are, I know, ready and willing to submit our lives and property to such discipline, because it makes possible a leadership which aims at a larger good. This I propose to offer, pledging that the larger purposes will bind upon us all as a sacred obligation with a unity of duty hitherto evoked only in time of armed strife.

With this pledge taken, I assume unhesitatingly the leadership of this great army of our people dedicated to a disciplined attack upon our common problems.

Action in this image and to this end is feasible under the form of government which we have inherited from our ancestors. Our Constitution is so simple and practical that it is possible always to meet extraordinary needs by changes in emphasis and arrangement without loss of essential form. That is why our constitutional system has proved itself the most superbly enduring political mechanism the modern world has produced. It has met every stress of vast expansion of territory, of foreign wars, of bitter internal strife, of world relations.

It is to be hoped that the normal balance of executive and legislative authority may be wholly adequate to meet the unprecedented task before us. But it may be that an unprecedented demand and need for undelayed action may call for temporary departure from that normal balance of public procedure.

I am prepared under my constitutional duty to recommend the measures that a stricken nation in the midst of a stricken world may require. These measures, or such other measures as the Congress may build out of its experience and wisdom, I shall seek, within my constitutional authority, to bring to speedy adoption.

But in the event that the Congress shall fail to take one of these two courses, and in the event that the national emergency is still critical, I shall not evade the clear course of duty that will then confront me. I shall ask the Congress for the one remaining instrument to meet the crisis—broad Executive power to wage a war against the emergency, as great as the power that would be given to me if we were in fact invaded by a foreign foe.

For the trust reposed in me I will return the courage and the devotion that befit the time. I can do no less.

We face the arduous days that lie before us in the warm courage of the national unity; with the clear consciousness of seeking old and precious moral values; with the clean satisfaction that comes from the stern performance of duty by old and young alike. We aim at the assurance of a rounded and permanent national life.

We do not distrust the future of essential democracy. The people of the United States have not failed. In their need they have registered a mandate that they want direct, vigorous action. They have asked for discipline and direction under leadership. They have made me the present instrument of their wishes. In the spirit of the gift I take it.

In this dedication of a Nation we humbly ask the blessing of God. May He protect each and every one of us. May He guide me in the days to come.

SECOND INAUGURAL ADDRESS
WEDNESDAY, JANUARY 20, 1937

WHEN four years ago we met to inaugurate a President, the Republic, single-minded in anxiety, stood in spirit here. We dedicated ourselves to the fulfillment of a vision—to speed the time when there would be for all the people that security and peace essential to the pursuit of happiness. We of the Republic pledged ourselves to drive from the temple of our ancient faith those who had profaned it; to end by action, tireless and unafraid, the stagnation and despair of that day. We did those first things first.

Our covenant with ourselves did not stop there. Instinctively we recognized a deeper need—the need to find through government the instrument of our united purpose to solve for the individual the ever-rising problems of a complex civilization. Repeated attempts at their solution without the aid of government had left us baffled and bewildered. For, without that aid, we had been unable to create those moral controls over the services of science which are necessary to make science a useful servant instead of a ruthless master of mankind. To do this we knew that we must find practical controls over blind economic forces and blindly selfish men.

We of the Republic sensed the truth that democratic government has innate capacity to protect its people against disasters once considered inevitable, to solve problems once considered unsolvable. We would not admit that we could not find a way to master economic epidemics just as, after centuries of fatalistic suffering, we had found a way to master epidemics of disease. We refused to leave the problems of our common welfare to be solved by the winds of chance and the hurricanes of disaster.

In this we Americans were discovering no wholly new truth; we were writing a new chapter in our book of self-government.

This year marks the one hundred and fiftieth anniversary of the Constitutional Convention which made us a nation. At that Convention our forefathers found the way out of the chaos which followed the Revolutionary War; they created a strong government with powers of united action sufficient then and now to solve problems utterly beyond individual or local solution. A century and a half ago they established the Federal Government in order to promote the general welfare and secure the blessings of liberty to the American people.

Today we invoke those same powers of government to achieve the same objectives.

Four years of new experience have not belied our historic instinct. They hold out the clear hope that government within communities, government within the separate States, and government of the United States can do the things the times require, without yielding its democracy. Our tasks in the last four years did not force democracy to take a holiday.

Nearly all of us recognize that as intricacies of human relationships increase, so power to govern them also must increase—power to stop evil; power to do good. The essential democracy of our Nation and the safety of our people depend not upon the absence of power, but upon lodging it with those whom the people can change or continue at stated intervals through an honest and free system of elections. The Constitution of 1787 did not make our democracy impotent.

In fact, in these last four years, we have made the exercise of all power more democratic; for we have begun to bring private autocratic powers into their proper subordination to the public's government. The legend that they were invincible—above and beyond the processes of a democracy—has been shattered. They have been challenged and beaten.

Our progress out of the depression is obvious. But that is not all that you and I mean by the new order of things. Our pledge was not merely to do a patchwork job with secondhand materials. By using the new materials of social justice we have undertaken to erect on the old foundations a more enduring structure for the better use of future generations.

In that purpose we have been helped by achievements of mind and spirit. Old truths have been relearned; untruths have been unlearned. We have always known that heedless self-interest was bad morals; we know now that it is bad economics. Out of the collapse of a prosperity whose builders boasted their practicality has come the conviction that in the long run economic morality pays. We are beginning to wipe out the line that divides the practical from the ideal; and in so doing we are fashioning an instrument of unimagined power for the establishment of a morally better world.

This new understanding undermines the old admiration of worldly success as such. We are beginning to abandon our tolerance of the abuse of power by those who betray for profit the elementary decencies of life.

In this process evil things formerly accepted will not be so easily condoned. Hard-headedness will not so easily excuse hardheartedness. We are moving toward an era of good feeling. But we realize that there can be no era of good feeling save among men of good will.

For these reasons I am justified in believing that the greatest change we have witnessed has been the change in the moral climate of America.

Among men of good will, science and democracy together offer an ever-richer life and ever-larger satisfaction to the individual. With this change in our moral climate and our rediscovered ability to improve our economic order, we have set our feet upon the road of enduring progress.

Shall we pause now and turn our back upon the road that lies ahead? Shall we call this the promised land? Or, shall we continue on our way? For "each age is a dream that is dying, or one that is coming to birth."

Many voices are heard as we face a great decision. Comfort says, "Tarry a while." Opportunism says, "This is a good spot." Timidity asks, "How difficult is the road ahead?"

True, we have come far from the days of stagnation and despair. Vitality has been preserved. Courage and confidence have been restored. Mental and moral horizons have been extended.

But our present gains were won under the pressure of more than ordinary circumstances. Advance became imperative under the goad of fear and suffering. The times were on the side of progress.

To hold to progress today, however, is more difficult. Dulled conscience, irresponsibility, and ruthless self-interest already reappear. Such symptoms of prosperity may become portents of disaster! Prosperity already tests the persistence of our progressive purpose.

Let us ask again: Have we reached the goal of our vision of that fourth day of March 1933? Have we found our happy valley?

I see a great nation, upon a great continent, blessed with a great wealth of natural resources. Its hundred and thirty million people are at peace among themselves; they are making their country a good neighbor among the nations. I see a United States which can demonstrate that, under democratic methods of government, national wealth can be translated into a spreading volume of human comforts hitherto unknown, and the lowest standard of living can be raised far above the level of mere subsistence.

But here is the challenge to our democracy: In this nation I see tens of millions of its citizens—a substantial part of its whole population—who at this very moment are denied the greater part of what the very lowest standards of today call the necessities of life.

I see millions of families trying to live on incomes so meager that the pall of family disaster hangs over them day by day.

I see millions whose daily lives in city and on farm continue under conditions labeled indecent by a so-called polite society half a century ago.

I see millions denied education, recreation, and the opportunity to better their lot and the lot of their children.

I see millions lacking the means to buy the products of farm and factory and by their poverty denying work and productiveness to many other millions.

I see one-third of a nation ill-housed, ill-clad, ill-nourished.

It is not in despair that I paint you that picture. I paint it for you in hope—because the Nation, seeing and understanding the injustice in it, proposes to paint it out. We are determined to make every American citizen the subject of his country's interest and concern; and we will never regard any faithful law-abiding group within our borders as superfluous. The test of our progress is not whether we add more to the abundance of those who have much; it is whether we provide enough for those who have too little.

If I know aught of the spirit and purpose of our Nation, we will not listen to Comfort, Opportunism, and Timidity. We will carry on.

Overwhelmingly, we of the Republic are men and women of good will; men and women who have more than warm hearts of dedication; men and women who have cool heads and willing hands of practical purpose as well. They will insist that every agency of popular government use effective instruments to carry out their will.

Government is competent when all who compose it work as trustees for the whole people. It can make constant progress when it keeps abreast of all the facts. It can obtain justified support and legitimate criticism when the people receive true information of all that government does.

If I know aught of the will of our people, they will demand that these conditions of effective government shall be created and maintained. They will demand a nation uncorrupted by cancers of injustice and, therefore, strong among the nations in its example of the will to peace.

Today we reconsecrate our country to long-cherished ideals in a suddenly changed civilization. In every land there are always at work forces that drive men apart and forces that draw men together. In our personal ambitions we are individualists. But in our seeking for economic and political progress as a nation, we all go up, or else we all go down, as one people.

To maintain a democracy of effort requires a vast amount of patience in dealing with differing methods, a vast amount of humility. But out of the confusion of many voices rises an understanding of dominant public need. Then political leadership can voice common ideals, and aid in their realization.

In taking again the oath of office as President of the United States, I assume the solemn obligation of leading the American people forward along the road over which they have chosen to advance.

While this duty rests upon me I shall do my utmost to speak their purpose and to do their will, seeking Divine guidance to help us each and every one to give light to them that sit in darkness and to guide our feet into the way of peace.

THE FOUR FREEDOMS: ADDRESS TO CONGRESS JANUARY 6, 1941

IN the future days, which we seek to make secure, we look forward to a world founded upon four essential human freedoms. The first is freedom of speech and expression — everywhere in the world.

The second is freedom of every person to worship God in his own way — everywhere in the world.

The third is freedom from want — which, translated into world terms, means economic understandings which will secure to every nation a healthy peacetime life for its inhabitants — everywhere in the world.

The fourth is freedom from fear — which, translated into world terms, means a world-wide reduction of armaments to such a point and in such a thorough fashion that no nation will be in a position to commit an act of physical aggression against any neighbor— anywhere in the world.

That is no vision of a distant millennium. It is a definite basis for a kind oi world attainable in our own time and generation. That kind of world is the very antithesis of the so-called new order of tyranny which the dictators seek to create with the crash of a bomb.

To that new order we oppose the greater conception — the moral order. A good society is able to face schemes of world domination and foreign revolutions alike without fear.

Since the beginning of our American history, we have been engaged in change — in a perpetual peaceful revolution — a revolution which goes on steadily, quietly adjusting itself to changing conditions — without the concentration camp or the quick-lime in the ditch. The world order which we seek is the cooperation of free countries, working together in a friendly, civilized society.

This nation has placed its destiny in the hands and heads

and hearts of its millions of free men and women; and its faith in freedom under the guidance of God. Freedom means the supremacy of human rights everywhere. Our support goes to those who struggle to gain those rights or keep them. Our strength is our unity of purpose.

To that high concept there can be no end save victory.

THIRD INAUGURAL ADDRESS
MONDAY, JANUARY 20, 1941

ON each national day of inauguration since 1789, the people have renewed their sense of dedication to the United States.

In Washington's day the task of the people was to create and weld together a nation.

In Lincoln's day the task of the people was to preserve that Nation from disruption from within.

In this day the task of the people is to save that Nation and its institutions from disruption from without.

To us there has come a time, in the midst of swift happenings, to pause for a moment and take stock—to recall what our place in history has been, and to rediscover what we are and what we may be. If we do not, we risk the real peril of inaction.

Lives of nations are determined not by the count of years, but by the lifetime of the human spirit. The life of a man is three-score years and ten: a little more, a little less. The life of a nation is the fullness of the measure of its will to live.

There are men who doubt this. There are men who believe that democracy, as a form of Government and a frame of life, is limited or measured by a kind of mystical and artificial fate that, for some unexplained reason, tyranny and slavery have become the surging wave of the future—and that freedom is an ebbing tide.

But we Americans know that this is not true.

Eight years ago, when the life of this Republic seemed frozen by a fatalistic terror, we proved that this is not true. We were in the midst of shock—but we acted. We acted quickly, boldly, decisively.

These later years have been living years—fruitful years for the people of this democracy. For they have brought to us greater security and, I hope, a better understanding that life's ideals are to be measured in other than material things.

Most vital to our present and our future is this experience of a democracy which successfully survived crisis at home; put away many evil things; built new structures on enduring lines; and, through it all, maintained the fact of its democracy.

For action has been taken within the three-way framework of the Constitution of the United States. The coordinate branches of the Government continue freely to function. The Bill of Rights remains inviolate. The freedom of elections is wholly maintained. Prophets of the downfall of American democracy have seen their dire predictions come to naught.

Democracy is not dying. We know it because we have seen it revive—and grow.

We know it cannot die—because it is built on the unhampered initiative of individual men and women joined together in a common enterprise—an enterprise undertaken and carried through by the free expression of a free majority.

We know it because democracy alone, of all forms of government, enlists the full force of men's enlightened will.

We know it because democracy alone has constructed an unlimited civilization capable of infinite progress in the improvement of human life.

We know it because, if we look below the surface, we sense it still spreading on every continent—for it is the most humane, the most advanced, and in the end the most unconquerable of all forms of human society.

A nation, like a person, has a body—a body that must be fed and clothed and housed, invigorated and rested, in a manner that measures up to the objectives of our time.

A nation, like a person, has a mind—a mind that must be kept informed and alert, that must know itself, that understands the hopes and the needs of its neighbors—all the other nations that live within the narrowing circle of the world.

And a nation, like a person, has something deeper, something more permanent, something larger than the sum of all its parts. It is that something which matters most to its future—which calls forth the most sacred guarding of its present.

It is a thing for which we find it difficult—even impossible—to hit upon a single, simple word.

And yet we all understand what it is—the spirit—the faith of America. It is the product of centuries. It was born in the multitudes of those who came from many lands—some of high degree, but mostly plain people, who sought here, early and late, to find freedom more freely.

The democratic aspiration is no mere recent phase in human history. It is human history. It permeated the ancient life of early peoples. It blazed anew in the middle ages. It was written in Magna Charta.

In the Americas its impact has been irresistible. America has been the New World in all tongues, to all peoples, not because this continent was a new-found land, but because all those who came here believed they could create upon this continent a new life—a life that should be new in freedom.

Its vitality was written into our own Mayflower Compact, into the Declaration of Independence, into the Constitution of the United States, into the Gettysburg Address.

Those who first came here to carry out the longings of their spirit, and the millions who followed, and the stock that sprang from them—all have moved forward constantly and consistently toward an ideal which in itself has gained stature and clarity with each generation.

The hopes of the Republic cannot forever tolerate either undeserved poverty or self-serving wealth.

We know that we still have far to go; that we must more greatly build the security and the opportunity and the knowledge of every citizen, in the measure justified by the resources and the capacity of the land.

But it is not enough to achieve these purposes alone. It is not enough to clothe and feed the body of this Nation, and instruct and inform its mind. For there is also the spirit. And of the three, the greatest is the spirit.

Without the body and the mind, as all men know, the Nation could not live.

But if the spirit of America were killed, even though the Nation's body and mind, constricted in an alien world, lived on, the America we know would have perished.

That spirit—that faith—speaks to us in our daily lives in ways often unnoticed, because they seem so obvious. It speaks to us here in the Capital of the Nation. It speaks to us through the processes of governing in the sovereignties of 48 States. It speaks to us in our counties, in our cities, in our towns, and in our villages. It speaks to us from the other nations of the hemisphere, and from those across the seas—the enslaved, as well as the free. Sometimes we fail to hear or heed these voices of freedom because to us the privilege of our freedom is such an old, old story.

The destiny of America was proclaimed in words of prophecy spoken by our first President in his first inaugural in 1789—words almost directed, it would seem, to this year of 1941: "The preservation of the sacred fire of liberty and the destiny of the republican model of government are justly considered ... deeply,... finally, staked on the experiment intrusted to the hands of the American people."

If we lose that sacred fire—if we let it be smothered with doubt and fear—then we shall reject the destiny which Washington strove so valiantly and so triumphantly to establish. The preservation of the spirit and faith of the Nation does, and will, furnish the highest justification for every sacrifice that we may make in the cause of national defense.

In the face of great perils never before encountered, our strong purpose is to protect and to perpetuate the integrity of democracy.

For this we muster the spirit of America, and the faith of America.

We do not retreat. We are not content to stand still. As Americans, we go forward, in the service of our country, by the will of God.

D-DAY PRAYER, JUNE 6, 1944

My Fellow Americans:

LAST night, when I spoke with you about the fall of Rome, I knew at that moment that troops of the United States and our Allies were crossing the Channel in another and greater operation. It has come to pass with success thus far.

And so, in this poignant hour, I ask you to join with me in prayer:

Almighty God: Our sons, pride of our nation, this day have set upon a mighty endeavor, a struggle to preserve our Republic, our religion, and our civilization, and to set free a suffering humanity.

Lead them straight and true; give strength to their arms, stoutness to their hearts, steadfastness in their faith.

They will need Thy blessings. Their road will be long and hard. For the enemy is strong. He may hurl back our forces. Success may not come with rushing speed, but we shall return again and again; and we know that by Thy grace, and by the righteousness of our cause, our sons will triumph.

They will be sore tried, by night and by day, without rest — until the victory is won. The darkness will be rent by noise and flame. Men?s souls will be shaken with the violences of war.

For these men are lately drawn from the ways of peace. They fight not for the lust of conquest. They fight to end conquest. They fight to liberate. They fight to let justice arise, and tolerance and goodwill among all Thy people. They yearn but for the end of battle, for their return to the haven of home.

Some will never return. Embrace these, Father, and receive them, Thy heroic servants, into Thy kingdom.

And for us at home — fathers, mothers, children, wives, sisters, and brothers of brave men overseas, whose thoughts and prayers are ever with them — help us, Almighty God, to rededicate ourselves in renewed faith in Thee in this hour of great sacrifice.

Many people have urged that I call the nation into a single day of special prayer. But because the road is long and the desire is great, I ask that our people devote themselves in a continuance of prayer. As we rise to each new day, and again when each day is spent, let words of prayer be on our lips, invoking Thy help to our efforts.

Give us strength, too strength in our daily tasks, to redouble the contributions we make in the physical and the material support of our armed forces.

And let our hearts be stout, to wait out the long travail, to bear sorrows that may come, to impart our courage unto our sons wheresoever they may be.

And, O Lord, give us faith. Give us faith in Thee; faith in our sons; faith in each other; faith in our united crusade. Let not the keeness of our spirit ever be dulled. Let not the impacts of temporary events, of temporal matters of but fleeting moment — let not these deter us in our unconquerable purpose.

With Thy blessing, we shall prevail over the unholy forces of our enemy. Help us to conquer the apostles of greed and racial arrogances. Lead us to the saving of our country, and with our sister nations into a world unity that will spell a sure peace — a peace invulnerable to the schemings of unworthy men. And a peace that will let all of men live in freedom, reaping the just rewards of their honest toil.

Thy will be done, Almighty God. Amen.

FOURTH INAUGURAL ADDRESS
SATURDAY, JANUARY 20, 1945

MR. Chief Justice, Mr. Vice President, my friends, you will understand and, I believe, agree with my wish that the form of this inauguration be simple and its words brief.

We Americans of today, together with our allies, are passing through a period of supreme test. It is a test of our courage—

of our resolve—of our wisdom—our essential democracy.

If we meet that test—successfully and honorably—we shall perform a service of historic importance which men and women and children will honor throughout all time.

As I stand here today, having taken the solemn oath of office in the presence of my fellow countrymen—in the presence of our God—I know that it is America's purpose that we shall not fail.

In the days and in the years that are to come we shall work for a just and honorable peace, a durable peace, as today we work and fight for total victory in war.

We can and we will achieve such a peace.

We shall strive for perfection. We shall not achieve it immediately—but we still shall strive. We may make mistakes—but they must never be mistakes which result from faintness of heart or abandonment of moral principle.

I remember that my old schoolmaster, Dr. Peabody, said, in days that seemed to us then to be secure and untroubled: "Things in life will not always run smoothly. Sometimes we will be rising toward the heights—then all will seem to reverse itself and start downward. The great fact to remember is that the trend of civilization itself is forever upward; that a line drawn through the middle of the peaks and the valleys of the centuries always has an upward trend."

Our Constitution of 1787 was not a perfect instrument; it is not perfect yet. But it provided a firm base upon which all manner of men, of all races and colors and creeds, could build our solid structure of democracy.

And so today, in this year of war, 1945, we have learned lessons—at a fearful cost—and we shall profit by them.

We have learned that we cannot live alone, at peace; that our own well-being is dependent on the well-being of other nations far away. We have learned that we must live as men, not as ostriches, nor as dogs in the manger.

We have learned to be citizens of the world, members of the human community.

We have learned the simple truth, as Emerson said, that "The only way to have a friend is to be one."

We can gain no lasting peace if we approach it with suspicion and mistrust or with fear. We can gain it only if we proceed with the understanding, the confidence, and the courage which flow from conviction.

The Almighty God has blessed our land in many ways. He has given our people stout hearts and strong arms with which to strike mighty blows for freedom and truth. He has given to our country a faith which has become the hope of all peoples in an anguished world.

So we pray to Him now for the vision to see our way clearly—to see the way that leads to a better life for ourselves and for all our fellow men—to the achievement of His will to peace on earth.

GEORGE W. BUSH

INTRODUCTION

President Bush was born on June 12, 1924, in in Milton, Massachusetts. On his 18th birthday he enlisted in the armed forces. The youngest pilot in the Navy when he received his wings, he flew 58 combat missions during World War II.

He was the 41st President of the United States. In 1980 Bush campaigned for the Republican nomination for President. He lost, but was chosen as a running mate by Ronald Reagan. As Vice President, Bush had responsibility in several domestic areas, including Federal deregulation and anti-drug programs, and visited scores of foreign countries. In 1988 Bush won the Republican nomination for President and, with Senator Dan Quayle of Indiana as his running mate, he defeated Massachusetts Governor Michael Dukakis in the general election. In 1992 he lost his bid for reelection to Democrat William Clinton.

INAUGURAL ADDRESS
FRIDAY, JANUARY 20, 1989

MR. Chief Justice, Mr. President, Vice President Quayle, Senator Mitchell, Speaker Wright, Senator Dole, Congressman Michel, and fellow citizens, neighbors, and friends:

There is a man here who has earned a lasting place in our hearts and in our history. President Reagan, on behalf of our Nation, I thank you for the wonderful things that you have done for America.

I have just repeated word for word the oath taken by George Washington 200 years ago, and the Bible on which I placed my hand is the Bible on which he placed his. It is right that the memory of Washington be with us today, not only because this is our Bicentennial Inauguration, but because Washington remains the Father of our Country. And he would, I think, be gladdened by this day; for today is the concrete expression of a stunning fact: our continuity these 200 years since our government began.

We meet on democracy's front porch, a good place to talk as neighbors and as friends. For this is a day when our nation is made whole, when our differences, for a moment, are suspended.

And my first act as President is a prayer. I ask you to bow your heads:

Heavenly Father, we bow our heads and thank You for Your love. Accept our thanks for the peace that yields this day and the shared faith that makes its continuance likely. Make us strong to do Your work, willing to heed and hear Your will, and write on our hearts these words: "Use power to help people." For we are given power not to advance our own purposes, nor to make a great show in the world, nor a name. There is but one just use of power, and it is to serve people. Help us to remember it, Lord. Amen.

I come before you and assume the Presidency at a moment rich with promise. We live in a peaceful, prosperous time, but we can make it better. For a new breeze is blowing, and a world refreshed by freedom seems reborn; for in man's heart, if not in fact, the day of the dictator is over. The totalitarian era is passing, its old ideas blown away like leaves from an ancient, lifeless tree. A new breeze is blowing, and a nation refreshed by freedom stands ready to push on. There is new ground to be broken, and new action to be taken. There are times when the future seems thick as a fog; you sit and wait, hoping the mists will lift and reveal the right path. But this is a time when the future seems a door you can walk right through into a room called tomorrow.

Great nations of the world are moving toward democracy through the door to freedom. Men and women of the world move toward free markets through the door to prosperity. The people of the world agitate for free expression and free thought through the door to the moral and intellectual satisfactions that only liberty allows.

We know what works: Freedom works. We know what's right: Freedom is right. We know how to secure a more just and prosperous life for man on Earth: through free markets, free speech, free elections, and the exercise of free will unhampered by the state.

For the first time in this century, for the first time in perhaps all history, man does not have to invent a system by which to live. We don't have to talk late into the night about which form of government is better. We don't have to wrest justice from the kings. We only have to summon it from within ourselves. We must act on what we know. I take as my guide the hope of a saint: In crucial things, unity; in important things, diversity; in all things, generosity.

America today is a proud, free nation, decent and civil, a place we cannot help but love. We know in our hearts, not loudly and proudly, but as a simple fact, that this country has meaning beyond what we see, and that our strength is a force for good. But have we changed as a nation even in our time? Are we enthralled with material things, less appreciative of the nobility of work and sacrifice?

My friends, we are not the sum of our possessions. They are not the measure of our lives. In our hearts we know what matters. We cannot hope only to leave our children a bigger car, a bigger bank account. We must hope to give them a sense of what it means to be a loyal friend, a loving parent, a citizen who leaves his home, his neighborhood and town better than he found it. What do we want the men and women who work with us to say when we are no longer there? That we were more driven to succeed than anyone around us? Or that we stopped to ask if a sick child had gotten better, and stayed a moment there to trade a word of friendship?

No President, no government, can teach us to remember

what is best in what we are. But if the man you have chosen to lead this government can help make a difference; if he can celebrate the quieter, deeper successes that are made not of gold and silk, but of better hearts and finer souls; if he can do these things, then he must.

America is never wholly herself unless she is engaged in high moral principle. We as a people have such a purpose today. It is to make kinder the face of the Nation and gentler the face of the world. My friends, we have work to do. There are the homeless, lost and roaming. There are the children who have nothing, no love, no normalcy. There are those who cannot free themselves of enslavement to whatever addiction—drugs, welfare, the demoralization that rules the slums. There is crime to be conquered, the rough crime of the streets. There are young women to be helped who are about to become mothers of children they can't care for and might not love. They need our care, our guidance, and our education, though we bless them for choosing life.

The old solution, the old way, was to think that public money alone could end these problems. But we have learned that is not so. And in any case, our funds are low. We have a deficit to bring down. We have more will than wallet; but will is what we need. We will make the hard choices, looking at what we have and perhaps allocating it differently, making our decisions based on honest need and prudent safety. And then we will do the wisest thing of all: We will turn to the only resource we have that in times of need always grows—the goodness and the courage of the American people.

I am speaking of a new engagement in the lives of others, a new activism, hands-on and involved, that gets the job done. We must bring in the generations, harnessing the unused talent of the elderly and the unfocused energy of the young. For not only leadership is passed from generation to generation, but so is stewardship. And the generation born after the Second World War has come of age.

I have spoken of a thousand points of light, of all the community organizations that are spread like stars throughout the Nation, doing good. We will work hand in hand, encouraging, sometimes leading, sometimes being led, rewarding. We will work on this in the White House, in the Cabinet agencies. I will go to the people and the programs that are the brighter points of light, and I will ask every member of my government to become involved. The old ideas are new again because they are not old, they are timeless: duty, sacrifice, commitment, and a patriotism that finds its expression in taking part and pitching in.

We need a new engagement, too, between the Executive and the Congress. The challenges before us will be thrashed out with the House and the Senate. We must bring the Federal budget into balance. And we must ensure that America stands before the world united, strong, at peace, and fiscally sound. But, of course, things may be difficult. We need compromise; we have had dissension. We need harmony; we have had a chorus of discordant voices.

For Congress, too, has changed in our time. There has grown a certain divisiveness. We have seen the hard looks and heard the statements in which not each other's ideas are challenged, but each other's motives. And our great parties have too often been far apart and untrusting of each other. It has been this way since Vietnam. That war cleaves us still. But, friends, that war began in earnest a quarter of a century ago; and surely the statute of limitations has been reached. This is a fact: The final lesson of Vietnam is that no great nation can long afford to be sundered by a memory. A new breeze is blowing, and the old bipartisanship must be made new again.

To my friends—and yes, I do mean friends—in the loyal opposition—and yes, I mean loyal: I put out my hand. I am putting out my hand to you, Mr. Speaker. I am putting out my hand to you, Mr. Majority Leader. For this is the thing: This is the age of the offered hand. We can't turn back clocks, and I don't want to. But when our fathers were young, Mr. Speaker, our differences ended at the water's edge. And we don't wish to turn back time, but when our mothers were young, Mr. Majority Leader, the Congress and the Executive were capable of working together to produce a budget on which this nation could live. Let us negotiate soon and hard. But in the end, let us produce. The American people await action. They didn't send us here to bicker. They ask us to rise above the merely partisan. "In crucial things, unity"—and this, my friends, is crucial.

To the world, too, we offer new engagement and a renewed vow: We will stay strong to protect the peace. The "offered hand" is a reluctant fist; but once made, strong, and can be used with great effect. There are today Americans who are held against their will in foreign lands, and Americans who are unaccounted for. Assistance can be shown here, and will be long remembered. Good will begets good will. Good faith can be a spiral that endlessly moves on.

Great nations like great men must keep their word. When America says something, America means it, whether a treaty or an agreement or a vow made on marble steps. We will always try to speak clearly, for candor is a compliment, but subtlety, too, is good and has its place. While keeping our alliances and friendships around the world strong, ever strong, we will continue the new closeness with the Soviet Union, consistent both with our security and with progress. One might say that our new relationship in part reflects the triumph of hope and strength over experience. But hope is good, and so are strength and vigilance.

Here today are tens of thousands of our citizens who feel the understandable satisfaction of those who have taken part in democracy and seen their hopes fulfilled. But my thoughts have been turning the past few days to those who would be watching at home, to an older fellow who will throw a salute by himself when the flag goes by, and the women who will tell her sons the words of the battle hymns. I don't mean this to be sentimental. I mean that on days like this, we remember that we are all part of a continuum, inescapably connected by the ties that bind.

Our children are watching in schools throughout our great land. And to them I say, thank you for watching democracy's big day. For democracy belongs to us all, and freedom is like a beautiful kite that can go higher and higher with the breeze. And to all I say: No matter what your circumstances or where you are, you are part of this day, you are part of the life of our great nation.

A President is neither prince nor pope, and I don't seek a window on men's souls. In fact, I yearn for a greater tolerance, an easy-goingness about each other's attitudes and way of life.

There are few clear areas in which we as a society must rise up united and express our intolerance. The most obvious now is drugs. And when that first cocaine was smuggled in on a ship, it may as well have been a deadly bacteria, so much has it hurt the body, the soul of our country. And there is much to be done and to be said, but take my word for it: This scourge will stop.

And so, there is much to do; and tomorrow the work begins. I do not mistrust the future; I do not fear what is ahead. For our problems are large, but our heart is larger. Our challenges are great, but our will is greater. And if our flaws are endless, God's love is truly boundless.

Some see leadership as high drama, and the sound of trumpets calling, and sometimes it is that. But I see history as a book with many pages, and each day we fill a page with acts of hopefulness and meaning. The new breeze blows, a page turns, the story unfolds. And so today a chapter begins, a small and stately story of unity, diversity, and generosity—shared, and written, together.

Thank you. God bless you and God bless the United States of America.

GEORGE WASHINGTON

INTRODUCTION

George Washington was born in 1732. He was Commander of American forces and First President of the USA.

Fought in the campaign of French and Indian War (1754-63); In 1787 he presided over the constitutional convention and became President, and in due course became a member of the Federalist Party.

FIRST INAUGURAL ADDRESS IN THE CITY OF NEW YORK, THURSDAY, APRIL 30, 1789

Fellow-Citizens of the Senate and of the House of Representatives:

AMONG the vicissitudes incident to life no event could have filled me with greater anxieties than that of which the notification was transmitted by your order, and received on the 14th day of the present month. On the one hand, I was summoned by my country, whose voice I can never hear but with veneration and love, from a retreat which I had chosen with the fondest predilection, and, in my flattering hopes, with an immutable decision, as the asylum of my declining years—a retreat which was rendered every day more necessary as well as more dear to me by the addition of habit to inclination, and of frequent interruptions in my health to the gradual waste committed on it by time. On the other hand, the magnitude and difficulty of the trust to which the voice of my country called me, being sufficient to awaken in the wisest and most experienced of her citizens a distrustful scrutiny into his qualifications, could not but overwhelm with despondence one who (inheriting inferior endowments from nature and unpracticed in the duties of civil administration) ought to be peculiarly conscious of his own deficiencies. In this conflict of emotions all I dare aver is that it has been my faithful study to collect my duty from a just appreciation of every circumstance by which it might be affected. All I dare hope is that if, in executing this task, I have been too much swayed by a grateful remembrance of former instances, or by an affectionate sensibility to this transcendent proof of the confidence of my fellow-citizens, and have thence too little consulted my incapacity as well as disinclination for the weighty and untried cares before me, my error will be palliated by the motives which mislead me, and its consequences be judged by my country with some share of the partiality in which they originated.

Such being the impressions under which I have, in obedience to the public summons, repaired to the present station, it would be peculiarly improper to omit in this first official act my fervent supplications to that Almighty Being who rules over the universe, who presides in the councils of nations, and whose providential aids can supply every human defect, that His benediction may consecrate to the liberties and happiness of the people of the United States a Government instituted by themselves for these essential purposes, and may enable every instrument employed in its administration to execute with success the functions allotted to his charge. In tendering this homage to the Great Author of every public and private good, I assure myself that it expresses your sentiments not less than my own, nor those of my fellow-citizens at large less than either. No people can be bound to acknowledge and adore the Invisible Hand which conducts the affairs of men more than those of the United States. Every step by which they have advanced to the character of an independent nation seems to have been distinguished by some token of providential agency; and in the important revolution just accomplished in the system of their united government the tranquil deliberations and voluntary consent of so many distinct communities from which the event has resulted can not be compared with the means by which most governments have been established without some return of pious gratitude, along with an humble anticipation of the future blessings which the past seem to presage. These reflections, arising out of the present crisis, have forced themselves too strongly on my mind to be suppressed. You will join with me, I trust, in thinking that there are none under the influence of which the proceedings of a new and free government can more auspiciously commence.

By the article establishing the executive department it is made the duty of the President "to recommend to your consideration such measures as he shall judge necessary and expedient." The circumstances under which I now meet you will acquit me from entering into that subject further than to refer to the great constitutional charter under which you are assembled, and which, in defining your powers, designates the objects to which your attention is to be given. It will be more consistent with those circumstances, and far more congenial with the feelings which actuate me, to substitute, in place of a recommendation of particular measures, the tribute that is due to the talents, the rectitude, and the patriotism which adorn the characters selected to devise and adopt them. In these honorable qualifications I behold the surest pledges that as on one side no local prejudices or attachments, no separate views nor party animosities, will misdirect the comprehensive and equal eye which ought to watch over this great assemblage of communities and interests, so, on another, that the foundation of our national policy will be laid in the pure and immutable principles of private morality, and the preeminence of free government be exemplified by all the attributes which can win the affections of its citizens and command the respect of the world. I dwell on this prospect with every satisfaction which an ardent love for my country can inspire, since there is no truth more thoroughly established than that there exists in the economy and course of nature an indissoluble union between virtue and happiness;

between duty and advantage; between the genuine maxims of an honest and magnanimous policy and the solid rewards of public prosperity and felicity; since we ought to be no less persuaded that the propitious smiles of Heaven can never be expected on a nation that disregards the eternal rules of order and right which Heaven itself has ordained; and since the preservation of the sacred fire of liberty and the destiny of the republican model of government are justly considered, perhaps, as *deeply,* as *finally,* staked on the experiment entrusted to the hands of the American people.

Besides the ordinary objects submitted to your care, it will remain with your judgment to decide how far an exercise of the occasional power delegated by the fifth article of the Constitution is rendered expedient at the present juncture by the nature of objections which have been urged against the system, or by the degree of inquietude which has given birth to them. Instead of undertaking particular recommendations on this subject, in which I could be guided by no lights derived from official opportunities, I shall again give way to my entire confidence in your discernment and pursuit of the public good; for I assure myself that whilst you carefully avoid every alteration which might endanger the benefits of an united and effective government, or which ought to await the future lessons of experience, a reverence for the characteristic rights of freemen and a regard for the public harmony will sufficiently influence your deliberations on the question how far the former can be impregnably fortified or the latter be safely and advantageously promoted.

To the foregoing observations I have one to add, which will be most properly addressed to the House of Representatives. It concerns myself, and will therefore be as brief as possible. When I was first honored with a call into the service of my country, then on the eve of an arduous struggle for its liberties, the light in which I contemplated my duty required that I should renounce every pecuniary compensation. From this resolution I have in no instance departed; and being still under the impressions which produced it, I must decline as inapplicable to myself any share in the personal emoluments which may be indispensably included in a permanent provision for the executive department, and must accordingly pray that the pecuniary estimates for the station in which I am placed may during my continuance in it be limited to such actual expenditures as the public good may be thought to require.

Having thus imparted to you my sentiments as they have been awakened by the occasion which brings us together, I shall take my present leave; but not without resorting once more to the benign Parent of the Human Race in humble supplication that, since He has been pleased to favor the American people with opportunities for deliberating in perfect tranquillity, and dispositions for deciding with unparalleled unanimity on a form of government for the security of their union and the advancement of their happiness, so His divine blessing may be equally *conspicuous* in the enlarged views, the temperate consultations, and the wise measures on which the success of this Government must depend.

SECOND INAUGURAL ADDRESS IN THE CITY OF PHILADELPHIA

MONDAY, MARCH 4, 1793

Fellow Citizens:

I AM again called upon by the voice of my country to execute the functions of its Chief Magistrate. When the occasion proper for it shall arrive, I shall endeavor to express the high sense I entertain of this distinguished honor, and of the confidence which has been reposed in me by the people of united America. Previous to the execution of any official act of the President the Constitution requires an oath of office. This oath I am now about to take, and in your presence: That if it shall be found during my administration of the Government I have in any instance violated willingly or knowingly the injunctions thereof, I may (besides incurring constitutional punishment) be subject to the upbraidings of all who are now witnesses of the present solemn ceremony.

HARRY S. TRUMAN

INTRODUCTION

Truman was born in Lamar, Missouri, in 1884. He grew up in Independence, and for 12 years prospered as a Missouri farmer.

He went to France during World War I as a captain in the Field Artillery. Returning, he married Elizabeth Virginia Wallace, and opened a haberdashery in Kansas City.

INAUGURAL ADDRESS
THURSDAY, JANUARY 20, 1949

MR. Vice President, Mr. Chief Justice, and fellow citizens, I accept with humility the honor which the American people have conferred upon me. I accept it with a deep resolve to do all that I can for the welfare of this Nation and for the peace of the world.

In performing the duties of my office, I need the help and prayers of every one of you. I ask for your encouragement and your support. The tasks we face are difficult, and we can accomplish them only if we work together.

Each period of our national history has had its special

challenges. Those that confront us now are as momentous as any in the past. Today marks the beginning not only of a new administration, but of a period that will be eventful, perhaps decisive, for us and for the world.

It may be our lot to experience, and in large measure to bring about, a major turning point in the long history of the human race. The first half of this century has been marked by unprecedented and brutal attacks on the rights of man, and by the two most frightful wars in history. The supreme need of our time is for men to learn to live together in peace and harmony.

The peoples of the earth face the future with grave uncertainty, composed almost equally of great hopes and great fears. In this time of doubt, they look to the United States as never before for good will, strength, and wise leadership.

It is fitting, therefore, that we take this occasion to proclaim to the world the essential principles of the faith by which we live, and to declare our aims to all peoples.

The American people stand firm in the faith which has inspired this Nation from the beginning. We believe that all men have a right to equal justice under law and equal opportunity to share in the common good. We believe that all men have the right to freedom of thought and expression. We believe that all men are created equal because they are created in the image of God.

From this faith we will not be moved.

The American people desire, and are determined to work for, a world in which all nations and all peoples are free to govern themselves as they see fit, and to achieve a decent and satisfying life. Above all else, our people desire, and are determined to work for, peace on earth—a just and lasting peace—based on genuine agreement freely arrived at by equals.

In the pursuit of these aims, the United States and other like-minded nations find themselves directly opposed by a regime with contrary aims and a totally different concept of life.

That regime adheres to a false philosophy which purports to offer freedom, security, and greater opportunity to mankind.

Misled by this philosophy, many peoples have sacrificed their liberties only to learn to their sorrow that deceit and mockery, poverty and tyranny, are their reward.

That false philosophy is communism.

Communism is based on the belief that man is so weak and inadequate that he is unable to govern himself, and therefore requires the rule of strong masters.

Democracy is based on the conviction that man has the moral and intellectual capacity, as well as the inalienable right, to govern himself with reason and justice.

Communism subjects the individual to arrest without lawful cause, punishment without trial, and forced labor as the chattel of the state. It decrees what information he shall receive, what art he shall produce, what leaders he shall follow, and what thoughts he shall think.

Democracy maintains that government is established for the benefit of the individual, and is charged with the responsibility of protecting the rights of the individual and his freedom in the exercise of his abilities.

Communism maintains that social wrongs can be corrected only by violence.

Democracy has proved that social justice can be achieved through peaceful change.

Communism holds that the world is so deeply divided into opposing classes that war is inevitable.

Democracy holds that free nations can settle differences justly and maintain lasting peace.

These differences between communism and democracy do not concern the United States alone. People everywhere are coming to realize that what is involved is material well-being, human dignity, and the right to believe in and worship God.

I state these differences, not to draw issues of belief as such, but because the actions resulting from the Communist philosophy are a threat to the efforts of free nations to bring about world recovery and lasting peace.

Since the end of hostilities, the United States has invested its substance and its energy in a great constructive effort to restore peace, stability, and freedom to the world.

We have sought no territory and we have imposed our will on none. We have asked for no privileges we would not extend to others.

We have constantly and vigorously supported the United Nations and related agencies as a means of applying democratic principles to international relations. We have consistently advocated and relied upon peaceful settlement of disputes among nations.

We have made every effort to secure agreement on effective international control of our most powerful weapon, and we have worked steadily for the limitation and control of all armaments.

We have encouraged, by precept and example, the expansion of world trade on a sound and fair basis.

Almost a year ago, in company with 16 free nations of Europe, we launched the greatest cooperative economic program in history. The purpose of that unprecedented effort is to invigorate and strengthen democracy in Europe, so that the free people of that continent can resume their rightful place in the forefront of civilization and can contribute once more to the security and welfare of the world.

Our efforts have brought new hope to all mankind. We have beaten back despair and defeatism. We have saved a number of countries from losing their liberty. Hundreds of millions of people all over the world now agree with us, that we need not have war—that we can have peace.

The initiative is ours.

We are moving on with other nations to build an even stronger structure of international order and justice. We shall have as our partners countries which, no longer solely concerned with the problem of national survival, are now working to improve the standards of living of all their people. We are ready to undertake new projects to strengthen the free world.

In the coming years, our program for peace and freedom will emphasize four major courses of action.

First, we will continue to give unfaltering support to the United Nations and related agencies, and we will continue to search for ways to strengthen their authority and increase their effectiveness. We believe that the United Nations will be strengthened by the new nations which are being formed in lands now advancing toward self-government under democratic principles.

Second, we will continue our programs for world economic recovery.

This means, first of all, that we must keep our full weight behind the European recovery program. We are confident of the success of this major venture in world recovery. We believe that our partners in this effort will achieve the status of self-supporting nations once again.

In addition, we must carry out our plans for reducing the barriers to world trade and increasing its volume. Economic recovery and peace itself depend on increased world trade.

Third, we will strengthen freedom-loving nations against the dangers of aggression.

We are now working out with a number of countries a joint agreement designed to strengthen the security of the North Atlantic area. Such an agreement would take the form of a collective defense arrangement within the terms of the United Nations Charter.

We have already established such a defense pact for the Western Hemisphere by the treaty of Rio de Janeiro.

The primary purpose of these agreements is to provide unmistakable proof of the joint determination of the free countries to resist armed attack from any quarter. Each country participating in these arrangements must contribute all it can to the common defense.

If we can make it sufficiently clear, in advance, that any armed attack affecting our national security would be met with overwhelming force, the armed attack might never occur.

I hope soon to send to the Senate a treaty respecting the North Atlantic security plan.

In addition, we will provide military advice and equipment to free nations which will cooperate with us in the maintenance of peace and security.

Fourth, we must embark on a bold new program for making the benefits of our scientific advances and industrial progress available for the improvement and growth of underdeveloped areas.

More than half the people of the world are living in conditions approaching misery. Their food is inadequate. They are victims of disease. Their economic life is primitive and stagnant. Their poverty is a handicap and a threat both to them and to more prosperous areas.

For the first time in history, humanity possesses the knowledge and the skill to relieve the suffering of these people.

The United States is pre-eminent among nations in the development of industrial and scientific techniques. The material resources which we can afford to use for the assistance of other peoples are limited. But our imponderable resources in technical knowledge are constantly growing and are inexhaustible.

I believe that we should make available to peace-loving peoples the benefits of our store of technical knowledge in order to help them realize their aspirations for a better life. And, in cooperation with other nations, we should foster capital investment in areas needing development.

Our aim should be to help the free peoples of the world, through their own efforts, to produce more food, more clothing, more materials for housing, and more mechanical power to lighten their burdens.

We invite other countries to pool their technological resources in this undertaking. Their contributions will be warmly welcomed. This should be a cooperative enterprise in which all nations work together through the United Nations and its specialized agencies wherever practicable. It must be a worldwide effort for the achievement of peace, plenty, and freedom.

With the cooperation of business, private capital, agriculture, and labor in this country, this program can greatly increase the industrial activity in other nations and can raise substantially their standards of living.

Such new economic developments must be devised and controlled to benefit the peoples of the areas in which they are established. Guarantees to the investor must be balanced by guarantees in the interest of the people whose resources and whose labor go into these developments.

The old imperialism—exploitation for foreign profit—has

no place in our plans. What we envisage is a program of development based on the concepts of democratic fair-dealing.

All countries, including our own, will greatly benefit from a constructive program for the better use of the world's human and natural resources. Experience shows that our commerce with other countries expands as they progress industrially and economically.

Greater production is the key to prosperity and peace. And the key to greater production is a wider and more vigorous application of modern scientific and technical knowledge.

Only by helping the least fortunate of its members to help themselves can the human family achieve the decent, satisfying life that is the right of all people.

Democracy alone can supply the vitalizing force to stir the peoples of the world into triumphant action, not only against their human oppressors, but also against their ancient enemies—hunger, misery, and despair.

On the basis of these four major courses of action we hope to help create the conditions that will lead eventually to personal freedom and happiness for all mankind.

If we are to be successful in carrying out these policies, it is clear that we must have continued prosperity in this country and we must keep ourselves strong.

Slowly but surely we are weaving a world fabric of international security and growing prosperity.

We are aided by all who wish to live in freedom from fear—even by those who live today in fear under their own governments.

We are aided by all who want relief from the lies of propaganda—who desire truth and sincerity.

We are aided by all who desire self-government and a voice in deciding their own affairs.

We are aided by all who long for economic security—for the security and abundance that men in free societies can enjoy.

We are aided by all who desire freedom of speech, freedom of religion, and freedom to live their own lives for useful ends.

Our allies are the millions who hunger and thirst after righteousness.

In due time, as our stability becomes manifest, as more and more nations come to know the benefits of democracy and to participate in growing abundance, I believe that those countries which now oppose us will abandon their delusions and join with the free nations of the world in a just settlement of international differences.

Events have brought our American democracy to new influence and new responsibilities. They will test our courage, our devotion to duty, and our concept of liberty.

But I say to all men, what we have achieved in liberty, we will surpass in greater liberty.

Steadfast in our faith in the Almighty, we will advance toward a world where man's freedom is secure.

To that end we will devote our strength, our resources, and our firmness of resolve. With God's help, the future of mankind will be assured in a world of justice, harmony, and peace.

HILLARY RODHAM CLINTON

INTRODUCTION

Hillary Diane Rodham, Dorothy and Hugh Rodham's first child, was born on October 26, 1947. Two brothers, Hugh and Tony, soon followed. Hillary's childhood in Park Ridge, Illinois, was happy and disciplined. She loved sports and her church, and was a member of the National Honor Society, and a student leader. Her parents encouraged her to study hard and to pursue any career that interested her.

She was elected United States Senator from New York on November 7, 2000. She is the first First Lady elected to the United States Senate and the first woman elected statewide in New York.

1969 STUDENT COMMENCEMENT SPEECH

MAY 31, 1969, WELLESLEY COLLEGE

I AM very glad that Miss Adams made it clear that what I am speaking for today is all of us — the 400 of us — and I find myself in a familiar position, that of reacting, something that our generation has been doing for quite a while now. We're not in the positions yet of leadership and power, but we do have that indispensable task of criticizing and constructive protest and I find myself reacting just briefly to some of the things that Senator Brooke said. This has to be brief because I do have a little speech to give. Part of the problem with empathy with professed goals is that empathy doesn't do us anything. We've had lots of empathy; we've had lots of sympathy, but we feel that for too long our leaders have used politics as the art of making what appears to be impossible, possible. What does it mean to hear that 13.3% of the people in this country are below the poverty line? That's a percentage. We're not interested in social reconstruction; it's human reconstruction. How can we talk about percentages and trends? The complexities are not lost in our analyses, but perhaps they're just put into what we consider a more human and eventually a more progressive perspective. The question about possible and impossible was one that we brought with us to Wellesley four years ago. We arrived not yet knowing what was not possible. Consequently, we expected a lot. Our attitudes are easily understood having grown up, having come to consciousness in the first five years of this decade — years dominated by men with dreams, men in the civil rights movement, the Peace Corps, the space program, so we arrived at Wellesley and we found, as all of us have found, that there was a gap between expectation and realities. But it wasn't a discouraging gap and it didn't turn us into cynical, bitter old women at the age of 18. It just inspired us to do something about that gap. What we did is often difficult for some people to understand. They ask us quite often: "Why, if you're dissatisfied, do you stay in a place?" Well, if you didn't care a lot about it you wouldn't stay. It's almost as though my mother used to say, "I'll always love you but there are times when I certainly won't like you." Our love for this place, this particular place, Wellesley College, coupled with our freedom from the burden of an inauthentic reality allowed us to question basic assumptions underlying our education. Before the days of the media orchestrated demonstrations, we had our own gathering over in Founder's parking lot. We protested against the rigid academic distribution requirement. We worked for a pass-fail system. We worked for a say in some of the process of academic decision making. And luckily we were in a place where, when we questioned the meaning of a liberal arts education there were people with enough imagination to respond to that questioning.

So we have made progress. We have achieved some of the things that initially saw as lacking in that gap between expectation and reality. Our concerns were not, of course, solely academic as all of us know. We worried about inside Wellesley questions of admissions, the kind of people that should be coming to Wellesley, the process for getting them here. We questioned about what responsibility we should have both for our lives as individuals and for our lives as members of a collective group.

Coupled with our concerns for the Wellesley inside here in the community were our concerns for what happened beyond Hathaway House. We wanted to know what relationship Wellesley was going to have to the outer world. We were lucky in that one of the first things Miss Adams did was to set up a cross-registration with MIT because everyone knows that education just can't have any parochial bounds any more. One of the other things that we did was the Upward Bound program. There are so many other things that we could talk about; so many attempts, at least the way we saw it, to pull ourselves into the world outside. And I think we've succeeded. There will be an Upward Bound program, just for one example, on the campus this summer.

Many of the issues that I've mentioned — those of sharing power and responsibility, those of assuming power and responsibility have been general concerns on campuses throughout the world. But underlying those concerns there is a theme, a theme which is so trite and so old because the words are so familiar. It talks about integrity and trust and respect. Words have a funny way of trapping our minds on the way to our tongues but there are necessary means even in this multimedia age for attempting to come to grasps with some of the inarticulate maybe even inarticulable things that we're feeling. We are, all of us, exploring a world that none of us even understands and attempting to create within that uncertainty. But there are some things we feel, feelings that our prevailing, acquisitive, and competitive corporate life, including tragically the universities, is not the way of life for us. We're searching for more immediate, ecstatic and penetrating mode of living. And so our questions, our questions about our institutions, about our colleges, about our churches, about our government continue. The questions about those institutions are familiar to all of us. We have seen heralded across the newspapers. Senator Brooke has suggested some of them this morning. But along with using these words "integrity, trust, and respect" in regard to institutions and leaders we're perhaps harshest with them in regard to ourselves.

Every protest, every dissent, whether it's an individual academic paper, Founder's parking lot demonstration, is unabashedly an attempt to forge an identity in this particular age. That attempt at forging for many of us over the past four years has meant coming to terms with our humanness. Within the context of a society that we perceive — now we can talk about reality, and I would like to talk about reality sometime, authentic reality, inauthentic reality, and what we have to accept of what we see — but our perception of it is that it hovers often between the possibility of disaster and the potentiality for imaginatively responding to men's needs. There's a very strange conservative strain that goes through a lot of New Left, collegiate protests that I find very intriguing because it harkens back to a lot of the old virtues, to the fulfillment of original ideas. And it's also a very unique American experience. It's such a great adventure. If the experiment in human living doesn't work in this country, in this age, it's not going to work anywhere.

But we also know that to be educated, the goal of it must be human liberation. A liberation enabling each of us to fulfill our capacity so as to be free to create within and around ourselves. To be educated to freedom must be evidenced in action, and here again is where we ask ourselves, as we have asked our parents and our teachers, questions about integrity, trust, and respect. Those three words mean different things to all of us. Some of the things they can mean, for instance: Integrity, the courage to be whole, to try to mold an entire person in this particular context, living in relation to one another in the full poetry of existence. If the only tool we have ultimately to use is our lives, so we use it in the way we can by choosing a way to live that will demonstrate the way we feel and the way we know. Integrity — a man like Paul Santmire. Trust. This is one word that when I asked the class at our rehearsal what it was they wanted me to say for them, everyone came up to me and said "Talk about trust, talk about the lack of trust both for us and the way we feel about others. Talk about the trust bust." What can you say about it? What can you say about a feeling that permeates a generation and that perhaps is not even understood by those who are distrusted? All they can do is keep trying again and again and again. There's that wonderful line in East Coker by Eliot about there's only the trying, again and again and again; to win again what we've lost before.

And then respect. There's that mutuality of respect between people where you don't see people as percentage points. Where you don't manipulate people. Where you're not interested in social engineering for people. The struggle for an integrated life existing in an atmosphere of communal trust and respect is one with desperately important political and social consequences. And the word "consequences" of course catapults us into the future. One of the most tragic things that happened yesterday, a beautiful day, was that I was talking to woman who said that she wouldn't want to be me for anything in the world. She wouldn't want to live today and look ahead to what it is she sees because she's afraid. Fear is always with us but we just don't have time for it. Not now.

There are two people that I would like to thank before concluding. That's Ellie Acheson, who is the spearhead for this, and also Nancy Scheibner who wrote this poem which is the last thing that I would like to read:

My entrance into the world of so-called "social problems". Must be with quiet laughter, or not at all. The hollow men of anger and bitterness, The bountiful ladies of righteous degradation All must be left to a bygone age. And the purpose of history is to provide a receptacle.

For all those myths and oddments Which oddly we have acquired.

And from which we would become unburdened To create a newer world.

To transform the future into the present.

We have no need of false revolutions

In a world where categories tend to tyrannize our minds.
And hang our wills up on narrow pegs.
It is well at every given moment to seek the limits in our lives.
And once those limits are understood
To understand that limitations no longer exist.
Earth could be fair. And you and I must be free
Not to save the world in a glorious crusade
Not to kill ourselves with a nameless gnawing pain
But to practice with all the skill of our being
The art of making possible.

WOMEN'S RIGHTS ARE HUMAN RIGHTS
SEPTEMBER 5, 1995, BEIJING, CHINA

THIS speech was given during the United Nations Fourth World Conference on Women.

Thank you very much Gertrude Mongella, for your dedicated work that has brought us to this point.

Distinguished delegates and guests, I would like to thank the Secretary General of the United Nations for inviting me to be part of this important United Nations Fourth World Conference on Women. This is truly a celebration — a celebration of the contributions women make in every aspect of life: in the home, on the job, in the community, as mothers, wives, sisters, daughters, learners, workers, citizens and leaders.

It is also a coming together, much the way women come together every day in every country.

We come together in fields and in factories. In village markets and supermarkets. In living rooms and board rooms.

Whether it is while playing with our children in the park, or washing clothes in a river, or taking a break at the office water cooler, we come together and talk about our aspirations and concerns. And time and again, our talk turns to our children and our families.

However different we may appear, there is far more that unites us than divides us. We share a common future. And we are here to find common ground so that we may help bring new dignity and respect to women and girls all over the world — and in so doing, bring new strength and stability to families as well.

By gathering in Beijing, we are focusing world attention on issues that matter most in the lives of women and their families: access to education, health care, jobs, and credit, the chance to enjoy basic legal and human rights and to participate fully in the political life of their countries.

There are some who question the reason for this conference. Let them listen to the voices of women in their homes, neighborhoods, and workplaces.

There are some who wonder whether the lives of women and girls matter to economic and political progress around the globe. ... Let them look at the women gathered here and at Hairou.... the homemakers, nurses, teachers, lawyers, policymakers, and women who run their own businesses.

It is conferences like this that compel governments and peoples everywhere to listen, look and face the world's most pressing problems.

Wasn't it after the women's conference in Nairobi ten years ago that the world focused for the first time on the crisis of domestic violence?

Earlier today, I participated in a World Health Organization forum. In that forum we talked about ways that where government officials, NGOs, and individual citizens are working on ways to address the health problems of women and girls.

Tomorrow, I will attend a gathering of the United Nations Development Fund for Women. There, the discussion will focus on local — and highly successful — programs that give hard_working women access to credit so they can improve their own lives and the lives of their families.

What we are learning around the world is that, if women are healthy and educated, their families will flourish. If women are free from violence, their families will flourish. If women have a chance to work and earn as full and equal partners in society, their families will flourish.

And when families flourish, communities and nations will flourish.

That is why every woman, every man, every child, every family, and every nation on our planet does have a stake in the discussion that takes place here.

Over the past 25 years, I have worked persistently on issues relating to women, children and families. Over the past two and a half years, I have had the opportunity to learn more about the challenges facing women in my own country and around the world.

I have met new mothers in Indonesia, who come together regularly in their village to discuss nutrition, family planning, and baby care.

I have met working parents in Denmark who talk about the comfort they feel in knowing that their children can be cared for in creative, safe, and nurturing after school centers.

I have met women in South Africa who helped lead the struggle to end apartheid and are now helping build a new democracy.

I have met with the leading women of my own hemisphere who are working every day to promote literacy and better health care for the children in their countries.

I have met women in India and Bangladesh who are taking out small loans to buy milk cows, rickshaws, thread and other materials to create a livelihood for themselves and their families.

I have met doctors and nurses in Belarus and Ukraine who are trying to keep children alive in the aftermath of Chernobyl.

The great challenge of this conference is to give voice to women everywhere whose experiences go unnoticed, whose words go unheard.

Women comprise more than half the world's population. Women are 70% percent of the world's poor, and two thirds of those who are not taught to read and write.

Women are the primary caretakers for most of the world's children and elderly. Yet much of the work we do is not valued — not by economists, not by historians, not by popular culture, not by government leaders.

At this very moment, as we sit here, women around the world are giving birth, raising children, cooking meals, washing clothes, cleaning houses, planting crops, working on assembly lines, running companies, and running countries.

Women also are dying from diseases that should have been prevented or treated; they are watching their children succumb to malnutrition caused by poverty and economic deprivation; they are being denied the right to go to school by their own fathers and brothers; they are being forced into prostitution, and they are being barred from the bank lending office and banned from the ballot box.

Those of us who have the opportunity to be here have the responsibility to speak for those who could not.

As an American, I want to speak up for women in my own country — women who are raising children on the minimum wage, women who can't afford health care or child care, women whose lives are threatened by violence, including violence in their own homes.

I want to speak up for mothers who are fighting for good schools, safe neighborhoods, clean air and clean airwaves.....for older women, some of them widows, who have raised their families and now find that their skills and life experiences are not valued in the workplace... for women who are working all night as nurses, hotel clerks, and fast food chefs so that they can be at home during the day with their kids... and for women everywhere who simply don't have time to do everything they are called upon to do each day.

Speaking to you today, I speak for them, just as each of us speaks for women around the world who are denied the chance to go to school, or see a doctor, or own property, or have a say about the direction of their lives, simply because they are women.

The truth is that most women around the world work both inside and outside the home, usually by necessity.

We need to understand that there is no one formula for how women should lead their lives.

That is why we must respect the choices that each woman makes for herself and her family. Every woman deserves the chance to realize her God given potential.

We also must recognize that women will never gain full dignity until their human rights are respected and protected.

Our goals for this conference, to strengthen families and societies by empowering women to take greater control over their own destinies, cannot be fully achieved unless all governments — here and around the world — accept their responsibility to protect and promote internationally recognized human rights.

The international community has long acknowledged — and recently affirmed at Vienna — that both women and men are entitled to a range of protections and personal freedoms, from the right of personal security to the right to determine freely the number and spacing of the children they bear.

No one should be forced to remain silent for fear of religious or political persecution, arrest, abuse or torture.

Tragically, women are most often the ones whose human rights are violated.

Even in the late 20th century, the rape of women continues to be used as an instrument of armed conflict. Women and children make up a large majority of the world's refugees. And when women are excluded from the political process, they become even more vulnerable to abuse.

I believe that, on the eve of a new millennium, it is time to break our silence. It is time for us to say here in Beijing; and the world to hear, that it is no longer acceptable to discuss women's rights as separate from human rights.

These abuses have continued because, for too long, the history of women has been a history of silence. Even today, there are those who are trying to silence our words.

The voices of this conference and of the women at Hairou must be heard loud and clear:

It is a violation of human rights when babies are denied food, or drowned, or suffocated, or their spines broken, simply because they are born girls.

It is a violation of human rights when women and girls are sold into the slavery of prostitution.

It is a violation of human rights when women are doused

with gasoline, set on fire and burned to death because their marriage dowries are deemed too small.

It is a violation of human rights when individual women are raped in their own communities and when thousands of women are subjected to rape as a tactic or prize of war.

It is a violation of human rights when a leading cause of death worldwide among women ages 14 to 44 is the violence they are subjected to in their own homes by their own relatives.

It is a violation of human rights when young girls are brutalized by the painful and degrading practice of genital mutilation.

It is a violation of human rights when women are denied the right to plan their own families, and that includes being forced to have abortions or being sterilized against their will.

If there is one message that echoes forth from this conference, let it be that human rights are women's rights.... And women's rights are human rights, once and for all.

Let us not forget that among those rights are the right to speak freely. And the right to be heard.

Women must enjoy the right to participate fully in the social and political lives of their countries if we want freedom and democracy to thrive and endure.

It is indefensible that many women in non_governmental organizations who wished to participate in this conference have not been able to attend — or have been prohibited from fully taking part.

Let me be clear. Freedom means the right of people to assemble, organize, and debate openly. It means respecting the views of those who may disagree with the views of their governments.

INDIRA GANDHI

INTRODUCTION

Indira Nehru Gandhi was born on November 19, 1917 and would be the only child of Jawaharlal and Kamala Nehru.

In 1938, Indira finally joined the Indian National Congress Party, something she always longed to do. Soon afterwards in 1942, she married journalist Feroze Gandhi to whom she eventually bore two sons. Soon after the couple was married, they were sent to prison on charges of subversion by the British. Her first and only imprisonment lasted from September 11, 1942 until May 13, 1943 at the Naini Central Jail in Allahabad. She was assassinated by her own guards on October 31, 1984.

WHAT EDUCATED WOMEN CAN DO AT THE GOLDEN JUBILEE CELEBRATIONS OF THE INDRAPRASTHA COLLEGE FOR WOMEN NEW DELHI, INDIA, NOVEMBER 23, 1974

AN ancient Sanskrit saying says, woman is the home and the home is the basis of society. It is as we build our homes that we can build our country. If the home is inadequate — either inadequate in material goods and necessities or inadequate in the sort of friendly, loving atmosphere that every child needs to grow and develop — then that country cannot have harm ony and no country which does not have harmony can grow in any direction at all.

That is why women's education is almost more important than the education of boys and men. We — and by "we" I do not mean only we in India but all the world — have neglected women education. It is fairly rece nt. Of course, not to you but when I was a child, the story of early days of women's education in England, for instance, was very current. Everybody remembered what had happened in the early days.

I remember what used to happen here. I still remember the days when living in old Delhi even as a small child of seven or eight. I had to go ou t in a doli if I left the house. We just did not walk. Girls did not walk in the streets. First, you had your sari with which you covered your head, then you had another shawl or something with which you covered your hand and all the body, then you had a white shawl, with which every thing was covered again although your face was open fortunately. Then you were i n the doli, which again was covered by another cloth. And this was in a family or community which did not observe purdah of any kind at all. In fact, all our social functions always were mixed functions but this was the atmosphere of the city and of the country.

Now, we have got education and there is a debate all over the country whether this education is adequate to the needs of society or the needs of our young people. I am one of those who always believe that education needs a thorough overhauling. But at the same time, I think that everything in our education is not bad, that even the present education has produced very fine men and women, specially scientists and experts in different fields, who are in great demand all over the world and even in the most affluent countries. Many of our young people leave us and go abroad because they get higher salaries, they get better conditions of work.

But it is not all a one-sided business because there are many who are persuaded and cajoled to go even when they are reluctant. We know of first class students, especially in medicine or nuclear energy for instance, they are approached long before they have passed out and offered all kinds of inducements to go out. Now, that shows that people do consider that they have a standard of knowledge and capability which will be useful any where in the world.

So, that is why I say that there is something worthwhile. It also shows that our own ancient philosophy has taught us that nothing in life is entirely bad or entirely good. Everything is somewhat of a mixture and it depends on us and our capability how we can extract the good, how we can make use of what is around us. There are people who through observation can learn from anything that is around them. There are others who can be surrounded by the most fascinating people, the most wonderful books, and other things and who yet remain quite closed in and they are unable to take anything from this wealth around them.

Our country is a very rich country. It is rich in culture, it is rich in many old traditions — old and even modern tradition. Of course, it has a lot of bad things too and some of the bad things are in the society — superstition, which has grown over the years and which sometimes clouds over the shining brightness of ancient thought and values, eternal values. Then, of course, there is the physical poverty of large numbers of our people. That is something which is ugly and that hampers the growth of millions of young boys and girls. Now, all these bad things we have to fight against and that is what we are doing since Independence.

But, we must not allow this dark side of the picture which, by the way, exists in every country in the world. Even the most rich country in the world has its dark side, but usually other people hide their dark sides and they try to project the shining side or the side of achievement. Here in India, we seem to want to project the worst side of society. Before anybody does anything, he has to have, of course, knowledge and capability, but along with it he has to have a certain amount of pride in what he or she is doing. He has to have self-confidence in his own ability. If your teacher tells, "You cannot do this," even if you are a very bright student I think every time you will find, it will be more and more difficult for you to do it. But if your teacher encourages saying, "Go along you have done very good work, now try a little harder," then you will try a little harder and you will be able to do it. And it is the same with societies and with countries.

This country, India, has had remarkable achievements to its credit, of course in ancient times, but even in modern times, I think there are a few modern stories, success stories, which are as fascinating as the success story of our country. It is true that we have not banished poverty, we have not banished many of our social ills, but if you compare us to what we were just about 27 years ago, I think that you will not find a single other country that has been able to achieve so much under the most difficult circumstances.

Today, we are passing through specially dark days. But these are not dark days for India alone. Except for the countries which call themselves socialist and about which we do not really know very much, every other country has the same sort of economic problems, which we have. Only a few countries, which have very small populations, have no unemployment. Otherwise, the rich countries also today have unemployment. They have shortages of essential articles. They have shortages even of food.

I do not know how many of you know that the countries of Western Europe and Japan import 41 per cent of their food needs, whereas India imports just under two per cent. Yet, somehow we ourselves project an image that India is out with the begging bowl. And naturally when we ourselves say it, other people will say it much louder and much stronger. It is true, of course, that our two per cent is pretty big because we are a very big country and we have a far bigger population than almost any country in the world with the exception of China. We have to see and you, the educated women, because it is great privilege for you to have higher education, you have to try and see our problems in the perspective of what has happened here in this country and what is happening all over the world.

There is today great admiration for certain things that have happened in other countries where the society is quite differently formed, where no dissent is allowed. The same people who admire that system or the achievements of that system are the ones who say there is dictatorship here even though, I think, nobody has yet been able to point out to me which country has more freedom of expression or action. So, something is said and a lot of people without thinking keep on repeating it with additions until an entirely distorted picture of the country and of our people is presented.

As I said, we do have many shortcomings, whether it is the government, whether it is the society. Some are due to our traditions because, as I said, not all tradition is good. And one of the biggest responsibilities of the educated women today is how to synthesise what has been valuable and timeless in our ancient traditions with what is good and valuable in modern thought. All that is modern is not good just as all that is old is neither all good nor all bad. We have to decide, not once and for all but almost every week, every month what is coming out that is good and useful to our country and what of the old we can keep and enshrine in our society. To be modern, most people think that it is something of a manner of dress or a manner of speaking or certain habits and customs, but that is not really being modern. It is a very superficial part of modernity.

For instance, when I cut my hair, it was because of the sort of life that I was leading. We were all in the movement. You simply could not have long hair and go in the villages and wash it every day. So, when you lead a life, a particular kind of life, your clothes, your everything has to fit into that life if you are to be efficient. If you have to go in the villages and you have to bother whether your clothes are going to be dirty, then you cannot be a good worker. You have to forget everything of that kind. That is why, gradually, clothes and so on have changed in some countries because of the changes in the life-style. Does it suit our life-style or what we want to do or not? If it does, maybe we have to adopt some of these things not merely because it is done in another country and perhaps for another purpose. But what clothes we wear is really quite unimportant. What is important is how we are thinking.

Sometimes, I am very sad that even people who do science are quite unscientific in their thinking and in their other actions — not what they are doing in the laboratories but how they live at home or their attitudes towards other people. Now, for India to become what we want it to become with a modern, rational society and firmly based on what is good in our ancient tradition and in our soil, for this we have to have a thinking public, thinking young women who are not content to accept what comes from any part of the world but are willing to listen to it, to analyse it and to decide whether it is to be accepted or whether it is to be thrown out and this is the sort of education which we want, which enables our young people to adjust to this changing world and to be able to contribute to it.

Some people think that only by taking up very high jobs, you are doing something important or you are doing national service. But we all know that the most complex machinery will be ineffective if one small screw is not working as it should and that screw is just as important as any big part. It is the same in national life. There is no job that is too small; there is no person who is too small. Everybody has something to do. And if he or she does it well, then the country will run well.

In our superstition, we have thought that some work is

dirty work. For instance, sweeping has been regarded as dirty. Only some people can do it; others should not do it. Now we find that manure is the most valuable thing that the world has today and many of the world's economies are shaking because there is not enough fertilizer — and not just the chemical fertilizer but the ordinary manure, night-soil and all that sort of thing, things which were considered dirty.

Now it shows how beautifully balanced the world was with everything fitted in with something else. Everything, whether dirty or small, had a purpose. We, with our science and technology, have tried to — not purposely, but somehow, we have created an imbalance and that is what is troubling, on a big scale, the economies of the world and also people and individuals. They are feeling alienated from their societies, not only in India but almost in every country in the world, except in places where the whole purpose of education and government has to be to make the people conform to just one idea. We are told that people there are very happy in whatever they are doing. If they are told to clean the streets, well, if he is a professor he has to clean the streets, if he is a scientist he has to do it, and we were told that they are happy doing it. Well, if they are happy, it is alright.

But I do not think in India we can have that kind of society where people are forced to do things because we think that they can be forced maybe for 25 years, maybe for 50 years, but sometime or the other there will be an explosion. In our society, we allow lots of smaller explosions because we think that that will guard the basic stability and progress of society and prevent it from having the kind of chaotic explosion which can retard our progress and harmony in the country.

So, I hope that all of you who have this great advantage of education will not only do whatever work you are doing keeping the national interests in view, but you will make your own contribution to creating peace and harmony, to bringing beauty in the lives of our people and our country. I think this is the special responsibility of the women of India. We want to do a great deal for our country, but we have never regarded India as isolated from the rest of the world. What we want to do is to make a better world. So, we have to see India's problems in the perspective of the larger world problems.

It has given me great pleasure to be with you here. I give my warm congratulations to those who are doing well and my very good wishes to all the others that they will also do much better. This college has had a high reputation but we must always see that we do better than those who were there before us. So, good luck and good wishes to you.

TRUE LIBERATION OF WOMEN
AT THE INAUGURATION OF THE ALL-INDIA WOMEN'S CONFERENCE BUILDING COMPLEX
NEW DELHI, INDIA, MARCH 26, 1980

FOR several decades the All-India Women's Conference has been the organized voice of the women of India. I have never been a member of any women's organization but have been interested enough to keep track of their activities and to lend the helping hand whenever I could.

I am glad that at long last the All-India Women's Conference has a home of its own and it is named after one of the best known and most remarkable women of our times, Sarojini Naidu, feminine to the core but well able to hold her own in the world of men, whether in letters or in politics.

To add to the importance of the occasion and to give it a touch of elegance, we have in our midst His Highness the Aga Khan and Her Highness the Begum Aga Khan. They are friends of India and have founded or encouraged many projects for education, health and other aspects of welfare. But for their timely and generous help, this complex would not have been ready today. Nor would we have before us the attractive Aga Khan Hall. We welcome them and wish them well in their work.

I see before me a number of eminent women who have distinguished themselves in various professions — in social work, in education, in science, in administration, in law and, of course, in politics. They must all feel gratified to see the completion of this building. I have often said that I am not a feminist. Yet, in my concern for the underprivileged, how can I ignore women who, since the beginning of history, have been dominated over and discriminated against in social customs and in laws. How insidious and all-pervasive is this attitude of male' superiority is revealed in the vocabulary of the languages the world over. And this is unquestioningly accepted and acquiesced in by all but a minuscule minority of men and also women. Currently I am reading a book titled *World and Women*. I learned from it what Mr. Ling White, the President of Mills College in the USA, wrote of the use of masculine generic pronouns. I quote: "The penetration of the habit of language into the minds of little girls as they grow up to be women is more profound than most people, including most women, have realized. For, it implies that personality is really a male attribute and that women are a sub or a human sub-species." The author goes on to say that it is time we looked more carefully where the thoughtless use of stereotypes is taking us. "Man as leader, woman as follower; man as producer, woman as consumer; man as strength, woman as weakness; this is the cosmography that has brought us to man as aggressor and humanity the victim."

Hence, by excluding women, men are depriving themselves of a fuller emancipation or growth for themselves.

In the West, women's so-called freedom is often equated with imitation of man. Frankly, I feel that is merely an exchange of one kind of bondage for another. To be liberated, woman must feel free to be herself, not in rivalry to man but in the context of her own capacity and her personality. We need women to be more interested, more alive and more active not because they are women but because they do comprise half the human race. Whether they like it or not, they cannot escape their responsibility nor should they be denied its benefits. Indian women are traditionally conservative but they also have the genius of synthesis, to adapt and to absorb. That is what gives them resilience to face suffering and to meet upheavals with a degree of calm, to change constantly and yet remain changeless, which is the quality of India herself.

Today's major concerns are: first, economic and social inequality and injustice between the affluent and developing countries and within countries. Secondly, the anxiety whether human wisdom will prevail over what can only be called a death wish in which the desire to dominate expresses itself in countless ways, the most dangerous being the armament race. And, thirdly, the need to protect this, our only Earth, from human rapacity and exploitation. Only recently have we awakened to the awareness of ancient truths regarding our own utter dependence on the balance of Nature and its resources.

These enormous challenges cannot be met only by some sections, however advanced they may be, while others pull in different directions or watch apathetically. The effort has to be a universal one, conscious and concerted, considering no one too small to contribute. The effort must embrace all nationalities and all classes regardless of religion, caste or sex.

There is no time to lose and it involves a tremendous task of educating. We want to walk together and in step with all others, but if men hesitate, should not women show the way? So, while complimenting the All-India Women's Conference, especially its President, Smt. Lakshmi Raghuramaiah, on their achievements, I dedicate to the nation this building complex of the All-India Women's Conference.

AT THE SEVENTH CONFERENCE OF HEADS OF STATE OR GOVERNMENT OF NON-ALIGNED COUNTRIES, NEW DELHI, MARCH 7, 1983

WHEN assuming the reins of government in 1946, my father, Jawaharlal Nehru, declared India's determination "to keep away from the power blocs or groups, aligned against one another, which have led in the past to world wars and which may again lead to disasters on an even vaster scale." Later, he explained that once "foreign relations go out of your hands into the charge of somebody else, to that extent and in that measure you are not independent... So our policy will continue to be not only to keep away from alignments, but also to try to make friendly co-operation possible. We approach the whole world on a friendly basis."

As more countries became free, the number of those who believed in peaceful coexistence and wished to keep out of military alliances increased steadily. It was natural for these nonaligned countries to come together, not to form another bloc but to raise the voices of the exploited millions through a moral and political movement.

The very growth in the membership of our Movement - twenty-five in Belgrade, a hundred now - proves that nonalignment meets a felt need of vast numbers of people In various continents.

Its significance is not to be measured by the number of divisions or the megatons of destructive power we command but by the intensity with which we desire peace and freedom, development and international justice.

Other governments may have conflicting opinions on right and wrong. We, the nonaligned have chosen peace, which surely is the right and inevitable choice. We have sought and continue to seek friendship with all, except governments which are racist or threaten the hard-earned freedom of others. Nonalignment is not vague, not negative, not neutral.

Nonalignment is national Independence and freedom. It stands for peace and the avoidance of confrontation. It aims at keeping away from military alliances. it means equality among nations and the democratization of international relations, economic and political. It wants global co-operation for development on the basis of mutual benefit. It is a strategy for the recognition and preservation of the world's diversity.

... Humankind is balancing on the brink of the collapse of the world economic system and annihilation through nuclear war. Should these tragedies occur, can anyone of us, large, small. rich or poor, from North or South, West or East, hope to escape? Let us analyze the economic crisis. We of the developing world have no margin of safety. We shall be the first and worst sufferers in any economic background. In this interdependent world, where you cannot "stir a flower without troubling a star," even the most affluent are not immune to such disturbances.

... Development, independence, disarmament and peace are closely related. Can there be peace alongside nuclear weapons? Without peace, my father said, all our dreams of development turn to ashes. It has been pointed out that global military expenditure is 20 times the total official development assistance. Each day, each hour, the size and the lethality of nuclear weapons increase. A nuclear aircraft carrier costs $ 4 billion, which is more than the GNP of 53 countries. The hood of the cobra is spread. Humankind watches in frozen fear, hoping against hope that it will not strike. Never before has the earth faced so much death and danger.

The destructive power contained in nuclear stockpiles can kill human life, indeed all life, many times over and might well prevent its reappearance for ages to come. Terrifying is the vividness of such descriptions by scientists. Yet, some statesmen and strategists art as though there is not much difference between these and the earlier artillery pieces. The arms race continues because of the pursuit of power and desire for one upmanship, and also because many industries and interests flourish on it. More recently, the notion has been propagated that tactial nuclear weapons are usable in "limited wars." Powerful States propagate the untenable doctrine of deterrence. New areas are being brought into the scope of strategic groupings, military blocs and alliances. New bases and facilities are being established. That is why our responses must be surer, swifter and sharper.

The desire for peace is universal even within countries which themselves produce nuclear weapons and in those where they are deployed. The Nonaligned Movement is history's biggest peace movement. It welcomes these spontaneous upsurges of peoples. But Governments persist in propounding, practicing and pursuing the self-same strategic interests, spheres of influence, balance of power, and tutelary relations reminiscent of the earlier theory of divine right.

The paradox of our age is that while weapons become increasingly sophisticated, minds remain imprisoned in ideas of simpler times. Technically, the colonial age has ended. But the wish to dominate persists. Neo-colonialism comes wrapped in all types of packages-in technology and communications, commerce and culture. It takes boldness and integrity to resist it. There are intense political and economic pressures. The limited economic viability, indeed the very survival of many of the nonaligned, especially those with small populations, is threatened through artificial barriers In trade, technology transfer and access to resources. It should be within our ability to devise measures to help these small nations to maintain their independence and nonalignment.

Only with coexistence can there be any existence. We regard non-interference and non-intervention as basic laws of international behavior. Yet different types of interventions, open or covert, do take place in Asia, in Africa, in Latin America. They are all intolerable and unacceptable. Interference leads to intervention and one intervention often attracts another. No single power or group of powers has the justification or moral authority to so interfere or intervene. You cannot condemn one instance but condone another. Each situation has its own origins. Whatever they be, solutions must be political and peaceful. All

States must abide by the principle that force or the threat of force will not be used against the territorial integrity or political independence of another state.

... Our plans for a better life for each of our peoples depend on world peace and the reversal of the arms race. Negotiations confined to a closed circle of nuclear-weapon powers have made little progress. We are non-nuclear States, who want nuclear energy used only for peace. But we too have a right to live and be heard. In the name of humanity and on behalf of us all, I call upon nuclear -weapon powers to give up the use of nuclear weapons in any circumstances; suspend all nuclear weapons: and resume disarmament negotiations with determination to reach agreement.

...Nationalism does not detach us from our common humanity. What a marvelous opportunity is ours with the immense knowledge and Increasing capability. Let us grasp it, though it be in the midst of dangers. Faith in the future has brought so many across the continents and the oceans to meet here. We are here because we do believe that minds and attitudes can and must be changed and the injustice and suffering can and must be diminished. Our world is small but it has room for all of us to live together and to improve the quality of the lives for our peoples in peace and beauty.

JAWAHARLAL NEHRU

INTRODUCTION

Jawaharlal Nehru was born in 14th November, 1889. His father Motilal Nehru being a reputed barrister.

He spent two years studying Law in London & returned home in 1912 as a barrister.

When India became Independent in 1947, he was asked to take over as the Prime Minister, which he did in 1951 when India became a republic. The great pillar of India's struggle for her freedom passed away on 27th May 1964, while in office. The whole country submerged into an ocean of grief & paid their last homage through prayers. After cremation his ashes were spread in the holy water of the Ganges.

SPEECH ON THE GRANTING OF INDIAN INDEPENDENCE, AUGUST 14, 1947

LONG years ago we made a tryst with destiny, and now the time comes when we shall redeem our pledge, not wholly or in full measure, but very substantially. At the stroke of the midnight hour, when the world sleeps, India will awake to life and freedom. A moment comes, which comes but rarely in history, when we step out from the old to the new, when an age ends, and when the soul of a nation, long supressed, finds utterance. It is fitting that at this solemn moment we take the pledge of dedication to the service of Inida and her people and to the still larger cause of humanity.

At the dawn of history India started on her unending quest, and trackless centuries are filled with her striving and the grandeur of her success and her failures. Through good and ill fortune alike she has never lost sight of that quest or forgotten the ideals which gave her strength. We end today a period of ill fortune and India discovers herself again. The achievement we celebrate today is but a step, an opening of opportunity, to the greater triumphs and achievements that await us. Are we brave enough and wise enough to grasp this opportunity and accept the challenge of the future?

Freedom and power bring responsibility. The responsibility rests upon this Assembly, a sovereign body representing the sovereign people of India. Before the birth of freedom we have endured all the pains of labour and our hearts are heavy with the memory of this sorrow. Some of those pains continue even now. Nevertheless, the past is over and it is the future that beckons to us now.

That future is not one of ease or resting but of incessant striving so that we may fulfil the pledges we have so often taken and the one we shall take today. The service of India means the service of the millions who suffer. It means the ending of poverty and ignorance and disease and inequality of opportunity. The ambition of the greatest man of our generation has been to wipe every tear from every eye. That may be beyond us, but as long as there are tears and suffering, so long our work will not be over.

And so we have to labour and to work, and work hard, to give reality to our dreams. Those dreams are for India, but they are also for the world, for all the nations and peoples are too closely knit together today for any one of them to imagine that it can live apart Peace has been said to be indivisible; so is freedom, so is prosperity now, and so also is disaster in this One World that can no longer be split into isolated fragments.

To the people of India, whose representatives we are, we

make an appeal to join us with faith and confidence in this great adventure. This is no time for petty and destructive criticism, no time for ill-will or blaming others. We have to build the noble mansion of free India where all her children may dwell.

SPEECH BEFORE A JOURNALISTS MEETING ON AUGUST 15, 1947

THE appointed day has come-the day appointed by destiny-and India stands forth again, after long slumber and struggle, awake, vital, free and independent. The past clings on to us still in some measure and we have to do much before we redeem the pledges we have so often taken. Yet the turning-point is past, and history begins anew for us, the history which we shall live and act and others will write about.

It is a fateful moment for us in India, for all Asia and for the world. A new star rises, the star of freedom in the East, a new hope comes into being, a vision long cherished materializes. May the star never set and that hope never be betrayed!

We rejoice in that freedom, even though clouds surround us, and many of our people are sorrowstricken and difficult problems encompass us. But freedom brings responsibilities and burdens and we have to face them in the spirit of a free and disciplined people.

On this day our first thoughts go to the architect of this freedom, the Father of our Nation [Gandhi], who, embodying the old spirit of India, held aloft the torch of freedom and lighted up the darkness that surrounded us. We have often been unworthy followers of his and have strayed from his message, but not only we but succeeding generations will remember this message and bear the imprint in their hearts of this great son of India, magnificent in his faith and strength and courage and humility. We shall never allow that torch of freedom to be blown out, however high the wind or stormy the tempest.

Our next thoughts must be of the unknown volunteers and

soldiers of freedom who, without praise or reward, have served India even unto death.

We think also of our brothers and sisters who have been cut off from us by political boundaries and who unhappily cannot share at present in the freedom that has come. They are of us and will remain of us whatever may happen, and we shall be sharers in their good [or] ill fortune alike.

The future beckons to us. Whither do we go and what shall be our endeavour? To bring freedom and opportunity to the common man, to the peasants and workers of India; to fight and end poverty and ignorance and disease; to build up a prosperous, democratic and progressive nation, and to create social, economic and political institutions which will ensure justice and fullness of life to every man and woman.

We have hard work ahead. There is no resting for any one of us till we redeem our pledge in full, till we make all the people of India what destiny intended them to be. We are citizens of a great country on the verge of bold advance, and we have to live up to that high standard. All of us, to whatever religion we may belong, are equally the children of India with equal rights, privileges and obligations. We cannot encourage communalism or narrow-mindedness, for no nation can be great whose people are narrow in thought or in action.

To the nations and peoples of the world we send greetings and pledge ourselves to cooperate with them in furthering peace, freedom and democracy.

And to India, our much-loved motherland, the ancient, the eternal and the ever-new, we pay our reverent homage and we bind ourselves afresh to her service.

JAI HIND.

AT THE UNITED NATIONS GENERAL ASSEMBLY, PARIS, NOVEMBER 3, 1948.

I COME from a country which, after a long struggle, though that struggle was a peaceful struggle, attained its freedom and its independence. In these long years of struggle we were taught by our great leader never to forget not only the objectives we had, but also the methods whereby we should achieve those objectives. Always he laid stress on this, that it was not good enough to have a good objective, that it was equally important that the means of attaining those objectives were good, means were always as important as ends. You will permit me to repeat that here, because I am convinced that, however good the ends, the larger ends of the United Nations, or the lesser objectives which we may from time to time have before us either as individual nations or as groups of nations, it is important that we should remember that the best of objectives may not be reached if our eyes are bloodshot and our minds clouded with passion.

Therefore, it becomes essential for us, for a while, to think more of how we are doing things than what we are aiming at, even though we should never forget what we are aiming at. It becomes necessary for us always to remember the principles and the purposes for which this great Assembly was formed.

Now, a mere repetition of those principles and purposes would perhaps indicate to us how sometimes, with passion and prejudice, we swerve away from that path. This Assembly took shape after two mighty wars and as a consequence of those wars. What has been the lesson of those wars? Surely the lesson of those wars has been that out of hatred and violence you will not build peace. It is a contradiction in terms. The lesson of history, the long course of history, and more especially the lesson of the last great wars which have devastated humanity, has been that out of hatred and violence only hatred and violence will come. We have got into a cycle of hatred and violence, and not the most brilliant debate will get us out of It, unless we look some other way and find some other means. It is obvious that if we continue in this cycle and have wars which this Assembly was especially meant to avoid and prevent, the result will not only be tremendous devastation all over the world, but non-achievement by any individual power or group of its objective.

It may be that it is difficult to get this hatred and prejudice and fear out of our minds. Nevertheless, unless we try to proceed in this way, to cast out this fear, we shall never succeed. Of that I am quite convinced.

I feel that today the world is tied up in fears and apprehensions, some of them justified, no doubt. But where a person feels fear, bad consequences and evil consequences follow. Fear is not a good companion. It is surprising to see that this sense of fear is pervading great countries fear, and grave fear of war, and fear of many things. I think that it is admitted, or it will be admitted, that no aggression of any kind can be tolerated, because the very idea of aggression must upset the balance and lead to conflict. Aggression of every type must be resisted. In existing circumstances it is difficult for people to say that they will not defend themselves, because if there is fear of aggression one has to defend oneself against aggression. We have to defend ourselves, but even in defending ourselves, we must not submit ourselves to this Assembly without clean hands.

I have no doubt that this Assembly is going to solve our problems. I am not afraid of the future. I have no fear in my mind, and I have no fear, even though India, from a military point of view, is of no great consequence. I am not afraid of the bigness of great powers, and their armies, their fleets and their atom bombs. That is the lesson which my Master taught me. We stood as an unarmed people against a great country and a powerful empire.

We were supported and strengthened, because throughout all this period we decided not to submit to evil, and I think that is the lesson which I have before me and which is before us today. I do not know if it is possible to apply this to the problems which face the world today. It is a terrible problem, but I think if we banish this fear, if we have confidence, even though we may take risks of trust rather than risk violent language, violent actions and in the end war, I think those risks are worth taking.

However, we do not think that the problems of the world or of India can be solved by thinking in terms of aggression or war or violence. We are frail mortals, and we cannot always live up to the teaching of the great man who led our nation to freedom. But that lesson has sunk deep into our souls and, so long as we remember it, I am sure we shall be on the right path. And, if I may venture to suggest this to the General Assembly, I think that if the essentials of that lesson are kept in mind, perhaps our approach to the problems of today will be different: perhaps the conflicts that always hang over us will appear a little less deep than they are and in fact gradually fade away.

I should like to state to this General Assembly, on behalf of my people and my Government, that we adhere completely and absolutely to the principles and purposes of the United Nations Charter and that we shall try, to the best of our ability. to work for the realisation of those principles and purposes.

AT THE UNITED NATIONS OF GENERAL ASSEMBLY, NEW YORK, NOVEMBER 10, 1961

WE talk about many problems like disarmament, and sometimes one has the feeling that although there is apparent agreement, really behind it there is not that faith in disarmament that is necessary, and that talks are more of some kind of attempt to put the other party in the wrong rather than to achieve something, while it is of the utmost importance that achievement should take place. I am convinced that the modern world cannot continue for long without full. disarmament. All these problems have come up again and again. Ultimately it is perhaps true that the material advance which has taken place in the world, and that is magnificent, has gone far ahead of the development of human minds, which lag behind. They do not fit in with the modem age, and the mind still thinks in its narrow terms of 100 to 200 years ago of how nations function, how diplomats function and how wars took place.

We know, we have heard and we have read about the new possibility of a nuclear war. Nevertheless, emotionally, we do not understand it fully. Otherwise it seems to me impossible why there should be these continuing deadlocks and impasses because the fact is that under modem conditions war must be ruled out or the world of civilisation or humanity has to submit to the ending of all it has laboured for thousands of years. if that is true, then surely it is important and urgent that we should approach this question with speed, deliberation and a determination to solve it rather than merely show that the other party is wrong.

I mentioned disarmament. This Assembly last year, I think decided almost unanimously in favour of general. widespread disarmament. The great nations of the world have all committed themselves to that. The United States, through its President, recently put forward proposals which are in line with what this Assembly has decided. The Soviet Union has put forward proposals to the same effect, varying slightly but essentially aiming at the same thing. Even in broad outline there is a good deal of commonness about them. If that is so, what comes in our way, why should we not grasp this opportunity when there is so much agreement and remove this fear and terror from people's minds and devote all the great energies and resources of the people to world advancement. I do not know except what I have said, that we are quite unable to get out Of old ways of thinking which ought to have no place in the modern world, old ways of hatred and violence of yesterday but a violence which could exterminate all of us, not realizing that there is no victory today for any country in a major war - only defeat and extermination for all. If that is so, then surely this major and outstanding question must be dealt with speed and those great countries, especially those which have the greatest responsibility because they possess the biggest weapons of warfare - nuclear weapons - should address themselves again and again to negotiations, to talks, to the consideration of this problem together to find some remedy, with the determination that they will not separate until they have come to some agreements, of course. Those agreements cannot be merely agreements of some countries, however great. They must represent all the members of this United Nations in this great body. But I do think that it is better for those countries - a few of them - to deal with this problem rather than for a larger body to deal with it to begin with. I feel rather strongly on this question although we in India are not situated in the major theatres of a possible war - probably not. Nevertheless, I feel that everything that man has striven for in the past thousands of years is at stake today. As strongly as I feel about these colonial matters, about the freedom of colonial countries and others, I do think that the major question and the biggest question of war and peace and disarmament. There is no conflict between those.

In fact, the whole atmosphere of the world will change if disarmament comes in and these present problems go towards solution. How then are we to do it? I do not know. The president was good enough the East or to my wisdom. It was kind of him to make that reference to me, but I possess no greater wisdom than each one of us here. Only perhaps in some matters, some of us may feel a little more, some of us who have experienced many ups and downs in their lives may think more deeply about them. But It is wisdom that we want, it Is the common wisdom that should come to everyone. It is no mystery. In the problems before us there are no mysteries. They are obvious problems, and the fear of war is obvious. The fear that grips mankind is obvious. How can we go on dealing with the secondary questions of the world, discussing them, etc., when this basic problem deludes us? As a part of this question of disarmament there is the particular question today of nuclear tests. The General Assembly passed a resolution recently about them. It was, I think, a great misfortune that after a period of abstinence from nuclear tests there was resumption. There can be no doubt that that turned the attention of the world in a wrong direction, apart from the harm it might do. Immediately the idea of a possible war became more prevalent. Immediately it became more difficult to have treaties for ending nuclear tests because while treaties are essential, are necessary for this. when the whole atmosphere becomes one of fear and apprehension, it becomes more difficult to get a treaty. I do think, and I would beg the countries concerned to realize, that they are doing a grave disservice to the world, to their countries even, by not putting an end to this business of nuclear tests by a treaty as rapidly as possible.

The Assembly has passed a resolution in favour of some

kind of moratorium. No one imagines that a voluntary moratorium is going to solve this question. There must be stricter controls by treaty and otherwise. But while that should be aimed at and worked for and achieved as rapidly as possible, one should not leave the door open, while you discuss It, for these nuclear tests, to go on. Arguments may be raised that one party or one country gets an advantage over.the other and these arguments may have substances. yet my own reaction to these nuclear tests is a very strong one. I think they are basically evil. They encourage evil. Therefore, the sooner this evil is dealt with the better.

JOHN F. KENNEDY

INTRODUCTION

U.S. statesman and 35th President (1961-63) received education at Harward and London. He was a great Intellectual when he wrote "Profiles In Courte" which won him a Pulitzer Prize (1956). Elected Democrat Representative (1947) and Senator (1952) for Massachussetts and youngest President In 1960. He displayed firmness and moderation in foreign policy. He Induced Russia to withdraw its missiles from Cuba and advised a partial nuclear test ban treaty in 1963. On November 22, 1963, he was assassinated by Lee Harvey Oswald while being driven in an open car.

INAUGURAL ADDRESS
FRIDAY, JANUARY 20, 1961

VICE President Johnson, Mr. Speaker, Mr. Chief Justice, President Eisenhower, Vice President Nixon, President Truman, reverend clergy, fellow citizens, we observe today not a victory of party, but a celebration of freedom—symbolizing an end, as well as a beginning—signifying renewal, as well as change. For I have sworn before you and Almighty God the same solemn oath our forebears prescribed nearly a century and three quarters ago.

The world is very different now. For man holds in his mortal hands the power to abolish all forms of human poverty and all forms of human life. And yet the same revolutionary beliefs for which our forebears fought are still at issue around the globe—the belief that the rights of man come not from the generosity of the state, but from the hand of God.

We dare not forget today that we are the heirs of that first revolution. Let the word go forth from this time and place, to friend and foe alike, that the torch has been passed to a new generation of Americans—born in this century, tempered by war, disciplined by a hard and bitter peace, proud of our ancient heritage—and unwilling to witness or permit the slow undoing of those human rights to which this Nation has always been committed, and to which we are committed today at home and around the world.

Let every nation know, whether it wishes us well or ill, that we shall pay any price, bear any burden, meet any hardship, support any friend, oppose any foe, in order to assure the survival and the success of liberty.

This much we pledge—and more.

To those old allies whose cultural and spiritual origins we share, we pledge the loyalty of faithful friends. United, there is little we cannot do in a host of cooperative ventures. Divided, there is little we can do—for we dare not meet a powerful challenge at odds and split asunder.

To those new States whom we welcome to the ranks of the free, we pledge our word that one form of colonial control shall not have passed away merely to be replaced by a far more iron tyranny. We shall not always expect to find them supporting our view. But we shall always hope to find them strongly supporting their own freedom—and to remember that, in the past, those who foolishly sought power by riding the back of the tiger ended up inside.

To those peoples in the huts and villages across the globe struggling to break the bonds of mass misery, we pledge our best efforts to help them help themselves, for whatever period is required—not because the Communists may be doing it, not because we seek their votes, but because it is right. If a free society cannot help the many who are poor, it cannot save the few who are rich.

To our sister republics south of our border, we offer a special pledge—to convert our good words into good deeds—in a new alliance for progress—to assist free men and free governments in casting off the chains of poverty. But this peaceful revolution of hope cannot become the prey of hostile powers. Let all our neighbors know that we shall join with them to oppose aggression or subversion anywhere in the Americas. And let every other power know that this Hemisphere intends to remain the master of its own house.

To that world assembly of sovereign states, the United Nations, our last best hope in an age where the instruments of war have far outpaced the instruments of peace, we renew our pledge of support—to prevent it from becoming merely a forum for invective—to strengthen its shield of the new and the weak—and to enlarge the area in which its writ may run.

Finally, to those nations who would make themselves our adversary, we offer not a pledge but a request: that both sides begin anew the quest for peace, before the dark powers of destruction unleashed by science engulf all humanity in planned or accidental self-destruction.

We dare not tempt them with weakness. For only when our arms are sufficient beyond doubt can we be certain beyond doubt that they will never be employed.

But neither can two great and powerful groups of nations take comfort from our present course—both sides overburdened by the cost of modern weapons, both rightly alarmed by the steady spread of the deadly atom, yet both racing to alter that uncertain balance of terror that stays the hand of mankind's final war.

So let us begin anew—remembering on both sides that civility is not a sign of weakness, and sincerity is always subject to proof. Let us never negotiate out of fear. But let us never fear to negotiate.

Let both sides explore what problems unite us instead of belaboring those problems which divide us.

Let both sides, for the first time, formulate serious and precise proposals for the inspection and control of arms—and bring the absolute power to destroy other nations under the absolute control of all nations.

Let both sides seek to invoke the wonders of science instead of its terrors. Together let us explore the stars, conquer the deserts, eradicate disease, tap the ocean depths, and encourage the arts and commerce.

Let both sides unite to heed in all corners of the earth the command of Isaiah—to "undo the heavy burdens ... and to let the oppressed go free."

And if a beachhead of cooperation may push back the jungle of suspicion, let both sides join in creating a new endeavor, not a new balance of power, but a new world of law, where the strong are just and the weak secure and the peace preserved.

All this will not be finished in the first 100 days. Nor will it be finished in the first 1,000 days, nor in the life of this Administration, nor even perhaps in our lifetime on this planet. But let us begin.

In your hands, my fellow citizens, more than in mine, will rest the final success or failure of our course. Since this country was founded, each generation of Americans has been summoned to give testimony to its national loyalty. The graves of young Americans who answered the call to service surround the globe.

Now the trumpet summons us again—not as a call to bear arms, though arms we need; not as a call to battle, though embattled we are—but a call to bear the burden of a long twilight struggle, year in and year out, "rejoicing in hope, patient in tribulation"—a struggle against the common enemies of man: tyranny, poverty, disease, and war itself.

Can we forge against these enemies a grand and global alliance, North and South, East and West, that can assure a more fruitful life for all mankind? Will you join in that historic effort?

In the long history of the world, only a few generations have been granted the role of defending freedom in its hour of maximum danger. I do not shrink from this responsibility—I welcome it. I do not believe that any of us would exchange places with any other people or any other generation. The energy, the faith, the devotion which we bring to this endeavor will light our country and all who serve it—and the glow from that fire can truly light the world.

And so, my fellow Americans: ask not what your country can do for you—ask what you can do for your country.

My fellow citizens of the world: ask not what America will do for you, but what together we can do for the freedom of man.

Finally, whether you are citizens of America or citizens of the world, ask of us the same high standards of strength and sacrifice which we ask of you. With a good conscience our only sure reward, with history the final judge of our deeds, let us go forth to lead the land we love, asking His blessing and His help, but knowing that here on earth God's work must truly be our own.

"WE CHOOSE TO GO TO THE MOON"
SEPTEMBER 12, 1962

PRESIDENT Pitzer, Mr. Vice President, Governor, Congressman Thomas, Senator Wiley, and Congressman Miller, Mr. Webb, Mr. Bell, scientists, distinguished guests, and ladies and gentlemen:

I appreciate your president having made me an honorary visiting professor, and I will assure you that my first lecture will be very brief.

I am delighted to be here and I'm particularly delighted to be here on this occasion.

We meet at a college noted for knowledge, in a city noted for progress, in a state noted for strength, and we stand in need of all three, for we meet in an hour of change and challenge, in a decade of hope and fear, in an age of both knowledge and ignorance. The greater our knowledge increases, the greater our ignorance unfolds.

Despite the striking fact that most of the scientists that the world has ever known are alive and working today, despite the fact that this Nation's own scientific manpower is doubling every 12 years in a rate of growth more than three times that of our population as a whole, despite that, the vast stretches of the unknown and the unanswered and the unfinished still far outstrip our collective comprehension.

No man can fully grasp how far and how fast we have come, but condense, if you will, the 50,000 years of man's recorded history in a time span of but a half-century. Stated in these terms, we know very little about the first 40 years, except at the end of them advanced man had learned to use the skins of animals to cover them. Then about 10 years ago, under this standard, man emerged from his caves to construct other kinds of shelter. Only five years ago man learned to write and use a cart with wheels. Christianity began less than two years ago. The printing press came this year, and then less than two months ago, during this whole 50-year span of human history, the steam engine provided a new source of power. Newton explored the meaning of gravity. Last month electric lights and telephones and automobiles and airplanes became available. Only last week did we develop penicillin and television and nuclear power, and now if America's new spacecraft succeeds in reaching Venus, we will have literally reached the stars before midnight tonight.

This is a breathtaking pace, and such a pace cannot help but create new ills as it dispels old, new ignorance, new problems, new dangers. Surely the opening vistas of space promise high costs and hardships, as well as high reward.

So it is not surprising that some would have us stay where we are a little longer to rest, to wait. But this city of Houston, this state of Texas, this country of the United States was not built by those who waited and rested and wished to look behind them. This country was conquered by those who moved forward—and so will space.

William Bradford, speaking in 1630 of the founding of the Plymouth Bay Colony, said that all great and honorable actions are accompanied with great difficulties, and both must be enterprised and overcome with answerable courage.

If this capsule history of our progress teaches us anything, it is that man, in his quest for knowledge and progress, is determined and cannot be deterred. The exploration of space will go ahead, whether we join in it or not, and it is one of the great adventures of all time, and no nation which expects to be the leader of other nations can expect to stay behind in this race for space.

Those who came before us made certain that this country rode the first waves of the industrial revolution, the first waves of modern invention, and the first wave of nuclear power, and this generation does not intend to founder in the backwash of the coming age of space. We mean to be a part of it—we mean to lead it. For the eyes of the world now look into space, to the moon and to the planets beyond, and we have vowed that we shall not see it governed by a hostile flag of conquest, but by a banner of freedom and peace. We have vowed that we shall not see space filled with weapons of mass destruction, but with instruments of knowledge and understanding.

Yet the vows of this Nation can only be fulfilled if we in this Nation are first, and, therefore, we intend to be first. In short, our leadership in science and industry, our hopes for peace and security, our obligations to ourselves as well as others, all require us to make this effort, to solve these mysteries, to solve them for the good of all men, and to become the world's leading space-faring nation.

We set sail on this new sea because there is new knowledge to be gained, and new rights to be won, and they must be won and used for the progress of all people. For space science, like nuclear science and all technology, has no conscience of its own. Whether it will become a force for good or ill depends on man, and only if the United States occupies a position of pre-eminence can we help decide whether this new ocean will be a sea of peace or a new terrifying theater of war. I do not say that we should or will go unprotected against the hostile misuse of space any more than we go unprotected against the hostile use of land or sea, but I do say that space can be explored and mastered without feeding the fires of war, without repeating the mistakes that man has made in extending his writ around this globe of ours.

There is no strife, no prejudice, no national conflict in outer space as yet. Its hazards are hostile to us all. Its conquest deserves the best of all mankind, and its opportunity for peaceful cooperation many never come again. But why, some say, the moon? Why choose this as our goal? And they may well ask why climb the highest mountain? Why, 35 years ago, fly the Atlantic? Why does Rice play Texas?

We choose to go to the moon. We choose to go to the moon in this decade and do the other things, not because they are easy, but because they are hard, because that goal will serve to organize and measure the best of our energies and skills, because that challenge is one that we are willing to accept, one we are unwilling to postpone, and one which we intend to win, and the others, too.

It is for these reasons that I regard the decision last year to shift our efforts in space from low to high gear as among the most important decisions that will be made during my incumbency in the office of the Presidency.

In the last 24 hours we have seen facilities now being created for the greatest and most complex exploration in man's history. We have felt the ground shake and the air shattered by the testing of a Saturn C-1 booster rocket, many times as powerful as the Atlas which launched John Glenn, generating power equivalent to 10,000 automobiles with their accelerators on the floor. We have seen the site where five F-1 rocket engines, each one as powerful as all eight engines of the Saturn combined, will be clustered together to make the advanced Saturn missile, assembled in a new building to be built at Cape Canaveral as tall as a 48 story structure, as wide as a city block, and as long as two lengths of this field.

Within these last 19 months at least 45 satellites have circled the earth. Some 40 of them were made in the United States of America and they were far more sophisticated and supplied far more knowledge to the people of the world than those of the Soviet Union.

The Mariner spacecraft now on its way to Venus is the most intricate instrument in the history of space science. The accuracy of that shot is comparable to firing a missile from Cape

Canaveral and dropping it in this stadium between the 40-yard lines.

Transit satellites are helping our ships at sea to steer a safer course. Tiros satellites have given us unprecedented warnings of hurricanes and storms, and will do the same for forest fires and icebergs.

We have had our failures, but so have others, even if they do not admit them. And they may be less public.

To be sure, we are behind, and will be behind for some time in manned flight. But we do not intend to stay behind, and in this decade, we shall make up and move ahead.

The growth of our science and education will be enriched by new knowledge of our universe and environment, by new techniques of learning and mapping and observation, by new tools and computers for industry, medicine, the home as well as the school. Technical institutions, such as Rice, will reap the harvest of these gains.

And finally, the space effort itself, while still in its infancy, has already created a great number of new companies, and tens of thousands of new jobs. Space and related industries are generating new demands in investment and skilled personnel, and this city and this state, and this region, will share greatly in this growth. What was once the furthest outpost on the old frontier of the West will be the furthest outpost on the new frontier of science and space. Houston, your city of Houston, with its Manned Spacecraft Center, will become the heart of a large scientific and engineering community. During the next 5 years the National Aeronautics and Space Administration expects to double the number of scientists and engineers in this area, to increase its outlays for salaries and expenses to $60 million a year; to invest some $200 million in plant and laboratory facilities; and to direct or contract for new space efforts over $1 billion from this center in this city.

To be sure, all this costs us all a good deal of money. This year's space budget is three times what it was in January 1961, and it is greater than the space budget of the previous eight years combined. That budget now stands at $5,400 million a year—a staggering sum, though somewhat less than we pay for cigarettes and cigars every year. Space expenditures will soon rise some more, from 40 cents per person per week to more than 50 cents a week for every man, woman and child in the United States, for we have given this program a high national priority—even though I realize that this is in some measure an act of faith and vision, for we do not now know what benefits await us. But if I were to say, my fellow citizens, that we shall send to the moon, 240,000 miles away from the control station in Houston, a giant rocket more than 300 feet tall, the length of this football field, made of new metal alloys, some of which have not yet been invented, capable of standing heat and stresses several times more than have ever been experienced, fitted together with a precision better than the finest watch, carrying all the equipment needed for propulsion, guidance, control, communications, food and survival, on an untried mission, to an unknown celestial body, and then return it safely to earth, re-entering the atmosphere at speeds of over 25,000 miles per hour, causing heat about half that of the temperature of the sun—almost as hot as it is here today—and do all this, and do it right, and do it first before this decade is out—then we must be bold.

I'm the one who is doing all the work, so we just want you to stay cool for a minute. [laughter]

However, I think we're going to do it, and I think that we must pay what needs to be paid. I don't think we ought to waste any money, but I think we ought to do the job. And this will be done in the decade of the Sixties. It may be done while some of you are still here at school at this college and university. It will be done during the terms of office of some of the people who sit here on this platform. But it will be done. And it will be done before the end of this decade.

And I am delighted that this university is playing a part in putting a man on the moon as part of a great national effort of the United States of America.

Many years ago the great British explorer George Mallory, who was to die on Mount Everest, was asked why did he want to climb it. He said, "Because it is there."

Well, space is there, and we're going to climb it, and the

moon and the planets are there, and new hopes for knowledge and peace are there. And, therefore, as we set sail we ask God's blessing on the most hazardous and dangerous and greatest adventure on which man has ever embarked.

Thank you.

CIVIL RIGHTS MESSAGE
JUNE 11, 1963

Good evening my fellow citizens:

THIS afternoon, following a series of threats and defiant statements, the presence of Alabama National Guardsmen was required on the University of Alabama to carry out the final and unequivocal order of the United States District Court of the Northern District of Alabama. That order called for the admission of two clearly qualified young Alabama residents who happened to have been born Negro.

That they were admitted peacefully on the campus is due in good measure to the conduct of the students of the University of Alabama, who met their responsibilities in a constructive way.

I hope that every American, regardless of where he lives, will stop and examine his conscience about this and other related incidents. This Nation was founded by men of many nations and backgrounds. It was founded on the principle that all men are created equal, and that the rights of every man are diminished when the rights of one man are threatened.

Today we are committed to a worldwide struggle to promote and protect the rights of all who wish to be free. And when Americans are sent to Viet Nam or West Berlin, we do not ask for whites only. It ought to be possible, therefore, for American students of any color to attend any public institution they select without having to be backed up by troops.

It ought to be possible for American consumers of any color to receive equal service in places of public accommodation, such as hotels and restaurants and theaters and retail stores, without being forced to resort to demonstrations in the street, and it ought to be possible for American citizens of any color to register and to vote in a free election without interference or fear of reprisal.

It ought to be possible, in short, for every American to enjoy the privileges of being American without regard to his race or his color. In short, every American ought to have the right to be treated as he would wish to be treated, as one would wish his children to be treated. But this is not the case.

The Negro baby born in America today, regardless of the section of the Nation in which he is born, has about one-half as much chance of completing a high school as a white baby born in the same place on the same day, one-third as much chance of completing college, one-third as much chance of becoming a professional man, twice as much chance of becoming unemployed, about one-seventh as much chance of earning $10,000 a year, a life expectancy which is 7 years shorter, and the prospects of earning only half as much.

This is not a sectional issue. Difficulties over segregation and discrimination exist in every city, in every State of the Union, producing in many cities a rising tide of discontent that threatens the public safety. Nor is this a partisan issue. In a time of domestic crisis men of good will and generosity should be able to unite regardless of party or politics. This is not even a legal or legislative issue alone. It is better to settle these matters in the courts than on the streets, and new laws are needed at every level, but law alone cannot make men see right.

We are confronted primarily with a moral issue. It is as old as the scriptures and is as clear as the American Constitution. The heart of the question is whether all Americans are to be afforded equal rights and equal opportunities, whether we are going to treat our fellow Americans as we want to be treated. If an American, because his skin is dark, cannot eat lunch in a restaurant open to the public, if he cannot send his children to the best public school available, if he cannot vote for the public officials who represent him, if, in short, he cannot enjoy the full and free life which all of us want, then who among us would be content to have the color of his skin changed and stand in his place?

Who among us would then be content with the counsels of patience and delay?

One hundred years of delay have passed since President Lincoln freed the slaves, yet their heirs, their grandsons, are not fully free. They are not yet freed from the bonds of injustice. They are not yet freed from social and economic oppression. And this Nation, for all its hopes and all its boasts, will not be fully free until all its citizens are free.

We preach freedom around the world, and we mean it, and we cherish our freedom here at home, but are we to say to the world, and much more importantly, to each other that this is a land of the free except for the Negroes; that we have no second-class citizens except Negroes; that we have no class or caste system, no ghettoes, no master race except with respect to Negroes?

Now the time has come for this Nation to fulfill its promise. The events in Birmingham and elsewhere have so increased the cries for equality that no city or State or legislative body can prudently choose to ignore them.

The fires of frustration and discord are burning in every city, North and South, where legal remedies are not at hand. Redress is sought in the streets, in demonstrations, parades, and protests which create tensions and threaten violence and threaten lives. We face, therefore, a moral crisis as a country and as a people. It cannot be met by repressive police action. It cannot be left to increased demonstrations in the streets. It cannot be quieted by token moves or talk. It is a time to act in the Congress, in your State and local legislative body and, above all, in all of our daily lives. It is not enough to pin the blame on others, to say this is a problem of one section of the country or another, or deplore the fact that we face. A great change is at hand, and our task, our obligation, is to make that revolution, that change, peaceful and constructive for all.

Those who do nothing are inviting shame as well as violence. Those who act boldly are recognizing right as well as reality. Next week I shall ask the Congress of the United States to act, to make a commitment it has not fully made in this century to the proposition that race has no place in American life or law. The Federal judiciary has upheld that proposition in a series of forthright cases. The executive branch has adopted that proposition in the conduct of its affairs, including the employment of Federal personnel, the use of Federal facilities, and the sale of federally financed housing.

But there are other necessary measures which only the Congress can provide, and they must be provided at this session. The old code of equity law under which we live commands for every wrong a remedy, but in too many communities, in too many parts of the country, wrongs are inflicted on Negro citizens and there are no remedies at law. Unless the Congress acts, their only remedy is in the street. I am, therefore, asking the Congress to enact legislation giving all Americans the right to be served in facilities which are open to the public hotels, restaurants, theaters, retail stores, and similar establishments.

This seems to me to be an elementary right. Its denial is an arbitrary indignity that no American in 1963 should have to endure, but many do.

I have recently met with scores of business leaders urging them to take voluntary action to end this discrimination and I have been encouraged by their response, and in the last 2 weeks over 75 cities have seen progress made in desegregating these kinds of facilities. But many are unwilling to act alone, and for this reason, nationwide legislation is needed if we are to move this problem from the streets to the courts.

I am also asking Congress to authorize the Federal Government to participate more fully in lawsuits designed to end segregation in public education. We have succeeded in persuading many districts to desegregate voluntarily. Dozens have admitted Negroes without violence. Today a Negro is attending a State-supported institution in every one of our 50 States, but the pace is very slow.

Too many Negro children entering segregated grade schools at the time of the Supreme Court's decision 9 years ago will enter segregated high schools this fall, having suffered a loss which can never be restored. The lack of an adequate education denies the Negro a chance to get a decent job.

The orderly implementation of the Supreme Court decision, therefore, cannot be left solely to those who may not have the economic resources to carry the legal action or who may be subject to harassment.

Other features will be also requested, including greater protection for the right to vote. But legislation, I repeat, cannot solve this problem alone. It must be solved in the homes of every American in every community across our country.

In this respect, I want to pay tribute to those citizens North and South who have been working in their communities to make life better for all. They are acting not out of a sense of legal duty but out of a sense of human decency.

Like our soldiers and sailors in all parts of the world they are meeting freedom's challenge on the firing line, and I salute them for their honor and their courage. My fellow Americans, this is a problem which faces us all — in every city of the North as well as the South. Today there are Negroes unemployed, two or three times as many compared to whites, inadequate in education, moving into the large cities, unable to find work, young people particularly out of work without hope, denied equal rights, denied the opportunity to eat at a restaurant or lunch counter or go to a movie theater, denied the right to a decent education, denied almost today the right to attend a State university even though qualified. It seems to me that these are matters which concern us all, not merely Presidents or Congressmen or Governors, but every citizen of the United States.

This is one country. It has become one country because all of us and all the people who came here had an equal chance to develop their talents.

We cannot say to 10 percent of the population that you can't have that right; that your children can't have the chance to develop whatever talents they have; that the only way that they are going to get their rights is to go into the streets and demonstrate. I think we owe them and we owe ourselves a better country than that. Therefore, I am asking for your help in making it easier for us to move ahead and to provide the kind of equality of treatment which we would want ourselves; to give a chance for every child to be educated to the limit of his talents.

As I have said before, not every child has an equal talent or an equal ability or an equal motivation, but they should have the equal right to develop their talent and their ability and their motivation, to make something of themselves.

We have a right to expect that the Negro community will be responsible, will uphold the law, but they have a right to expect that the law will be fair, that the Constitution will be color blind, as Justice Harlan said at the turn of the century.

This is what we are talking about and this is a matter which concerns this country and what it stands for, and in meeting it I ask the support of all our citizens.

Thank you very much.

LAL BAHADUR SHASTRI

INTRODUCTION

Lal Bahadur Shastri was born in 1905 in Prayag. On May 27, 1964 Pandit Jawaharlal Nehru died. May of that year Lal Bahadur Shastri became India's second Prime Minister.

In 1966 a cease-fire was issued as a result of international pressure. Lal Bahadur Shastri went to Tashkent to hold talks with Ayub Khan and an agreement was soon signed. Lal Bahadur passed away in Tashkent before returning home on January 11, 1966. He was posthumously conferred with the Bharat Ratna Award.

EXCERPTS FROM HIS REPLY TO THE DEBATE ON THE MOTION OF THANKS FOR THE PRESIDENT'S ADDRESS IN THE RAJYA SABHA ON MARCH 9, 1965.

Vital Issues

THERE has been a prolonged discussion on the President's Address and except perhaps for a couple of very critical speeches, on the whole I must say that they were set in the proper key. The most important problem before us today is the economic development of our country, and we have naturally to concentrate our utmost attention on that problem. Sometimes an impression is given that there is no progress or no adequate development in the economic field. I would not go into the past history but during the last decade or twelve years, we have touched almost every vital item of industry. The essential ingredients of industry like oil, mines and minerals, steel, power, all these items have been not only fully explored but after giving some time to the exploration part of it, the Government has made definite progress and the industrial production has considerably gone up. There have been bottlenecks in the development of cement and steel. I might say that cement production during the next twelve months is expected to increase by about I million tonnes. Steel production between this year and the next two is expected to increase by 1/2 million tonnes. Fertilizer output is also expected to go up by 100,000 tonnes with the Trombay fertiliser plant going into production.

Then in regard to power, there will be an increase of nearly 3 million kilowatts in the power generating capacity of the country. In regard to steel, we have signed the Bokaro agreement. Two additional blast furnaces are being constructed at Bhilai in respect of steel plant expansion in the Fourth Plan. The Bhadravati Steel Works is being converted to produce alloy, tool and special steel, and a separate plant for it at Durgapur is nearing completion. In regard to petroleum, the Barauni refinery has just been commissioned. Construction of the third public sector refinery at Koyali is progressing and it should be completed by the end of 1965. Cochin refinery is also expected to be completed by the end of 1965.

About petro-chemicals, large petro-chemical complexes have been planned so far, one in the public sector around Koyali refinery in Gujarat and the other in the private sector near Bombay.

In the matter of machinery making, the Tiruchi Boiler Factory will start production in 1965. The fifth unit of the Hindustan Machine Tools at Hyderabad will also go into production this year. The surgical Instruments Plant at Madras will be commissioned in the middle of 1965. There is the Heavy Structural Works in regard to which we have entered into an agreement with Austria. And then there is the Czech Foundry Forge at Wardha, which is also to be constructed. These are some of the examples which indicate what is being done and what we would achieve in the course of about a couple of years in regard to certain plants and in a longer period in regard to other plants. This is a sector in which we have naturally to depend more on the public sector.

The public sector has to expand considerably both as a matter of policy and also because it is not possible for outsiders to invest huge sums of money which are needed for setting up these basic industries. It is also in a way easier for the Government to enter into collaboration with other governments on government-to-government basis. And, therefore, we have to expand our public sector and these public sector projects will come to fruition to serve as the base of our industries and the industrial economy in the country. I would also like the private sector to grow, and naturally, they have to function in the background of our social objectives. It is also true that they will have to be given every opportunity to develop. And incentives may also have to be given so that they can increase their production.

Our fiscal policy is oriented towards greater production as also towards helping the weaker elements of our society. The various measures of proposals of our Budget indicate that for greater production incentives will be provided. The incentives are given mainly on the basis of production.

There may be—there may not have been—a large reduction or any special reduction in the corporate sector so far as taxes are concerned, but what is most important is increased production and for that, the Budget proposals do contain various incentives.

In regard to agriculture, there is no doubt that we had to face a difficult food situation a few months back. I do not say that everything is now all right. Things are still difficult. Yet, it must be said that we have turned the corner. There are foodgrains available in the market, and the prices also have not gone up recently. It is, of course, unfortunate that we have to continue to import and there seems to be no alternative for us for some time to come except to add to our indigenous production through imports and serve the needs of our people. It is essential especially in order to build up a buffer stock. It helps in getting over the lean periods and it also acts as a check and some kind of regulation on the trends of the market. Luckily, we have had very good rice crops, over 39 million tonnes, perhaps the highest production of rice, this year. We expect that we will have a good wheat crop also. And in the matter of rice, we have procured rice, and our target of procurement is about 19 lakh tonnes. We have so far procured about eight lakh tonnes but this procurement will continue and this will help us in building up a buffer stock. In regard to wheat, we have not yet taken a final decision but we will be building up stocks of foodgrains. Naturally, they will have to be procured from the surplus States. It is open to the deficit States also to make purchases, if they so like. We have our Food Corporation set-up which would also enter into the market. There is going to be no monopoly procurement by the Food corporation but it would also enter into the field along with others. I, therefore, hope, sir, that in this year (1965) we would have solved one of our most intricate problems and that there will be an easy situation so far as foodgrains are concerned. Of course, imports are there but in fact the Government of India does not want that we should have to import for a long time to come. We have naturally to increase our agricultural production and for that it is essential that the necessary inputs, the necessary ingredients for agricultural production should be provided to the farmer, whether it is fertiliser or water or good seeds or similar other things. These things are very important and it has to be seen that these things reach the farmers in time. And it is important for the administration, the district administration, to take a special interest in it. There should be better coordination between the departments concerned, particularly those which deal with the panchayats.

Our target of foodgrains production for the Third Five Year Plan was 92 million tonnes. I am sorry to say that last year it has only been 80 million tonnes.

This indicates that we have to go very far. In fact, the Memorandum of the Fourth Five Year Plan has fixed the target at 120 million tonnes. Well, I do not think that it is impossible to achieve it.

Yet great efforts will have to be made and everyone of us will have to cooperate in the matter. I say "us" because Members of Parliament can help in this matter a great deal. They are the representatives of the people and they have to create an atmosphere in which the farmer, the peasant, will be interested in increasing agricultural production. It is essential that we generate a feeling in him that it is good for him to produce more and it is in the best interests of the country to have greater agricultural production. Sometimes it is not the physical need but perhaps a mental resolve, a mental resolution that he will do his utmost to increase the production in the larger interest of the country which would work as a magic. We have to create the mental resolution amongst our farmers. I have no doubt that if we increase our production, it would lead to stability in prices and it would also help in creating general prosperity all round, and then naturally it would mean less of dependence on foreign countries.

Sir, in regard to external affairs, we have always tried that the Geneva Agreement on Indochina should be adhered to; that there should be no breach of the Agreement and that there should be no conflict. Unfortunately, recently a new development has already arisen and the position seems to be fairly delicate. In that context we had appealed and expressed our views that two things are absolutely essential to resolve this problem : First, the hostilities which are going on at present should come to an end and the two parties should stop fighting. Secondly, there should be a Geneva-type conference. We feel that those who are not directly interested might also meet so that there is a dialogue, there is a talk, there is a discussion and there might be mutual consultations and talks also which would lead us to finding some kind of solution. We have also written to different Governments, different countries in this regard, and I might say that there is a generally favourable response from those countries. They have generally supported the idea that there should be some kind of joint appeal in order to end the present hostilities, and they also feel that there should be some kind of a conference. I think it is in the interest of world peace that these suggestions are accepted, and we will do our level best to move in this matter and see that something positive is done.

Our policy of non-alignment and peaceful co-existence is strongly and fully endorsed and is going to continue as our basic policy. As a non-aligned country we should have the authority to think independently. Secondly, non-alignment helps us in expanding the sphere of peace. It is essential that if we want to have peace it would be better for as large a number of countries as possible to keep out of the power blocs. And we, therefore, feel that our policy of non-alignment is necessary, useful and good for the country. Peaceful co-existence means that we do believe that it is not possible to have one kind of pattern throughout the world. It is not possible to regiment the thinking of man. The human being has got this special faculty of thinking and, therefore, there will be different patterns, different systems of administration and different forms of government. It is therefore, important that in spite of the different ways of thinking, different approaches, different ideologies, the world should live in peace and different countries should live as good neighbours.

The United Nations, in spite of its failings, has been a hope for the world. It has done many useful things and averted a number of critical moments when the world might have plunged into war. But recently, in regard to article 19, a new difficulty, a new complication has arisen. I do not want to go into that particular matter in detail because the House is aware of the developments. Recently they have formed a Committee to go into this matter. India is also a member of this Committee. We will try to contribute our mite.

We have had a number of distinguished guests from abroad during the last five or six months in our country. I am glad to say that our relations with our neighbouring countries have considerably improved. There may be some differences still remaining but by and large our relations are better and it is essential that we should have the best of relations with our neighbouring countries—Ceylon, Nepal, Burma, Afghanistan. The dignitaries, the Heads of these States, the Prime Ministers of these countries, have visited India. We have met them, have had talks and discussions with them and I must say that these talks have been very useful and we have definitely come closer to each other. I might also say that I have received invitations from a number of countries. It is not possible for me to visit all the countries from where I have received invitations but I have decided to visit the Soviet Republic and I have also received an invitation from the President of the United States and I would also be going there.

In regard to the language question, I would say that it is a very delicate issue. It has aroused feelings throughout the country, especially in the southern parts of India. People are naturally deeply attached to their mother-tongue and there is absolutely no question of displacing or replacing the mother-tongue spoken in different States. When I referred to misapprehension, I said it especially in regard to the use of the State language, or the mother-tongue, because some Tamil papers and some other pamphlets, etc., wrote that Tamil goes and Hindi comes, that Hindi will replace Tamil. There were even slogans to this effect shouted by some people in Madras. So this was a clear case of misapprehension. In so far as the State language is concerned, it is there, it has to be there and the Government of India will naturally like to give all possible encouragement to the development of the State languages. It is essential and we have certainly no objection to it. Almost all the State Governments have accepted or adopted the policy of introducing the State language as the official language of the State, and I know that in course of time all the State languages will become the principal languages for official purposes. As to the medium of instruction, of course, it is left to the State Governments. So therefore, in so far as the State languages are concerned, there can be no doubt at all in the mind of anyone that there is any question of replacing those languages by Hindi.

The second point is about the use of English. On January 26, 1965, it was, of course, officially announced, in terms of the provisions of the constitution, Hindi would be the official language of the Union and, if the Hon'ble members will see, there was no other action taken which could create any kind of confusion. I am told about some circulars in Hindi. Well, even if some circulars were issued, it should not have resulted in such violent action. Our mistakes could have been pointed out. I remember, when I was in charge of the Communications Ministry, a money order form was brought to my knowledge ; it was printed in Hindi only. Immediately I got it rectified and money order forms in Hindi were completely stopped from being sent to the south; forms in English were introduced there. So, even if there were certain discrepancies, or some mistakes made, it should have been pointed out to us, and we would have immediately rectified it. So there has been some cause for misapprehension, and as Mr. Annadurai rightly said, there has been a genuine apprehension also of the imposition of Hindi. I have made it categorically clear that we will abide by the wishes of and the assurances given by the late Prime Minister, Pandit Jawaharlal Nehru. I stand by it and we will certainly consider as to how to do it, how to implement it. That is one point which is under our consideration. Along with that, of course, we will have to realise that this country should have a link language. I am glad that Mr. Annadurai has said that he is not against Hindi as such, but he wants that it should not be spread through the help of the Government. Well, I would not like to say anything about that, but I do wish and hope that after some time he might like to reconsider his view even in regard to this particular matter. I do agree that there should be non-official effort, as big an effort as possible., for the teaching and propagation of Hindi. All the same it is important that English has to continue, it will continue. In terms of the Official Languages Act, English is to continue as an associate language, and there will be no difficulty at all for anyone who does not know Hindi, whether he is functioning here in the Secretariat, or in any other all-India office in any other part of the country. There will be no handicap at all in the matter of recruitment. There will be no handicap at all in the matter of promotion etc., because the officer does not know Hindi. I mean, these assurances are there. And then, between one State and the other English could be used, and is to be used, but in regard to the Center it is again open to the State Governments to use English. Between one State and another, if they agree to correspond with each other in a particular language, they are free to do so. For example, between Rajasthan and Uttar Pradesh, if they want to correspond with each other in Hindi, they might do so. But so far as the Centre is concerned, it has to be both in English as well as in Hindi.

With these assurances, Sir, I do not think there should be any kind of fear or apprehension in the minds of the people of

Madras. I would like to say that we are considering several matters in this connection. The question of the three-language formula is there; then some other matters, for example, the medium of examination in different languages. Well, we will examine all these matters; we will study them and then come to definite conclusions. The issue of language is such that it is better to take a cool and calculated view of things, and we must consider its various aspects and implications. I do hope that the students of Madras will now at least see things in the correct perspective. They have by and large withdrawn their strike, and I have extended my congratulations to them. Still there is some trouble somewhere; it may not be especially due to the language problem as such; it perhaps might be because of the cases of the detentions, etc. I would appeal to them that they must wait and see. They should not take any hurried action. I have no doubt that the Madras Government will consider all their suggestions more sympathetically. It would be in the best interests of the students as well as the State and the country that they do not resort to any kind of direct action.

I am glad that Shri Annadurai said that he did not want to interfere with the students or that he did not want to encourage them. It is indeed, from my point of view, very good and very satisfactory. I also do not believe that students as such should take direct part in politics. For youth outside the colleges and schools it is different. But so long as students are studying in universities and colleges and schools, they should not take an active part or associate themselves with any political organisation. They may study peacefully and quietly, and after they have completed their studies, they will be free to associate themselves with any political party or political organisation. I would humbly appeal that language should serve as a cementing force. Language is to unite; it is not to disunite. Language has to integrate and not to disintegrate, and, therefore, we have to keep the question of unity first and foremost in our minds. I would without taking much time of this House, Sir, appeal to Members of Parliament that they should always have the vision of a united India. In their mind's eye, they should carry an image of the whole country a map which has no internal dividing lines but only the frontiers of this vast and varied and yet united land.

MARTIN LUTHER KING, JR.

INTRODUCTION

Michael Luther King, Jr. was born in January 15, 1929, but later had his name changed to Martin. He fought aginst the racism and it ultimately saw the whites and blacks at par. Today the American society is dominated by the blacks. He died on April 4, 1968.

I HAVE A DREAM
APRIL 23, 1963
LINCOLN MEMORIAL, WASHINGTON, D.C.

FIVE score years ago, a great American, in whose symbolic shadow we stand signed the Emancipation Proclamation. This momentous decree came as a great beacon light of hope to millions of Negro slaves who had been seared in the flames of withering injustice. It came as a joyous daybreak to end the long night of captivity. But one hundred years later, we must face the tragic fact that the Negro is still not free. men, Jews and Gentiles, Protestants and Catholics, will be able to join hands and sing in the words of the old Negro spiritual, "Free at last!

free at last! thank God Almighty, we are free at last!"

One hundred years later, the life of the Negro is still sadly crippled by the manacles of segregation and the chains of discrimination. One hundred years later, the Negro lives on a lonely island of poverty in the midst of a vast ocean of material prosperity. One hundred years later, the Negro is still languishing in the corners of American society and finds himself an exile in his own land. So we have come here today to dramatize an appalling condition. In a sense we have come to our nation's capital to cash a check. When the architects of our republic wrote the magnificent words of the Constitution and the Declaration of Independence, they were signing a promissory note to which every American was to fall heir. men, Jews and Gentiles, Protestants and Catholics, will be able to join hands and sing in the words of the old Negro spiritual, "Free at last! free at last! thank God Almighty, we are free at last!"

This note was a promise that all men would be guaranteed the inalienable rights of life, liberty, and the pursuit of happiness. It is obvious today that America has defaulted on this promissory note insofar as her citizens of color are concerned. Instead of honoring this sacred obligation, America has given the Negro people a bad check which has come back marked "insufficient funds." But we refuse to believe that the bank of justice is bankrupt. We refuse to believe that there are insufficient funds in the great vaults of opportunity of this nation. men, Jews and Gentiles, Protestants and Catholics, will be able to join hands and sing in the words of the old Negro spiritual, "Free at last! free at last! thank God Almighty, we are free at last!"

So we have come to cash this check — a check that will give us upon demand the riches of freedom and the security of justice. We have also come to this hallowed spot to remind America of the fierce urgency of now. This is no time to engage in the luxury of cooling off or to take the tranquilizing drug of gradualism. Now is the time to rise from the dark and desolate valley of segregation to the sunlit path of racial justice. Now is the time to open the doors of opportunity to all of God's children. Now is the time to lift our nation from the quicksands of racial injustice to the solid rock of brotherhood. men, Jews and

Gentiles, Protestants and Catholics, will be able to join hands and sing in the words of the old Negro spiritual, "Free at last! free at last! thank God Almighty, we are free at last!"

It would be fatal for the nation to overlook the urgency of the moment and to underestimate the determination of the Negro. This sweltering summer of the Negro's legitimate discontent will not pass until there is an invigorating autumn of freedom and equality. Nineteen sixty-three is not an end, but a beginning. Those who hope that the Negro needed to blow off steam and will now be content will have a rude awakening if the nation returns to business as usual. There will be neither rest nor tranquility in America until the Negro is granted his citizenship rights. men, Jews and Gentiles, Protestants and Catholics, will be able to join hands and sing in the words of the old Negro spiritual, "Free at last! free at last! thank God Almighty, we are free at last!"

The whirlwinds of revolt will continue to shake the foundations of our nation until the bright day of justice emerges. But there is something that I must say to my people who stand on the warm threshold which leads into the palace of justice. In the process of gaining our rightful place we must not be guilty of wrongful deeds. Let us not seek to satisfy our thirst for freedom by drinking from the cup of bitterness and hatred. men, Jews and Gentiles, Protestants and Catholics, will be able to join hands and sing in the words of the old Negro spiritual, "Free at last! free at last! thank God Almighty, we are free at last!"

We must forever conduct our struggle on the high plane of dignity and discipline. we must not allow our creative protest to degenerate into physical violence. Again and again we must rise to the majestic heights of meeting physical force with soul force, The marvelous new militancy which has engulfed the Negro community must not lead us to distrust of all white people, for many of our white brothers, as evidenced by their presence here today, have come to realize that their destiny is tied up with our destiny and their freedom is inextricably bound to our freedom. men, Jews and Gentiles, Protestants and Catholics, will be able to join hands and sing in the words of the old Negro spiritual, "Free at last! free at last! thank God Almighty, we are free at last!"

We cannot walk alone. And as we walk, we must make the pledge that we shall march ahead. We cannot turn back. There are those who are asking the devotees of civil rights, "When will you be satisfied?" we can never be satisfied as long as our bodies, heavy with the fatigue of travel, cannot gain lodging in the motels of the highways and the hotels of the cities. We cannot be satisfied as long as the Negro's basic mobility is from a smaller ghetto to a larger one. We can never be satisfied as long as a Negro in Mississippi cannot vote and a Negro in New York believes he has nothing for which to vote. No, no, we are not satisfied, and we will not be satisfied until justice rolls down like waters and righteousness like a mighty stream. men, Jews and Gentiles, Protestants and Catholics, will be able to join hands and sing in the words of the old Negro spiritual, "Free at last! free at last! thank God Almighty, we are free at last!"

I am not unmindful that some of you have come here out of great trials and tribulations. Some of you have come fresh from narrow cells. Some of you have come from areas where your quest for freedom left you battered by the storms of persecution and staggered by the winds of police brutality. You have been the veterans of creative suffering. Continue to work with the faith that unearned suffering is redemptive. men, Jews and Gentiles, Protestants and Catholics, will be able to join hands and sing in the words of the old Negro spiritual, "Free at last! free at last! thank God Almighty, we are free at last!"

Go back to Mississippi, go back to Alabama, go back to Georgia, go back to Louisiana, go back to the slums and ghettos of our northern cities, knowing that somehow this situation can and will be changed. Let us not wallow in the valley of despair. I say to you today, my friends, that in spite of the difficulties and frustrations of the moment, I still have a dream. It is a dream deeply rooted in the American dream. men, Jews and Gentiles, Protestants and Catholics, will be able to join hands and sing in the words of the old Negro spiritual, "Free at last! free at last! thank God Almighty, we are free at last!"

I have a dream that one day this nation will rise up and

live out the true meaning of its creed: "We hold these truths to be self-evident: that all men are created equal." I have a dream that one day on the red hills of Georgia the sons of former slaves and the sons of former slaveowners will be able to sit down together at a table of brotherhood. I have a dream that one day even the state of Mississippi, a desert state, sweltering with the heat of injustice and oppression, will be transformed into an oasis of freedom and justice. I have a dream that my four children will one day live in a nation where they will not be judged by the color of their skin but by the content of their character. I have a dream today. men, Jews and Gentiles, Protestants and Catholics, will be able to join hands and sing in the words of the old Negro spiritual, "Free at last! free at last! thank God Almighty, we are free at last!"

I have a dream that one day the state of Alabama, whose governor's lips are presently dripping with the words of interposition and nullification, will be transformed into a situation where little black boys and black girls will be able to join hands with little white boys and white girls and walk together as sisters and brothers. I have a dream today. I have a dream that one day every valley shall be exalted, every hill and mountain shall be made low, the rough places will be made plain, and the crooked places will be made straight, and the glory of the Lord shall be revealed, and all flesh shall see it together. This is our hope. This is the faith with which I return to the South. With this faith we will be able to hew out of the mountain of despair a stone of hope. With this faith we will be able to transform the jangling discords of our nation into a beautiful symphony of brotherhood. With this faith we will be able to work together, to pray together, to struggle together, to go to jail together, to stand up for freedom together, knowing that we will be free one day. men, Jews and Gentiles, Protestants and Catholics, will be able to join hands and sing in the words of the old Negro spiritual, "Free at last! free at last! thank God Almighty, we are free at last!"

This will be the day when all of God's children will be able to sing with a new meaning, "My country, 'tis of thee, sweet land of liberty, of thee I sing. Land where my fathers died, land of the pilgrim's pride, from every mountainside, let freedom ring." And if America is to be a great nation, this must become true. So let freedom ring from the prodigious hilltops of New Hampshire. Let freedom ring from the mighty mountains of New York. Let freedom ring from the heightening Alleghenies of Pennsylvania! Let freedom ring from the snowcapped Rockies of Colorado! Let freedom ring from the curvaceous peaks of California! But not only that; let freedom ring from Stone Mountain of Georgia! Let freedom ring from Lookout Mountain of Tennessee! Let freedom ring from every hill and every molehill of Mississippi. From every mountainside, let freedom ring. men, Jews and Gentiles, Protestants and Catholics, will be able to join hands and sing in the words of the old Negro spiritual, "Free at last! free at last! thank God Almighty, we are free at last!"

When we let freedom ring, when we let it ring from every village and every hamlet, from every state and every city, we will be able to speed up that day when all of God's children, black men and white men, Jews and Gentiles, Protestants and Catholics, will be able to join hands and sing in the words of the old Negro spiritual, "Free at last! free at last! thank God Almighty, we are free at last!"

I SEE THE PROMISED LAND
APRIL 3, 1968
MEMPHIS, TENNESSEE

THANK you very kindly, my friends. As I listened to Ralph Abernathy in his eloquent and generous introduction and then thought about myself, I wondered who he was talking about. It's always good to have your closest friend and associate say something good about you. And Ralph is the best friend that I have in the world.

I'm delighted to see each of you here tonight in spite of a storm warning. You reveal that you are determined to go on anyhow. Something is happening in Memphis, something is happening in our world.

As you know, if I were standing at the beginning of time, with the possibility of general and panoramic view of the whole human history up to now, and the Almighty said to me, "Martin Luther King, which age would you like to live in?" — I would take my mental flight by Egypt through, or rather across the Red Sea, through the wilderness on toward the promised land. And in spite of its magnificence, I wouldn't stop there. I would move on by Greece, and take my mind to Mount Olympus. And I would see Plato, Aristotle, Socrates, Euripides and Aristophanes assembled around the Parthenon as they discussed the great and eternal issues of reality.

But I wouldn't stop there. I would go on, even to the great heyday of the Roman Empire. And I would see developments around there, through various emperors and leaders. But I wouldn't stop there. I would even come up to the day of the Renaissance, and get a quick picture of all that the Renaissance did for the cultural and esthetic life of man. But I wouldn't stop there. I would even go by the way that the man for whom I'm named had his habitat. And I would watch Martin Luther as he tacked his ninety-five theses on the door at the church in Wittenberg.

But I wouldn't stop there. I would come on up even to 1863, and watch a vacillating president by the name of Abraham Lincoln finally come to the conclusion that he had to sign the Emancipation Proclamation. But I wouldn't stop there. I would even come up the early thirties, and see a man grappling with the problems of the bankruptcy of his nation. And come with an eloquent cry that we have nothing to fear but fear itself.

But I wouldn't stop there. Strangely enough, I would turn to the Almighty, and say, "If you allow me to live just a few years in the second half of the twentieth century, I will be happy." Now that's a strange statement to make, because the world is all messed up. The nation is sick. Trouble is in the land. Confusion all around. That's a strange statement. But I know, somehow, that only when it is dark enough, can you see the stars. And I see God working in this period of the twentieth century in a way that men, in some strange way, are responding—something is happening in our world. The masses of people are rising up. And wherever they are assembled today, whether they are in Johannesburg, South Africa; Nairobi, Kenya: Accra, Ghana; New York City; Atlanta, Georgia; Jackson, Mississippi; or Memphis, Tennessee — the cry is always the same — "We want to be free."

And another reason that I'm happy to live in this period is that we have been forced to a point where we're going to have to grapple with the problems that men have been trying to grapple with through history, but the demands didn't force them to do it. Survival demands that we grapple with them. Men, for years now, have been talking about war and peace. But now, no longer can they just talk about it. It is no longer a choice between violence and nonviolence in this world; it's nonviolence or nonexistence.

That is where we are today. And also in the human rights revolution, if something isn't done, and in a hurry, to bring the colored peoples of the world out of their long years of poverty, their long years of hurt and neglect, the whole world is doomed. Now, I'm just happy that God has allowed me to live in this period, to see what is unfolding. And I'm happy that he's allowed me to be in Memphis.

I can remember, I can remember when Negroes were just going around as Ralph has said, so often, scratching where they didn't itch, and laughing when they were not tickled. But that day is all over. We mean business now, and we are determined to gain our rightful place in God's world.

And that's all this whole thing is about. We aren't engaged in any negative protest and in any negative arguments with anybody. We are saying that we are determined to be men. We are determined to be people. We are saying that we are God's children. And that we don't have to live like we are forced to live.

Now, what does all of this mean in this great period of history? It means that we've got to stay together. We've got to stay together and maintain unity. You know, whenever Pharaoh wanted to prolong the period of slavery in Egypt, he had a favorite, favorite formula for doing it. What was that? He kept the slaves fighting among themselves. But whenever the slaves get together, something happens in Pharaoh's court, and he cannot hold the slaves in slavery. When the slaves get together, that's the beginning of getting out of slavery. Now let us maintain unity.

Secondly, let us keep the issues where they are. The issue is injustice. The issue is the refusal of Memphis to be fair and honest in its dealings with its public servants, who happen to be sanitation workers. Now, we've got to keep attention on that. That's always the problem with a little violence. You know what happened the other day, and the press dealt only with the window-breaking. I read the articles. They very seldom got around to mentioning the fact that one thousand, three hundred sanitation workers were on strike, and that Memphis is not being fair to them, and that Mayor Loeb is in dire need of a doctor. They didn't get around to that.

Now we're going to march again, and we've got to march again, in order to put the issue where it is supposed to be. And force everybody to see that there are thirteen hundred of God's children here suffering, sometimes going hungry, going through dark and dreary nights wondering how this thing is going to come out. That's the issue. And we've got to say to the nation: we know it's coming out. For when people get caught up with that which is right and they are willing to sacrifice for it, there is no stopping point short of victory.

We aren't going to let any mace stop us. We are masters in our nonviolent movement in disarming police forces; they don't know what to do. I've seen them so often. I remember in Birmingham, Alabama, when we were in that majestic struggle there we would move out of the 16th Street Baptist Church day after day; by the hundreds we would move out. And Bull Connor would tell them to send the dogs forth and they did come; but we just went before the dogs singing, "Ain't gonna let nobody turn me round." Bull Connor next would say, "Turn the fire hoses on." And as I said to you the other night, Bull

Connor didn't know history. He knew a kind of physics that somehow didn't relate to the transphysics that we knew about. And that was the fact that there was a certain kind of fire that no water could put out. And we went before the fire hoses; we had known water. If we were Baptist or some other denomination, we had been immersed. If we were Methodist, and some others, we had been sprinkled, but we knew water.

That couldn't stop us. And we just went on before the dogs and we would look at them; and we'd go on before the water hoses and we would look at it, and we'd just go on singing. "Over my head I see freedom in the air." And then we would be thrown in the paddy wagons, and sometimes we were stacked in there like sardines in a can. And they would throw us in, and old Bull would say, "Take them off," and they did; and we would just go in the paddy wagon singing, "We Shall Overcome." And every now and then we'd get in the jail, and we'd see the jailers looking through the windows being moved by our prayers, and being moved by our words and our songs. And there was a power there which Bull Connor couldn't adjust to; and so we ended up transforming Bull into a steer, and we won our struggle in Birmingham.

Now we've got to go on to Memphis just like that. I call upon you to be with us Monday. Now about injunctions: We have an injunction and we're going into court tomorrow morning to fight this illegal, unconstitutional injunction. All we say to America is, "Be true to what you said on paper." If I lived in China or even Russia, or any totalitarian country, maybe I could understand the denial of certain basic First Amendment privileges, because they hadn't committed themselves to that over there. But somewhere I read of the freedom of assembly. Somewhere I read of the freedom of speech. Somewhere I read of the freedom of the press. Somewhere I read that the greatness of America is the right to protest for right. And so just as I say, we aren't going to let any injunction turn us around. We are going on.

We need all of you. And you know what's beautiful to me, is to see all of these ministers of the Gospel. It's a marvelous picture. Who is it that is supposed to articulate the longings and aspirations of the people more than the preacher? Somehow the preacher must be an Amos, and say, "Let justice roll down like waters and righteousness like a mighty stream." Somehow, the preacher must say with Jesus, "The spirit of the Lord is upon me, because he hath anointed me to deal with the problems of the poor."

And I want to commend the preachers, under the leadership of these noble men: James Lawson, one who has been in this struggle for many years; he's been to jail for struggling; but he's still going on, fighting for the rights of his people. Rev. Ralph Jackson, Billy Kiles; I could just go right on down the list, but time will not permit. But I want to thank them all. And I want you to thank them, because so often, preachers aren't concerned about anything but themselves. And I'm always happy to see a relevant ministry.

It's alright to talk about "long white robes over yonder," in all of its symbolism. But ultimately people want some suits and dresses and shoes to wear down here. It's alright to talk about "streets flowing with milk and honey," but God has commanded us to be concerned about the slums down here, and his children who can't eat three square meals a day. It's alright to talk about the new Jerusalem, but one day, God's preacher must talk about the New York, the new Atlanta, the new Philadelphia, the new Los Angeles, the new Memphis, Tennessee. This is what we have to do.

Now the other thing we'll have to do is this: Always anchor our external direct action with the power of economic withdrawal. Now, we are poor people, individually, we are poor when you compare us with white society in America. We are poor.

Never stop and forget that collectively, that means all of us together, collectively we are richer than all the nation in the world, with the exception of nine. Did you ever think about that? After you leave the United States, Soviet Russia, Great Britain, West Germany, France, and I could name the others, the Negro collectively is richer than most nations of the world. We have an annual income of more than thirty billion dollars a year, which is more than all of the exports of the United States, and more than the national budget of Canada. Did you know that? That's power right there, if we know how to pool it.

We don't have to argue with anybody. We don't have to curse and go around acting bad with our words. We don't need any bricks and bottles, we don't need any Molotov cocktails, we just need to go around to these stores, and to these massive industries in our country, and say, "God sent us by here, to say to you that you're not treating his children right. And we've come by here to ask you to make the first item on your agenda—fair treatment, where God's children are concerned. Now, if you are not prepared to do that, we do have an agenda that we must follow. And our agenda calls for withdrawing economic support from you."

And so, as a result of this, we are asking you tonight, to go out and tell your neighbors not to buy Coca-Cola in Memphis. Go by and tell them not to buy Sealtest milk. Tell them not to buy—what is the other bread?—Wonder Bread. And what is the other bread company, Jesse? Tell them not to buy Hart's bread. As Jesse Jackson has said, up to now, only the garbage men have been feeling pain; now we must kind of redistribute the pain. We are choosing these companies because they haven't been fair in their hiring policies; and we are choosing them because they can begin the process of saying, they are going to support the needs and the rights of these men who are on strike. And then they can move on downtown and tell Mayor Loeb to do what is right.

But not only that, we've got to strengthen black institutions. I call upon you to take you money out of the banks downtown and deposit you money in Tri-State Bank—we want a "bank-in" movement in Memphis. So go by the savings and loan association. I'm not asking you something that we don't do ourselves at SCLC. Judge Hooks and others will tell you that we have an account here in the savings and loan association from the Southern Christian Leadership Conference. We're just telling you to follow what we're doing. Put your money there. You have six or seven black insurance companies in Memphis. Take out your insurance there. We want to have an "insurance-in."

Now there are some practical things we can do. We begin the process of building a greater economic base. And at the same time, we are putting pressure where it really hurts. I ask you to follow through here.

Now, let me say as I move to my conclusion that we've got to give ourselves to this struggle until the end. Nothing would be more tragic than to stop at this point, in Memphis. We've got to see it through. And when we have our march, you need to be there. Be concerned about your brother. You may not be on strike. But either we go up together, or we go down together.

Let us develop a kind of dangerous unselfishness. One day a man came to Jesus; and he wanted to raise some questions about some vital matters in life. At points, he wanted to trick Jesus, and show him that he knew a little more than Jesus knew, and through this, throw him off base. Now that question could have easily ended up in a philosophical and theological debate. But Jesus immediately pulled that question from mid-air, and placed it on a dangerous curve between Jerusalem and Jericho. And he talked about a certain man, who fell among thieves. You remember that a Levite and a priest passed by on the other side. They didn't stop to help him. And finally a man of another race came by. He got down from his beast, decided not to be compassionate by proxy. But with him, administered first aid, and helped the man in need. Jesus ended up saying, this was the good man, because he had the capacity to project the "I" into the "thou," and to be concerned about his brother. Now you know, we use our imagination a great deal to try to determine why the priest and the Levite didn't stop. At times we say they were busy going to church meetings — an ecclesiastical gathering — and they had to get on down to Jerusalem so they wouldn't be late for their meeting. At other times we would speculate that there was a religious law that "One who was engaged in religious ceremonials was not to touch a human body twenty-four hours before the ceremony." And every now and then we begin to wonder whether maybe they were not going down to Jerusalem, or down to Jericho, rather to organize a "Jericho Road Improvement Association." That's a possibility. Maybe they felt that it was better to deal with the problem from the casual root, rather than to get bogged down with an individual effort.

But I'm going to tell you what my imagination tells me. It's possible that these men were afraid. You see, the Jericho road is a dangerous road. I remember when Mrs. King and I were first in Jerusalem. We rented a car and drove from Jerusalem down to Jericho. And as soon as we got on that road, I said to my wife, "I can see why Jesus used this as a setting for his parable." It's a winding, meandering road. It's really conducive for ambushing. You start out in Jerusalem, which is about 1200 miles, or rather 1200 feet above sea level. And by the time you get down to Jericho, fifteen or twenty minutes later, you're about 2200 feet below sea level. That's a dangerous road. In the day of Jesus it came to be known as the "Bloody Pass." And you know, it's possible that the priest and the Levite looked over that man on the ground and wondered if the robbers were still around. Or it's possible that they felt that the man on the ground was merely faking. And he was acting like he had been robbed and hurt, in order to seize them over there, lure them there for quick and easy seizure. And so the first question that the Levite asked was, "If I stop to help this man, what will happen to me?" But then the Good Samaritan came by. And he reversed the question: "If I do not stop to help this man, what will happen to him?".

That's the question before you tonight. Not, "If I stop to help the sanitation workers, what will happen to all of the hours that I usually spend in my office every day and every week as a pastor?" The question is not, "If I stop to help this man in need, what will happen to me?" "If I do no stop to help the sanitation workers, what will happen to them?" That's the question.

Let us rise up tonight with a greater readiness. Let us stand with a greater determination. And let us move on in these powerful days, these days of challenge to make America what it ought to be. We have an opportunity to make America a better nation. And I want to thank God, once more, for allowing me to be here with you.

You know, several years ago, I was in New York City

autographing the first book that I had written. And while sitting there autographing books, a demented black woman came up. The only question I heard from her was, "Are you Martin Luther King?"

And I was looking down writing, and I said yes. And the next minute I felt something beating on my chest. Before I knew it I had been stabbed by this demented woman. I was rushed to Harlem Hospital. It was a dark Saturday afternoon. And that blade had gone through, and the X-rays revealed that the tip of the blade was on the edge of my aorta, the main artery. And once that's punctured, you drown in your own blood—that's the end of you.

It came out in the New York Times the next morning, that if I had sneezed, I would have died. Well, about four days later, they allowed me, after the operation, after my chest had been opened, and the blade had been taken out, to move around in the wheel chair in the hospital. They allowed me to read some of the mail that came in, and from all over the states, and the world, kind letters came in. I read a few, but one of them I will never forget. I had received one from the President and the Vice-President. I've forgotten what those telegrams said. I'd received a visit and a letter from the Governor of New York, but I've forgotten what the letter said. But there was another letter that came from a little girl, a young girl who was a student at the White Plains High School. And I looked at that letter, and I'll never forget it. It said simply, "Dear Dr. King: I am a ninth-grade student at the Whites Plains High School." She said, "While it should not matter, I would like to mention that I am a white girl. I read in the paper of your misfortune, and of your suffering. And I read that if you had sneezed, you would have died. And I'm simply writing you to say that I'm so happy that you didn't sneeze."

And I want to say tonight, I want to say that I am happy that I didn't sneeze. Because if I had sneezed, I wouldn't have been around here in 1960, when students all over the South started sitting-in at lunch counters. And I knew that as they were sitting in, they were really standing up for the best in the American dream. And taking the whole nation back to those great wells of democracy which were dug deep by the Founding

Fathers in the Declaration of Independence and the Constitution. If I had sneezed, I wouldn't have been around in 1962, when Negroes in Albany, Georgia, decided to straighten their backs up. And whenever men and women straighten their backs up, they are going somewhere, because a man can't ride your back unless it is bent. If I had sneezed, I wouldn't have been here in 1963, when the black people of Birmingham, Alabama, aroused the conscience of this nation, and brought into being the Civil Rights Bill. If I had sneezed, I wouldn't have had a chance later that year, in August, to try to tell America about a dream that I had had. If I had sneezed, I wouldn't have been down in Selma, Alabama, to see the great movement there. If I had sneezed, I wouldn't have been in Memphis to see a community rally around those brothers and sisters who are suffering. I'm so happy that I didn't sneeze.

And they were telling me, now it doesn't matter now. It really doesn't matter what happens now. I left Atlanta this morning, and as we got started on the plane, there were six of us, the pilot said over the public address system, "We are sorry for the delay, but we have Dr. Martin Luther King on the plane. And to be sure that all of the bags were checked, and to be sure that nothing would be wrong with the plane, we had to check out everything carefully. And we've had the plane protected and guarded all night."

And then I got into Memphis. And some began to say that threats, or talk about the threats that were out. What would happen to me from some of our sick white brothers?

Well, I don't know what will happen now. We've got some difficult days ahead. But it doesn't matter with me now. Because I've been to the mountaintop. And I don't mind. Like anybody, I would like to live a long life. Longevity has its place. But I'm not concerned about that now. I just want to do God's will. And He's allowed me to go up to the mountain. And I've looked over. And I've seen the promised land. I may not get there with you. But I want you to know tonight, that we, as a people will get to the promised land. And I'm happy, tonight. I'm not worried about anything. I'm not fearing any man. Mine eyes have seen the glory of the coming of the Lord.

MARK TWAIN

INTRODUCTION

"Mark Twain," was born in Florida, Missouri, on November 30, 1835.

He was one of the foremost American philosophers of his day; he was the world's most famous humorist of any day.

ANNUAL MEETING OF THE HEBREW TECHNICAL SCHOOL FOR GIRLS, JANUARY 20, 1901

LADIES and Gentlemen, — It is a small help that I can afford, but it is just such help that one can give as coming from the heart through the mouth. The report of Mr. Meyer was admirable, and I was as interested in it as you have been. Why, I'm twice as old as he, and I've had so much experience that I would say to him, when he makes his appeal for help: "Don't make it for today or tomorrow, but collect the money on the spot."

We are all creatures of sudden impulse. We must be worked up by steam, as it were. Get them to write their wills now, or it may be too late by-and-by. Fifteen or twenty years ago I had an experience I shall never forget. I got into a church which was crowded by a sweltering and panting multitude. The city missionary of our town — Hartford — made a telling appeal for help. He told of personal experiences among the poor in cellars and top lofts requiring instances of devotion and help. The poor are always good to the poor. When a person with his millions gives a hundred thousand dollars it makes a great noise in the world, but he does not miss it; it's the widow's mite that makes no noise but does the best work.

I remember on that occasion in the Hartford church the collection was being taken up. The appeal had so stirred me that I could hardly wait for the hat or plate to come my way. I had four hundred dollars in my pocket, and I was anxious to drop it in the plate and wanted to borrow more. But the plate was so long in coming my way that the fever-heat of beneficence was going down lower and lower — going down at the rate of a hundred dollars a minute. The plate was passed too late. When it finally came to me, my enthusiasm had gone down so much that I kept my four hundred dollars — and stole a dime from the plate. So, you see, time sometimes leads to crime. Oh, many a time have I thought of that and regretted it, and I adjure you all to give while the fever is on you.

Referring to woman's sphere in life, I'll say that woman is always right. For twenty-five years I've been a woman's rights man. I have always believed, long before my mother died, that, with her gray hairs and admirable intellect, perhaps she knew as much as I did. Perhaps she knew as much about voting as I.

I should like to see the time come when women shall help to make the laws. I should like to see that whiplash, the ballot, in the hands of women. As for this city's government, I don't want to say much, except that it is a shame — a shame; but if I should live twenty-five years longer — and there is no reason why I shouldn't — I think I'll see women handle the ballot. If women had the ballot to-day, the state of things in this town would not exist. If all the women in this town had a vote today they would elect a mayor at the next election, and they would rise in their might and change the awful state of things now existing here.

MOHANDAS KARAMCHAND GANDHI

INTRODUCTION

Mohandas Karamchand Gandhi was born on 2nd October in 1869. His family belonged to the the Hindu religion and practiced the ahimsa principle of never injuring a living thing.

He was one of the great personalities of the 50th century. When In South Africa (1873 to 1914) he fought legal battle with the White Minority government and secured several civil rights for Asians living there. On return to India, he led the freedom movement against the British rule until the country secured Independence in August 1947.

WHILE LEADING THE CHAMPARAN INDIGO MOVEMENT, HE MADE THE FOLLOWING SPEECH

MY object is to inquire into the condition of the Champaran agriculturists and understand their grievances against the indigo planters. For this purpose it is necessary that I should meet thousands of the ryots. But I deem it essential, before starting on my inquiry, to know the planters' side of the case and see the Commissioner of the Division. •I sought and was granted appointments with both.

The Secretary of the Planters' Association told me plainly

that I was an outsider and that I had no business to come between the planters and their tenants, but if I had any representation to make, I might submit it in writing. I politely told him that I did* not regard myself as an outsider, and that I had every right to inquire into the condition of the tenants if they desired me to do so.

The Commissioner, on whom I called, proceeded to bully me, and advised me forthwith to leave Tirhut.

I acquainted my co-workers with all this, and told them that there was a likelihood of Government stopping me from proceeding further, and that I might have to go to jail earlier than I had expected, and that, if I was to be arrested, it would be best that the arrest should take place in Motihari or if possible in Bettiah. It was advisable, therefore, that I should go to those places as early as possible.

Champaran is a district of the Tirhut division and Motihari is its headquarters. Rajkumar Shukla's place was in the vicinity of Bettiah, and the tenants belonging to the kothis in its neighbourhood were the poorest in the district. Rajkumar Shukla wanted me to see them and I was equally anxious to do so.

So I started with my co-workers for Motihari the same day. Babu Gorakh Prasad harboured us in his home, which became a caravan serai- It could hardly contain us all. The very same day we heard that about five miles from Motihari a tenant had been ill-treated. It was decided that, in company with Babu Dharanidhar Prasad, I should go and see him the next morning, and we accordingly set off for the place on elephant's back. An elephant, by the way, is about as common in Champaran as a bullock-cart in Gujarat. We had scarcely gone half way when a messenger from the Police Superintendent overtook us and said that the latter had sent his compliments. I saw what he meant. Having left Dharanidharbabu to proceed to the original destination, I got into the hired carriage which the messenger had brought. He then served on me a notice to leave Champaran, and drove me to my place. On his asking me to acknowledge the service of the notice, I wrote to the effect that I did not propose to comply with it and leave Champaran till my inquiry was finished. There upon I received a summons to take my trial the next day for disobeying the order to leave Champaran.

I kept awake that whole night writing letters and giving necessary instructions to Babu Brajkishore Prasad.

The news of the notice and the summons spread like wildfire, and I was told that Motihari that day witnessed unprecedented scenes. Gorakhbabu's house and the court house overflowed with men. Fortunately I had finished all my work during the night and so was able to cope with the crowds. My companions proved the greatest help. They occupied themselves with regulating the crowds, for the latter followed me wherever I went.

A sort of friendliness sprang up between the officials—Collector, Magistrate, Police Superintendent—and myself. I might have legally resisted the notices served on me. Instead I accepted them all, and my conduct towards the officials was correct. They thus saw that I did not want to offend them personally, but that I wanted to offer civil resistance to their orders. In this way they were put at ease, and instead of harassing me they gladly availed themselves of my and my co-workers' co-operation in regulating the crowds. But it was an ocular demonstration to them of the fact that their authority was shaken. The people had for the moment lost all fear of punishment and yielded obedience to the power of love which their new friend exercised.

It should be remembered that no one knew me in Champaran. The peasants were all ignorant, Champaran, being far up north of the Ganges, and right at the foot of the Himalayas in close proximity to Nepal, was cut off from the rest of India. The Congress was practically unknown in those parts. Even those who had heard the name of the Congress shrank from joining it or even mentioning it. And now the Congress and its members had entered this land though not in the name of the Congress, yet in a far more real sense.

In consultation with my co-workers I had decided that nothing should be done in the name of the Congress. What we wanted was work and not name, substance and not shadow. For the name of the Congress was the bete noire of the government and their controllers—the planters. To them the Congress was a byword for lawyers' wrangles, evasion of law through legal loopholes, a byword for bomb and anarchical crime and for diplomacy and hypocrisy. We had to disillusion them both. Therefore we bad decided not to mention the name of the Congress and not to acquaint the peasants with the organization called the Congress. It was enough, we thought, if they understood and followed the spirit of the Congress instead of its letter.

No emissaries had therefore been sent there, openly or secretly, on behalf of the Congress to prepare the ground for our arrival. Rajkumar Shukla was incapable of reaching the thousands of peasants. No political work had yet been done amongst them. The world outside Champaran was not known to them. And yet they received me as though we had been age-long friends. It is no exaggeration, but the

literal truth, to say that in this meeting with the peasants, I was face to face with God, Ahimsa and Truth.

When I come to examine my title to this realization, I find nothing but my love for the people. And this in turn is nothing but an expression of my unshakable faith in Ahimsa.

That day in Champaran was an unforgettable event in my life and a red-letter day for the peasants and for me.

According to the law, I was to be on my trial, but truly speaking Government was to be on its trial. The Commissioner only succeeded in trapping Government in the net which he had spread for me.

The trial began. The Government pleader, the Magistrate and other officials were on tenterhooks. They were at a loss to know what to do. The Government pleader was pressing the Magistrate to postpone the case. But I interfered and requested the Magistrate not to postpone the case, as I wanted to plead guilty to having disobeyed the order to leave Champaran and read a brief statement as follows :

With the permission of the Court I would like to make a brief statement showing why I have taken the very serious step of seemingly disobeying the order passed under Sec. 144 of Cr. P.C. In my humble opinion it is a question of difference of opinion between the Local Administration and myself. I have entered the country with motives of rendering humanitarian and national service. I have done so in response to a pressing invitation to come and help the ryots, who urge they are not being fairly treated by the indigo planters. I could not render any help without studying the problem. I have, therefore, come to study it with the assistance, if possible, of the Administration and the planters. I have no other motive, and cannot believe that my coming can be any claim to have considerable experience in such matters. The Administration, however, have thought differently. I fully appreciate their difficulty, and I admit too that they can only proceed upon information they received. As a law-abiding citizen my first instinct would be, as it was, to obey the order served upon me. But I could not do so without doing violence to my sense of duty to those for whom I have come.

I feel that I could just now serve them only by remaining in their midst. I could not, therefore, voluntarily retire. Amid this conflict of duties I could only throw the responsibility of removing me from them on the Administration. I am fully conscious of the fact that a person, holding, in the public life of India, a position such as I do, has to be most careful in setting an example. It is my firm belief that in the complex constitution under which we are living, the only safe and honourable course for a self-respecting man is, in the circumstances such as face me, to do what I have decided to do. that is, to submit without protest to the penalty of disobedience.

I venture to make this statement not in any way in extenuation of the penalty to be awarded against me, but to show that I have disregarded the order served upon me not for want of respect for lawful authority, but in obedience to the higher law of our being, the voice of conscience.'

There was now no occasion to postpone the hearing, but as both the Magistrate and the Government pleader had been taken by surprise, the Magistrate postponed the judgment. Meanwhile I had wired full details to the Viceroy, to Patna friends, as also to Pandit Madan Mohan Malaviya and others.

Before I could appear before the Court to receive the

sentence, the Magistrate sent a written message that the Lieutenant Governor had ordered the case against me to be withdrawn, and the Collector wrote to me saying that I was at liberty to conduct the proposed inquiry, and that I might count on whatever help I needed from the officials. None of us was prepared for this prompt and happy action.

I called on the Collector Mr. Heycock. He seemed to be a good man, anxious to do justice. He told me that I might ask for whatever papers I desired to see, and that I was at liberty to see him whenever I liked.

The country thus had its first direct object-lesson in Civil Disobedience. The affair was freely discussed both locally and in the press, and my inquiry got unexpected publicity.

It was necessary for my inquiry that the Government should remain neutral. But the inquiry did not need support from press reporters or leading articles in the press. Indeed the situation in Champaran was so delicate and difficult that over-energetic criticism or highly coloured reports might easily damage the cause which I was seeking to espouse. So I wrote to the editors of the principal papers requesting them not to trouble to send any reporters, as I should send them whatever might be necessary for publication and keep them informed.

I knew that the Government attitude countenancing my presence had displeased the Champaran planters, and I knew that even the officials, though they could say nothing openly, could hardly have liked it. Incorrect or misleading reports, therefore, were likely to incense them all the more, and their ire, instead of descending on me, would be sure to descend on the poor fear-stricken ryots and seriously hinder my search for the truth about the case.

In spite of these precautions the planters engineered against me a poisonous agitation. All sorts of falsehoods appeared in the press about my co-workers and myself. But my extreme cautiousness and my insistence on truth, even to the minutest detail, turned the edge of their sword.

The planters left no stone unturned in maligning Brajkishorebabu. but the more they maligned him, the more he rose in the estimation of the people.

In such a delicate situation as this I did not think it proper to invite any leaders from other provinces. Pandit Malaviyaji had sent me an assurance that whenever I wanted him, I had only to send him word, but I did nor trouble him. I thus prevented the struggle from assuming a political accent. But I sent to the leaders and the principal papers occasional reports, not for publication, but merely for their information. I had seen that, even where the end might be political, but where the cause was non-political. one damaged it by giving it a political accent and helped it by keeping it within its non-political limit. The Champaran struggle was a proof of the fact that disinterested service of the people of any sphere ultimately helps the country politically.

NELSON ROLIHLAHLA MANDELA

INTRODUCTION

Nelson Rolihlahla Mandela was born in 1918. He earned (1942) a law degree from the University of South Africa and was prominent in Johannesburg's youth wing of the African National Congress (ANC). In 1952 he became ANC deputy national president, advocating nonviolent resistance to apartheid. However, after a group of peaceful demonstrators were massacred (1960) in Sharpeville, Mandela organized a paramilitary branch of the ANC to carry out guerrilla warfare against the white government. After being acquitted (1962) on charges of treason, he was arrested (1964) and convicted of sabotage and sentenced to life in prison, where he became the leading symbol of South Africa's oppressed black majority. Released in 1990 as an expression of President de Klerk's committment to change, Mandela was elected (July, 1991) ANC president after a triumphal global tour. Mandela and de Klerk were jointly awarded the Nobel peace prize in 1993. In South Africa's first multiracial elections (1994), Mandela was elected president, and served until 1999, when Thabo Mbeki succeeded him, after Mandela decided not to contest.

"I AM PREPARED TO DIE"

APRIL 20, 1964

I AM the First Accused.

I hold a Bachelor's Degree in Arts and practised as an attorney in Johannesburg for a number of years in partnership with Oliver Tambo. I am a convicted prisoner serving five years for leaving the country without a permit and for inciting people to go on strike at the end of May 1961.

At the outset, I want to say that the suggestion made by the State in its opening that the struggle in South Africa is under the influence of foreigners or communists is wholly incorrect. I have done whatever I did, both as an individual and as a leader of my people, because of my experience in South Africa and my own proudly felt African background, and not because of what any outsider might have said.

In my youth in the Transkei I listened to the elders of my tribe telling stories of the old days. Amongst the tales they related to me were those of wars fought by our ancestors in defence of the fatherland. The names of Dingane and Bambata, Hintsa and Makana, Squngthi and Dalasile, Moshoeshoe and Sekhukhuni, were praised as the glory of the entire African nation. I hoped then that life might offer me the opportunity to serve my people and make my own humble contribution to their freedom struggle. This is what has motivated me in all that I have done in relation to the charges made against me in this case.

Having said this, I must deal immediately and at some length with the question of violence. Some of the things so far told to the Court are true and some are untrue. I do not, however, deny that I planned sabotage. I did not plan it in a spirit of recklessness, nor because I have any love of violence. I planned it as a result of a calm and sober assessment of the political situation that had arisen after many years of tyranny, exploitation, and oppression of my people by the Whites.

I admit immediately that I was one of the persons who helped to form Umkhonto we Sizwe, and that I played a prominent role in its affairs until I was arrested in August 1962.

In the statement which I am about to make I shall correct certain false impressions which have been created by State witnesses. Amongst other things, I will demonstrate that certain of the acts referred to in the evidence were not and could not have been committed by Umkhonto. I will also deal with the relationship between the African National Congress and Umkhonto, and with the part which I personally have played in the affairs of both organizations. I shall deal also with the part played by the Communist Party. In order to explain these matters properly, I will have to explain what Umkhonto set out to achieve; what methods it prescribed for the achievement of these objects, and why these methods were chosen. I will also have to explain how I became involved in the activities of these organizations.

I deny that Umkhonto was responsible for a number of acts which clearly fell outside the policy of the organization, and which have been charged in the indictment against us. I do not know what justification there was for these acts, but to demonstrate that they could not have been authorized by Umkhonto, I want to refer briefly to the roots and policy of the organization.

I have already mentioned that I was one of the persons who helped to form Umkhonto. I, and the others who started the organization, did so for two reasons. Firstly, we believed that as a result of Government policy, violence by the African people had become inevitable, and that unless responsible leadership was given to canalize and control the feelings of our people, there would be outbreaks of terrorism which would produce an intensity of bitterness and hostility between the various races of this country which is not produced even by war. Secondly, we felt that without violence there would be no way open to the African people to succeed in their struggle against the principle of white supremacy. All lawful modes of expressing opposition to this principle had been closed by legislation, and we were placed in a position in which we had either to accept a permanent state of inferiority, or to defy the Government. We chose to defy the law. We first broke the law in a way which avoided any recourse to violence; when this form was legislated against, and then the Government resorted to a show of force to crush opposition to its policies, only then did we decide to answer violence with violence.

But the violence which we chose to adopt was not terrorism. We who formed Umkhonto were all members of the African National Congress, and had behind us the ANC tradition of non-violence and negotiation as a means of solving political disputes. We believe that South Africa belongs to all the people who live in it, and not to one group, be it black or white. We did not want an interracial war, and tried to avoid it to the last minute. If the Court is in doubt about this, it will be seen that the whole history of our organization bears out what I have said, and what I will subsequently say, when I describe the tactics which Umkhonto decided to adopt. I want, therefore, to say something about the African National Congress.

The African National Congress was formed in 1912 to defend the rights of the African people which had been seriously curtailed by the South Africa Act, and which were then being threatened by the Native Land Act. For thirty-seven years - that is until 1949 - it adhered strictly to a constitutional struggle. It put forward demands and resolutions; it sent delegations to the Government in the belief that African grievances could be settled through peaceful discussion and that Africans could advance gradually to full political rights. But White Governments remained unmoved, and the rights of Africans became less instead of becoming greater. In the words of my leader, Chief Lutuli, who became President of the ANC in 1952, and who was later awarded the Nobel Peace Prize:

"Who will deny that thirty years of my life have been spent knocking in vain, patiently, moderately, and modestly at a closed and barred door? What have been the fruits of moderation? The past thirty years have seen the greatest number of laws restricting our rights and progress, until today we have reached a stage where we have almost no rights at all."

Even after 1949, the ANC remained determined to avoid violence. At this time, however, there was a change from the strictly constitutional means of protest which had been employed in the past. The change was embodied in a decision which was taken to protest against apartheid legislation by peaceful, but unlawful, demonstrations against certain laws. Pursuant to this policy the ANC launched the Defiance Campaign, in which I was placed in charge of volunteers. This campaign was based on the principles of passive resistance. More than 8,500 people defied apartheid laws and went to jail. Yet there was not a single instance of violence in the course of this campaign on the part of any defier. I and nineteen colleagues were convicted for the role which we played in organizing the campaign, but our sentences were suspended mainly because the Judge found that discipline and non-violence had been stressed throughout. This was the time when the volunteer section of the ANC was established, and when the word 'Amadelakufa' was first used: this was the time when the volunteers were asked to take a pledge to uphold certain principles. Evidence dealing with volunteers and their pledges has been introduced into this case, but completely out of context. The volunteers were not, and are not, the soldiers of a black army pledged to fight a civil war against the whites. They were, and are, dedicated workers who are prepared to lead campaigns initiated by the ANC to distribute leaflets, to organize strikes, or do whatever the particular campaign required. They are called volunteers because they volunteer to face the penalties of imprisonment and whipping which are now prescribed by the legislature for such acts.

During the Defiance Campaign, the Public Safety Act and the Criminal Law Amendment Act were passed. These Statutes provided harsher penalties for offences committed by way of protests against laws. Despite this, the protests continued and the ANC adhered to its policy of non-violence. In 1956, 156 leading members of the Congress Alliance, including myself, were arrested on a charge of high treason and charges under the Suppression of Communism Act. The non-violent policy of the ANC was put in issue by the State, but when the Court gave judgement some five years later, it found that the ANC did not have a policy of violence. We were acquitted on all counts, which included a count that the ANC sought to set up a communist state in place of the existing regime. The Government has always sought to label all its opponents as communists. This allegation has been repeated in the present case, but as I will show, the ANC is not, and never has been, a communist organization.

In 1960 there was the shooting at Sharpeville, which resulted in the proclamation of a state of emergency and the declaration of the ANC as an unlawful organization. My colleagues and I, after careful consideration, decided that we would not obey this decree. The African people were not part of the Government and did not make the laws by which they were governed. We believed in the words of the Universal Declaration of Human Rights, that 'the will of the people shall be the basis of authority of the Government,' and for us to accept the banning was equivalent to accepting the silencing of the Africans for all time. The ANC refused to dissolve, but instead went underground. We believed it was our duty to preserve this organization which had been built up with almost fifty years of unremitting toil. I have no doubt that no self-respecting White political organization would disband itself if declared illegal by a government in which it had no say.

In 1960 the Government held a referendum which led to the establishment of the Republic. Africans, who constituted approximately 70 per cent of the population of South Africa, were not entitled to vote, and were not even consulted about the proposed constitutional change. All of us were apprehensive of our future under the proposed White Republic, and a resolution was taken to hold an All-In African Conference to call for a National Convention, and to organize mass demonstrations on the eve of the unwanted Republic, if the Government failed to call the Convention. The conference was attended by Africans of various political persuasions. I was the Secretary of the conference and undertook to be responsible for organizing the national stay-at-home which was subsequently called to coincide with the declaration of the Republic. As all strikes by Africans are illegal, the person organizing such a strike must avoid arrest. I was chosen to be this person, and consequently I had to leave my home and family and my practice and go into hiding to avoid arrest.

The stay-at-home, in accordance with ANC policy, was to be a peaceful demonstration. Careful instructions were given to organizers and members to avoid any recourse to violence. The Government's answer was to introduce new and harsher laws, to mobilize its armed forces, and to send Saracens, armed vehicles, and soldiers into the townships in a massive show of force designed to intimidate the people. This was an indication that the Government had decided to rule by force alone, and this decision was a milestone on the road to Umkhonto.

Some of this may appear irrelevant to this trial. In fact, I believe none of it is irrelevant because it will, I hope, enable the Court to appreciate the attitude eventually adopted by the various persons and bodies concerned in the National Liberation Movement. When I went to jail in 1962, the dominant idea was that loss of life should be avoided. I now know that this was still so in 1963.

I must return to June 1961. What were we, the leaders of our people, to do? Were we to give in to the show of force and the implied threat against future action, or were we to fight it and, if so, how?

We had no doubt that we had to continue the fight. Anything else would have been abject surrender. Our problem was not whether to fight, but was how to continue the fight. We of the ANC had always stood for a non-racial democracy, and we shrank from any action which might drive the races further apart than they already were. But the hard facts were that fifty years of non-violence had brought the African people nothing but more and more repressive legislation, and fewer and fewer rights. It may not be easy for this Court to understand, but it is a fact that for a long time the people had been talking of violence - of the day when they would fight the White man and win back their country - and we, the leaders of the ANC, had nevertheless always prevailed upon them to avoid violence and to pursue peaceful methods. When some of us discussed this in May and June of 1961, it could not be denied that our policy to achieve a non-racial State by non-violence had achieved nothing, and that our followers were beginning to lose confidence in this policy and were developing disturbing ideas of terrorism.

It must not be forgotten that by this time violence had, in fact, become a feature of the South African political scene. There had been violence in 1957 when the women of Zeerust were ordered to carry passes; there was violence in 1958 with the enforcement of cattle culling in Sekhukhuniland; there was violence in 1959 when the people of Cato Manor protested against pass raids; there was violence in 1960 when the Government attempted to impose Bantu Authorities in Pondoland. Thirty-nine Africans died in these disturbances. In 1961 there had been riots in Warmbaths, and all this time the Transkei had been a seething mass of unrest. Each disturbance pointed clearly to the inevitable growth among Africans of the belief that violence was the only way out - it showed that a

Government which uses force to maintain its rule teaches the oppressed to use force to oppose it. Already small groups had arisen in the urban areas and were spontaneously making plans for violent forms of political struggle. There now arose a danger that these groups would adopt terrorism against Africans, as well as Whites, if not properly directed. Particularly disturbing was the type of violence engendered in places such as Zeerust, Sekhukhuniland, and Pondoland amongst Africans. It was increasingly taking the form, not of struggle against the Government - though this is what prompted it - but of civil strife amongst themselves, conducted in such a way that it could not hope to achieve anything other than a loss of life and bitterness.

At the beginning of June 1961, after a long and anxious assessment of the South African situation, I, and some colleagues, came to the conclusion that as violence in this country was inevitable, it would be unrealistic and wrong for African leaders to continue preaching peace and non-violence at a time when the Government met our peaceful demands with force.

This conclusion was not easily arrived at. It was only when all else had failed, when all channels of peaceful protest had been barred to us, that the decision was made to embark on violent forms of political struggle, and to form Umkhonto we Sizwe. We did so not because we desired such a course, but solely because the Government had left us with no other choice. In the Manifesto of Umkhonto published on 16 December 1961, which is Exhibit AD, we said:

"The time comes in the life of any nation when there remain only two choices - submit or fight. That time has now come to South Africa. We shall not submit and we have no choice but to hit back by all means in our power in defence of our people, our future, and our freedom."

This was our feeling in June of 1961 when we decided to press for a change in the policy of the National Liberation Movement. I can only say that I felt morally obliged to do what I did.

We who had taken this decision started to consult leaders of various organizations, including the ANC. I will not say whom we spoke to, or what they said, but I wish to deal with the role of the African National Congress in this phase of the struggle, and with the policy and objectives of Umkhonto we Sizwe.

As far as the ANC was concerned, it formed a clear view which can be summarized as follows:

- It was a mass political organization with a political function to fulfil. Its members had joined on the express policy of non-violence.
- Because of all this, it could not and would not undertake violence. This must be stressed. One cannot turn such a body into the small, closely knit organization required for sabotage. Nor would this be politically correct, because it would result in members ceasing to carry out this essential activity: political propaganda and organization. Nor was it permissible to change the whole nature of the organization.
- On the other hand, in view of this situation I have described, the ANC was prepared to depart from its fifty-year-old policy of non-violence to this extent that it would no longer disapprove of properly controlled violence. Hence members who undertook such activity would not be subject to disciplinary action by the ANC.

I say 'properly controlled violence' because I made it clear that if I formed the organization I would at all times subject it to the political guidance of the ANC and would not undertake any different form of activity from that contemplated without the consent of the ANC. And I shall now tell the Court how that form of violence came to be determined.

As a result of this decision, Umkhonto was formed in November 1961. When we took this decision, and subsequently formulated our plans, the ANC heritage of non-violence and racial harmony was very much with us. We felt that the country was drifting towards a civil war in which Blacks and Whites would fight each other. We viewed the situation with alarm. Civil war could mean the destruction of what the ANC stood for; with civil war, racial peace would be more difficult than ever to achieve. We already have examples in South African history of the results of war. It has taken more than fifty years for the scars of the South African War to disappear. How much longer would it take to eradicate the scars of inter-racial civil war, which could not be fought without a great loss of life on both sides?

The avoidance of civil war had dominated our thinking for

many years, but when we decided to adopt violence as part of our policy, we realized that we might one day have to face the prospect of such a war. This had to be taken into account in formulating our plans. We required a plan which was flexible and which permitted us to act in accordance with the needs of the times; above all, the plan had to be one which recognized civil war as the last resort, and left the decision on this question to the future. We did not want to be committed to civil war, but we wanted to be ready if it became inevitable.

Four forms of violence were possible. There is sabotage, there is guerrilla warfare, there is terrorism, and there is open revolution. We chose to adopt the first method and to exhaust it before taking any other decision.

In the light of our political background the choice was a logical one. Sabotage did not involve loss of life, and it offered the best hope for future race relations. Bitterness would be kept to a minimum and, if the policy bore fruit, democratic government could become a reality. This is what we felt at the time, and this is what we said in our Manifesto (Exhibit AD):

"We of Umkhonto we Sizwe have always sought to achieve liberation without bloodshed and civil clash. We hope, even at this late hour, that our first actions will awaken everyone to a realization of the disastrous situation to which the Nationalist policy is leading. We hope that we will bring the Government and its supporters to their senses before it is too late, so that both the Government and its policies can be changed before matters reach the desperate state of civil war."

The initial plan was based on a careful analysis of the political and economic situation of our country. We believed that South Africa depended to a large extent on foreign capital and foreign trade. We felt that planned destruction of power plants, and interference with rail and telephone communications, would tend to scare away capital from the country, make it more difficult for goods from the industrial areas to reach the seaports on schedule, and would in the long run be a heavy drain on the economic life of the country, thus compelling the voters of the country to reconsider their position.

Attacks on the economic life-lines of the country were to be linked with sabotage on Government buildings and other symbols of apartheid. These attacks would serve as a source of inspiration to our people. In addition, they would provide an outlet for those people who were urging the adoption of violent methods and would enable us to give concrete proof to our followers that we had adopted a stronger line and were fighting back against Government violence.

In addition, if mass action were successfully organized, and mass reprisals taken, we felt that sympathy for our cause would be roused in other countries, and that greater pressure would be brought to bear on the South African Government.

This then was the plan. Umkhonto was to perform sabotage, and strict instructions were given to its members right from the start, that on no account were they to injure or kill people in planning or carrying out operations. These instructions have been referred to in the evidence of 'Mr. X' and 'Mr. Z.'

The affairs of the Umkhonto were controlled and directed by a National High Command, which had powers of co-option and which could, and did, appoint Regional Commands. The High Command was the body which determined tactics and targets and was in charge of training and finance. Under the High Command there were Regional Commands which were responsible for the direction of the local sabotage groups. Within the framework of the policy laid down by the National High Command, the Regional Commands had authority to select the targets to be attacked. They had no authority to go beyond the prescribed framework and thus had no authority to embark upon acts which endangered life, or which did not fit into the overall plan of sabotage. For instance, Umkhonto members were forbidden ever to go armed into operation. Incidentally, the terms High Command and Regional Command were an importation from the Jewish national underground organization Irgun Zvai Leumi, which operated in Israel between 1944 and 1948.

Umkhonto had its first operation on 16 December 1961, when Government buildings in Johannesburg, Port Elizabeth and Durban were attacked. The selection of targets is proof of the policy to which I have referred. Had we intended to attack life we would have selected targets where people congregated and not empty buildings and power stations. The sabotage which was committed before 16 December 1961 was the work of isolated groups and had no connection whatever with Umkhonto. In fact, some of these and a number of later acts were claimed by other organizations.

The Manifesto of Umkhonto was issued on the day that operations commenced. The response to our actions and Manifesto among the white population was characteristically violent. The Government threatened to take strong action, and called upon its supporters to stand firm and to ignore the demands of the Africans. The Whites failed to respond by suggesting change; they responded to our call by suggesting the laager.

In contrast, the response of the Africans was one of encouragement. Suddenly there was hope again. Things were happening. People in the townships became eager for political news. A great deal of enthusiasm was generated by the initial successes, and people began to speculate on how soon freedom would be obtained.

But we in Umkhonto weighed up the white response with anxiety. The lines were being drawn. The whites and blacks were moving into separate camps, and the prospects of avoiding a civil war were made less. The white newspapers carried reports that sabotage would be punished by death. If this was so, how could we continue to keep Africans away from terrorism?

Already scores of Africans had died as a result of racial friction. In 1920 when the famous leader, Masabala, was held in Port Elizabeth jail, twenty-four of a group of Africans who had gathered to demand his release were killed by the police and white civilians. In 1921 more than one hundred Africans died in the Bulhoek affair. In 1924 over two hundred Africans were killed when the Administrator of South-West Africa led a force against a group which had rebelled against the imposition of dog tax. On 1 May 1950, eighteen Africans died as a result of police shootings during the strike. On 21 March 1960, sixty-nine unarmed Africans died at Sharpeville.

How many more Sharpevilles would there be in the history of our country? And how many more Sharpevilles could the country stand without violence and terror becoming the order of the day? And what would happen to our people when that stage was reached? In the long run we felt certain we must succeed, but at what cost to ourselves and the rest of the country?

And if this happened, how could black and white ever live together again in peace and harmony? These were the problems that faced us, and these were our decisions.

Experience convinced us that rebellion would offer the Government limitless opportunities for the indiscriminate slaughter of our people. But it was precisely because the soil of South Africa is already drenched with the blood of innocent Africans that we felt it our duty to make preparations as a long-term undertaking to use force in order to defend ourselves against force. If war were inevitable, we wanted the fight to be conducted on terms most favorable to our people. The fight which held out prospects best for us and the least risk of life to both sides was guerrilla warfare. We decided, therefore, in our preparations for the future, to make provision for the possibility of guerrilla warfare.

All whites undergo compulsory military training, but no such training was given to Africans. It was in our view essential to build up a nucleus of trained men who would be able to provide the leadership which would be required if guerrilla warfare started. We had to prepare for such a situation before it became too late to make proper preparations. It was also necessary to build up a nucleus of men trained in civil administration and other professions, so that Africans would be equipped to participate in the government of this country as soon as they were allowed to do so.

At this stage it was decided that I should attend the Conference of the Pan-African Freedom Movement for Central, East, and Southern Africa, which was to be held early in 1962 in Addis Ababa, and, because of our need for preparation, it was also decided that, after the conference, I would undertake a tour of the African States with a view to obtaining facilities for the training of soldiers, and that I would also solicit scholarships for the higher education of matriculated Africans. Training in both fields would be necessary, even if changes came about by peaceful means. Administrators would be necessary who would be willing and able to administer a non-racial State and so would men be necessary to control the army and police force of such a State.

It was on this note that I left South Africa to proceed to Addis Ababa as a delegate of the ANC. My tour was a success.

Wherever I went I met sympathy for our cause and promises of help. All Africa was united against the stand of White South Africa, and even in London I was received with great sympathy by political leaders, such as Mr. Gaitskell and Mr. Grimond. In Africa I was promised support by such men as Julius Nyerere, now President of Tanganyika; Mr. Kawawa, then Prime Minister of Tanganyika; Emperor Haile Selassie of Ethiopia; General Abboud, President of the Sudan; Habib Bourguiba, President of Tunisia; Ben Bella, now President of Algeria; Modibo Keita, President of Mali; Leopold Senghor, President of Senegal; Sekou Toure, President of Guinea; President Tubman of Liberia; and Milton Obote, Prime Minister of Uganda. It was Ben Bella who invited me to visit Oujda, the Headquarters of the Algerian Army of National Liberation, the visit which is described in my diary, one of the Exhibits.

I started to make a study of the art of war and revolution and, whilst abroad, underwent a course in military training. If there was to be guerrilla warfare, I wanted to be able to stand and fight with my people and to share the hazards of war with them. Notes of lectures which I received in Algeria are contained in Exhibit 16, produced in evidence. Summaries of books on guerrilla warfare and military strategy have also been produced. I have already admitted that these documents are in my writing, and I acknowledge that I made these studies to equip myself for the role which I might have to play if the struggle drifted into guerrilla warfare. I approached this question as every African Nationalist should do. I was completely objective. The Court will see that I attempted to examine all types of authority on the subject - from the East and from the West, going back to the classic work of Clausewitz, and covering such a variety as Mao Tse Tung and Che Guevara on the one hand, and the writings on the Anglo-Boer War on the other. Of course, these notes are merely summaries of the books I read and do not contain my personal views.

I also made arrangements for our recruits to undergo military training. But here it was impossible to organize any scheme without the co-operation of the ANC offices in Africa. I consequently obtained the permission of the ANC in South Africa to do this. To this extent then there was a departure from the original decision of the ANC, but it applied outside South Africa only. The first batch of recruits actually arrived in Tanganyika when I was passing through that country on my way back to South Africa.

I returned to South Africa and reported to my colleagues on the results of my trip. On my return I found that there had been little alteration in the political scene save that the threat of a death penalty for sabotage had now become a fact. The attitude of my colleagues in Umkhonto was much the same as it had been before I left. They were feeling their way cautiously and felt that it would be a long time before the possibilities of sabotage were exhausted. In fact, the view was expressed by some that the training of recruits was premature. This is recorded by me in the document which is Exhibit R.14. After a full discussion, however, it was decided to go ahead with the plans for military training because of the fact that it would take many years to build up a sufficient nucleus of trained soldiers to start a guerrilla campaign, and whatever happened, the training would be of value.

I wish to turn now to certain general allegations made in this case by the State. But before doing so, I wish to revert to certain occurrences said by witnesses to have happened in Port Elizabeth and East London. I am referring to the bombing of private houses of pro-Government persons during September, October and November 1962. I do not know what justification there was for these acts, nor what provocation had been given. But if what I have said already is accepted, then it is clear that these acts had nothing to do with the carrying out of the policy of Umkhonto.

One of the chief allegations in the indictment is that the ANC was a party to a general conspiracy to commit sabotage. I have already explained why this is incorrect but how, externally, there was a departure from the original principle laid down by the ANC. There has, of course, been overlapping of functions internally as well, because there is a difference between a resolution adopted in the atmosphere of a committee room and the concrete difficulties that arise in the field of practical activity. At a later stage the position was further affected by bannings and house arrests, and by persons leaving the country to take up political work abroad. This led to individuals having to do work in different capacities. But though this may have blurred the distinction between Umkhonto and the ANC, it by no means abolished that distinction. Great care was taken to keep the activities of the two organizations in South Africa distinct. The ANC remained a mass political body of Africans only carrying on the type of political work they had conducted prior to 1961. Umkhonto remained a small organization recruiting its members from different races and organizations and trying to achieve its own particular object. The fact that members of Umkhonto were recruited from the ANC, and the fact that persons served both organizations, like Solomon Mbanjwa, did not, in our view, change the nature of the ANC or give it a policy of violence. This overlapping of officers, however, was more the exception than the rule. This is why persons such as 'Mr. X' and 'Mr. Z,' who were on the Regional Command of their respective areas, did not participate in any of the ANC committees or activities, and why people such as Mr. Bennett Mashiyana and Mr. Reginald Ndubi did not hear of sabotage at their ANC meetings.

Another of the allegations in the indictment is that Rivonia was the headquarters of Umkhonto. This is not true of the time when I was there. I was told, of course, and knew that certain of the activities of the Communist Party were carried on there. But this is no reason (as I shall presently explain) why I should not use the place.

I came there in the following manner:

- As already indicated, early in April 1961 I went underground to organize the May general strike. My work entailed travelling throughout the country, living now in African townships, then in country villages and again in cities.
- During the second half of the year I started visiting the Parktown home of Arthur Goldreich, where I used to meet my family privately. Although I had no direct political association with him, I had known Arthur Goldreich socially since 1958.
- In October, Arthur Goldreich informed me that he was moving out of town and offered me a hiding place there. A few days thereafter, he arranged for Michael Harmel to take me to Rivonia. I naturally found Rivonia an ideal place for the man who lived the life of an outlaw. Up to that time I had been compelled to live indoors during the daytime and could only venture out under cover of darkness. But at Liliesleaf [farm,

Rivonia,] I could live differently and work far more efficiently.

· For obvious reasons, I had to disguise myself and I assumed the fictitious name of David. In December, Arthur Goldreich and his family moved in. I stayed there until I went abroad on 11 January 1962. As already indicated, I returned in July 1962 and was arrested in Natal on 5 August.

· Up to the time of my arrest, Liliesleaf farm was the headquarters of neither the African National Congress nor Umkhonto. With the exception of myself, none of the officials or members of these bodies lived there, no meetings of the governing bodies were ever held there, and no activities connected with them were either organized or directed from there. On numerous occasions during my stay at Liliesleaf farm I met both the Executive Committee of the ANC, as well as the NHC, but such meetings were held elsewhere and not on the farm.

· Whilst staying at Liliesleaf farm, I frequently visited Arthur Goldreich in the main house and he also paid me visits in my room. We had numerous political discussions covering a variety of subjects. We discussed ideological and practical questions, the Congress Alliance, Umkhonto and its activities generally, and his experiences as a soldier in the Palmach, the military wing of the Haganah. Haganah was the political authority of the Jewish National Movement in Palestine.

· Because of what I had got to know of Goldreich, I recommended on my return to South Africa that he should be recruited to Umkhonto. I do not know of my personal knowledge whether this was done.

Another of the allegations made by the State is that the aims and objects of the ANC and the Communist Party are the same. I wish to deal with this and with my own political position, because I must assume that the State may try to argue from certain Exhibits that I tried to introduce Marxism into the ANC. The allegation as to the ANC is false. This is an old allegation which was disproved at the Treason Trial and which has again reared its head. But since the allegation has been made again, I shall deal with it as well as with the relationship between the ANC and the Communist Party and Umkhonto and that party.

The ideological creed of the ANC is, and always has been, the creed of African Nationalism. It is not the concept of African

Nationalism expressed in the cry, 'Drive the White man into the sea.' The African Nationalism for which the ANC stands is the concept of freedom and fulfilment for the African people in their own land. The most important political document ever adopted by the ANC is the 'Freedom Charter.' It is by no means a blueprint for a socialist state. It calls for redistribution, but not nationalization, of land; it provides for nationalization of mines, banks, and monopoly industry, because big monopolies are owned by one race only, and without such nationalization racial domination would be perpetuated despite the spread of political power. It would be a hollow gesture to repeal the Gold Law prohibitions against Africans when all gold mines are owned by European companies. In this respect the ANC's policy corresponds with the old policy of the present Nationalist Party which, for many years, had as part of its programme the nationalization of the gold mines which, at that time, were controlled by foreign capital. Under the Freedom Charter, nationalization would take place in an economy based on private enterprise. The realization of the Freedom Charter would open up fresh fields for a prosperous African population of all classes, including the middle class. The ANC has never at any period of its history advocated a revolutionary change in the economic structure of the country, nor has it, to the best of my recollection, ever condemned capitalist society.

As far as the Communist Party is concerned, and if I understand its policy correctly, it stands for the establishment of a State based on the principles of Marxism. Although it is prepared to work for the Freedom Charter, as a short term solution to the problems created by white supremacy, it regards the Freedom Charter as the beginning, and not the end, of its program.

The ANC, unlike the Communist Party, admitted Africans only as members. Its chief goal was, and is, for the African people to win unity and full political rights. The Communist Party's main aim, on the other hand, was to remove the capitalists and to replace them with a working-class government. The Communist Party sought to emphasize class distinctions whilst the ANC seeks to harmonize them. This is a vital distinction.

It is true that there has often been close co-operation

between the ANC and the Communist Party. But co-operation is merely proof of a common goal - in this case the removal of white supremacy - and is not proof of a complete community of interests.

The history of the world is full of similar examples. Perhaps the most striking illustration is to be found in the co-operation between Great Britain, the United States of America, and the Soviet Union in the fight against Hitler. Nobody but Hitler would have dared to suggest that such co-operation turned Churchill or Roosevelt into communists or communist tools, or that Britain and America were working to bring about a communist world.

Another instance of such co-operation is to be found precisely in Umkhonto. Shortly after Umkhonto was constituted, I was informed by some of its members that the Communist Party would support Umkhonto, and this then occurred. At a later stage the support was made openly.

I believe that communists have always played an active role in the fight by colonial countries for their freedom, because the short-term objects of communism would always correspond with the long-term objects of freedom movements. Thus communists have played an important role in the freedom struggles fought in countries such as Malaya, Algeria, and Indonesia, yet none of these States today are communist countries. Similarly in the underground resistance movements which sprung up in Europe during the last World War, communists played an important role. Even General Chiang Kai-Shek, today one of the bitterest enemies of communism, fought together with the communists against the ruling class in the struggle which led to his assumption of power in China in the 1930s.

This pattern of co-operation between communists and non-communists has been repeated in the National Liberation Movement of South Africa. Prior to the banning of the Communist Party, joint campaigns involving the Communist Party and the Congress movements were accepted practice. African communists could, and did, become members of the ANC, and some served on the National, Provincial, and local committees. Amongst those who served on the National Executive are Albert Nzula, a former Secretary of the Communist Party, Moses Kotane, another former Secretary, and

J. B. Marks, a former member of the Central Committee.

I joined the ANC in 1944, and in my younger days I held the view that the policy of admitting communists to the ANC, and the close co-operation which existed at times on specific issues between the ANC and the Communist Party, would lead to a watering down of the concept of African Nationalism. At that stage I was a member of the African National Congress Youth League, and was one of a group which moved for the expulsion of communists from the ANC. This proposal was heavily defeated. Amongst those who voted against the proposal were some of the most conservative sections of African political opinion. They defended the policy on the ground that from its inception the ANC was formed and built up, not as a political party with one school of political thought, but as a Parliament of the African people, accommodating people of various political convictions, all united by the common goal of national liberation. I was eventually won over to this point of view and I have upheld it ever since.

It is perhaps difficult for white South Africans, with an ingrained prejudice against communism, to understand why experienced African politicians so readily accept communists as their friends. But to us the reason is obvious. Theoretical differences amongst those fighting against oppression is a luxury we cannot afford at this stage. What is more, for many decades communists were the only political group in South Africa who were prepared to treat Africans as human beings and their equals; who were prepared to eat with us; talk with us, live with us, and work with us. They were the only political group which was prepared to work with the Africans for the attainment of political rights and a stake in society. Because of this, there are many Africans who, today, tend to equate freedom with communism. They are supported in this belief by a legislature which brands all exponents of democratic government and African freedom as communists and bans many of them (who are not communists) under the Suppression of Communism Act. Although I have never been a member of the Communist Party, I myself have been named under that pernicious Act because of the role I played in the Defiance Campaign. I have also been banned and imprisoned under that Act.

It is not only in internal politics that we count communists as amongst those who support our cause. In the international field, communist countries have always come to our aid. In the United Nations and other Councils of the world the communist bloc has supported the Afro-Asian struggle against colonialism and often seems to be more sympathetic to our plight than some of the Western powers. Although there is a universal condemnation of apartheid, the communist bloc speaks out against it with a louder voice than most of the white world. In these circumstances, it would take a brash young politician, such as I was in 1949, to proclaim that the Communists are our enemies.

I turn now to my own position. I have denied that I am a communist, and I think that in the circumstances I am obliged to state exactly what my political beliefs are.

I have always regarded myself, in the first place, as an African patriot. After all, I was born in Umtata, forty-six years ago. My guardian was my cousin, who was the acting paramount chief of Tembuland, and I am related both to the present paramount chief of Tembuland, Sabata Dalindyebo, and to Kaizer Matanzima, the Chief Minister of the Transkei.

Today I am attracted by the idea of a classless society, an attraction which springs in part from Marxist reading and, in part, from my admiration of the structure and organization of early African societies in this country. The land, then the main means of production, belonged to the tribe. There were no rich or poor and there was no exploitation.

It is true, as I have already stated, that I have been influenced by Marxist thought. But this is also true of many of the leaders of the new independent States. Such widely different persons as Gandhi, Nehru, Nkrumah, and Nasser all acknowledge this fact. We all accept the need for some form of socialism to enable our people to catch up with the advanced countries of this world and to overcome their legacy of extreme poverty. But this does not mean we are Marxists.

Indeed, for my own part, I believe that it is open to debate whether the Communist Party has any specific role to play at this particular stage of our political struggle. The basic task at the present moment is the removal of race discrimination and the attainment of democratic rights on the basis of the Freedom Charter. In so far as that Party furthers this task, I welcome its assistance. I realize that it is one of the means by which people of all races can be drawn into our struggle.

From my reading of Marxist literature and from conversations with Marxists, I have gained the impression that communists regard the parliamentary system of the West as undemocratic and reactionary. But, on the contrary, I am an admirer of such a system.

The Magna Carta, the Petition of Rights, and the Bill of Rights are documents which are held in veneration by democrats throughout the world.

I have great respect for British political institutions, and for the country's system of justice. I regard the British Parliament as the most democratic institution in the world, and the independence and impartiality of its judiciary never fails to arouse my admiration.

The American Congress, that country's doctrine of separation of powers, as well as the independence of its judiciary, arouses in me similar sentiments.

I have been influenced in my thinking by both West and East. All this has led me to feel that in my search for a political formula, I should be absolutely impartial and objective. I should tie myself to no particular system of society other than of socialism. I must leave myself free to borrow the best from the West and from the East . . .

There are certain Exhibits which suggest that we received financial support from abroad, and I wish to deal with this question.

Our political struggle has always been financed from internal sources - from funds raised by our own people and by our own supporters. Whenever we had a special campaign or an important political case - for example, the Treason Trial - we received financial assistance from sympathetic individuals and organizations in the Western countries. We had never felt it necessary to go beyond these sources.

But when in 1961 the Umkhonto was formed, and a new phase of struggle introduced, we realized that these events would make a heavy call on our slender resources, and that the scale of our activities would be hampered by the lack of funds. One of my instructions, as I went abroad in January 1962, was to raise funds from the African states.

I must add that, whilst abroad, I had discussions with leaders of political movements in Africa and discovered that almost every single one of them, in areas which had still not attained independence, had received all forms of assistance from the socialist countries, as well as from the West, including that of financial support. I also discovered that some well-known African states, all of them non-communists, and even anti-communists, had received similar assistance.

On my return to the Republic, I made a strong recommendation to the ANC that we should not confine ourselves to Africa and the Western countries, but that we should also send a mission to the socialist countries to raise the funds which we so urgently needed.

I have been told that after I was convicted such a mission was sent, but I am not prepared to name any countries to which it went, nor am I at liberty to disclose the names of the organizations and countries which gave us support or promised to do so.

As I understand the State case, and in particular the evidence of 'Mr. X,' the suggestion is that Umkhonto was the inspiration of the Communist Party which sought by playing upon imaginary grievances to enroll the African people into an army which ostensibly was to fight for African freedom, but in reality was fighting for a communist state. Nothing could be further from the truth. In fact the suggestion is preposterous. Umkhonto was formed by Africans to further their struggle for freedom in their own land. Communists and others supported the movement, and we only wish that more sections of the community would join us.

Our fight is against real, and not imaginary, hardships or, to use the language of the State Prosecutor, 'so-called hardships.' Basically, we fight against two features which are the hallmarks of African life in South Africa and which are entrenched by legislation which we seek to have repealed. These features are poverty and lack of human dignity, and we do not need communists or so-called 'agitators' to teach us about these things.

South Africa is the richest country in Africa, and could be one of the richest countries in the world. But it is a land of extremes and remarkable contrasts. The whites enjoy what may well be the highest standard of living in the world, whilst Africans live in poverty and misery. Forty per cent of the Africans live in hopelessly overcrowded and, in some cases, drought-stricken Reserves, where soil erosion and the overworking of the soil makes it impossible for them to live properly off the land. Thirty per cent are laborers, labor tenants, and squatters on white farms and work and live under conditions similar to those of the serfs of the Middle Ages. The other 30 per cent live in towns where they have developed economic and social habits which bring them closer in many respects to white standards. Yet most Africans, even in this group, are impoverished by low incomes and high cost of living.

The highest-paid and the most prosperous section of urban African life is in Johannesburg. Yet their actual position is desperate. The latest figures were given on 25 March 1964 by Mr. Carr, Manager of the Johannesburg Non-European Affairs Department. The poverty datum line for the average African family in Johannesburg (according to Mr. Carr's department) is R42.84 per month. He showed that the average monthly wage is R32.24 and that 46 per cent of all African families in Johannesburg do not earn enough to keep them going.

Poverty goes hand in hand with malnutrition and disease. The incidence of malnutrition and deficiency diseases is very high amongst Africans. Tuberculosis, pellagra, kwashiorkor, gastro-enteritis, and scurvy bring death and destruction of health. The incidence of infant mortality is one of the highest in the world. According to the Medical Officer of Health for Pretoria, tuberculosis kills forty people a day (almost all Africans), and in 1961 there were 58,491 new cases reported. These diseases not only destroy the vital organs of the body, but they result in retarded mental conditions and lack of initiative, and reduce powers of concentration. The secondary results of such conditions affect the whole community and the standard of work performed by African laborers.

The complaint of Africans, however, is not only that they are poor and the whites are rich, but that the laws which are made by the whites are designed to preserve this situation. There are two ways to break out of poverty. The first is by formal education, and the second is by the worker acquiring a greater skill at his work and thus higher wages. As far as Africans are concerned, both these avenues of advancement are deliberately curtailed by legislation.

The present Government has always sought to hamper Africans in their search for education. One of their early acts, after coming into power, was to stop subsidies for African school feeding. Many African children who attended schools depended on this supplement to their diet. This was a cruel act.

There is compulsory education for all white children at virtually no cost to their parents, be they rich or poor. Similar facilities are not provided for the African children, though there are some who receive such assistance. African children, however, generally have to pay more for their schooling than whites. According to figures quoted by the South African Institute of Race Relations in its 1963 journal, approximately 40 per cent of African children in the age group between seven to fourteen do not attend school. For those who do attend school, the standards are vastly different from those afforded to white children. In 1960-61 the per capita Government spending on African students at State-aided schools was estimated at R12.46. In the same years, the per capita spending on white children in the Cape Province (which are the only figures available to me) was R144.57. Although there are no figures available to me, it can be stated, without doubt, that the white children on whom R144.57 per head was being spent all came from wealthier homes than African children on whom R12.46 per head was being spent.

The quality of education is also different. According to the Bantu Educational Journal, only 5,660 African children in the whole of South Africa passed their Junior Certificate in 1962, and in that year only 362 passed matric. This is presumably consistent with the policy of Bantu education about which the present Prime Minister said, during the debate on the Bantu Education Bill in 1953:

"When I have control of Native education I will reform it so that Natives will be taught from childhood to realize that equality with Europeans is not for them . . . People who believe in equality are not desirable teachers for Natives. When my

Department controls Native education it will know for what class of higher education a Native is fitted, and whether he will have a chance in life to use his knowledge."

The other main obstacle to the economic advancement of the African is the industrial color-bar under which all the better jobs of industry are reserved for Whites only. Moreover, Africans who do obtain employment in the unskilled and semi-skilled occupations which are open to them are not allowed to form trade unions which have recognition under the Industrial Conciliation Act. This means that strikes of African workers are illegal, and that they are denied the right of collective bargaining which is permitted to the better-paid White workers. The discrimination in the policy of successive South African Governments towards African workers is demonstrated by the so-called 'civilized labor policy' under which sheltered, unskilled Government jobs are found for those white workers who cannot make the grade in industry, at wages which far exceed the earnings of the average African employee in industry.

The Government often answers its critics by saying that Africans in South Africa are economically better off than the inhabitants of the other countries in Africa. I do not know whether this statement is true and doubt whether any comparison can be made without having regard to the cost-of-living index in such countries. But even if it is true, as far as the African people are concerned it is irrelevant. Our complaint is not that we are poor by comparison with people in other countries, but that we are poor by comparison with the white people in our own country, and that we are prevented by legislation from altering this imbalance.

The lack of human dignity experienced by Africans is the direct result of the policy of white supremacy. White supremacy implies black inferiority. Legislation designed to preserve white supremacy entrenches this notion. Menial tasks in South Africa are invariably performed by Africans. When anything has to be carried or cleaned the white man will look around for an African to do it for him, whether the African is employed by him or not. Because of this sort of attitude, whites tend to regard Africans as a separate breed. They do not look upon them as people with families of their own; they do not realize that they have emotions - that they fall in love like white people do; that they want to be with their wives and children like white people want to be with theirs; that they want to earn enough money to support their families properly, to feed and clothe them and send them to school. And what 'house-boy' or 'garden-boy' or laborer can ever hope to do this?

Pass laws, which to the Africans are among the most hated bits of legislation in South Africa, render any African liable to police surveillance at any time. I doubt whether there is a single African male in South Africa who has not at some stage had a brush with the police over his pass. Hundreds and thousands of Africans are thrown into jail each year under pass laws. Even worse than this is the fact that pass laws keep husband and wife apart and lead to the breakdown of family life.

Poverty and the breakdown of family life have secondary effects. Children wander about the streets of the townships because they have no schools to go to, or no money to enable them to go to school, or no parents at home to see that they go to school, because both parents (if there be two) have to work to keep the family alive. This leads to a breakdown in moral standards, to an alarming rise in illegitimacy, and to growing violence which erupts not only politically, but everywhere. Life in the townships is dangerous. There is not a day that goes by without somebody being stabbed or assaulted. And violence is carried out of the townships in the white living areas. People are afraid to walk alone in the streets after dark. Housebreakings and robberies are increasing, despite the fact that the death sentence can now be imposed for such offences. Death sentences cannot cure the festering sore.

Africans want to be paid a living wage. Africans want to perform work which they are capable of doing, and not work which the Government declares them to be capable of. Africans want to be allowed to live where they obtain work, and not be endorsed out of an area because they were not born there. Africans want to be allowed to own land in places where they work, and not to be obliged to live in rented houses which they can never call their own. Africans want to be part of the general population, and not confined to living in their own ghettoes. African men want to have their wives and children to live with them where they work, and not be forced into an unnatural existence in men's hostels. African women want to be with their menfolk and not be left permanently widowed in the Reserves. Africans want to be allowed out after eleven o'clock at night and not to be confined to their rooms like little children. Africans want to be allowed to travel in their own country and to seek work where they want to and not where the Labor Bureau tells them to. Africans want a just share in the whole of South Africa; they want security and a stake in society.

Above all, we want equal political rights, because without them our disabilities will be permanent. I know this sounds revolutionary to the whites in this country, because the majority of voters will be Africans. This makes the white man fear democracy.

But this fear cannot be allowed to stand in the way of the only solution which will guarantee racial harmony and freedom for all. It is not true that the enfranchisement of all will result in racial domination. Political division, based on color, is entirely artificial and, when it disappears, so will the domination of one color group by another. The ANC has spent half a century fighting against racialism. When it triumphs it will not change that policy.

This then is what the ANC is fighting. Their struggle is a truly national one. It is a struggle of the African people, inspired by their own suffering and their own experience. It is a struggle for the right to live.

During my lifetime I have dedicated myself to this struggle of the African people. I have fought against white domination, and I have fought against black domination. I have cherished the ideal of a democratic and free society in which all persons live together in harmony and with equal opportunities. It is an ideal which I hope to live for and to achieve. But if needs be, it is an ideal for which I am prepared to die.

NAPOLEON BONAPARTE

INTRODUCTION

French Emperor and general. His victories over Austria and Russia made him practically the master of Europe. He, however, experienced a disastrous retreat from Moscow in 1812.

The Allies forced him to abdicate and retire to Elba. He emerged alone in 1815 but was defeated by the British at Waterloo and exiled to St. Helene where he died.

FAREWELL TO THE OLD GUARD

APRIL 20, 1814

SOLDIERS of my Old Guard: I bid you farewell. For twenty years I have constantly accompanied you on the road to honor and glory. In these latter times, as in the days of our prosperity, you have invariably been models of courage and fidelity. With men such as you our cause could not be lost; but the war would have been interminable; it would have been civil war, and that would have entailed deeper misfortunes on France.

I have sacrificed all of my interests to those of the country.

I go, but you, my friends, will continue to serve France.

Her happiness was my only thought. It will still be the object of my wishes. Do not regret my fate; if I have consented to survive, it is to serve your glory. I intend to write the history of the great achievements we have performed together. Adieu, my friends, wish I could press you all to my heart. I embrance you all in the person of your general. Come, General Petit, that I may press you to my heart! Bring me the eagle that I may embrance it also! Adieu, my children! Be always gallant and good. Do not forget me.

ON THE OCCASION OF THE ITALIAN CAMPAIGN

SOLDIERS, you are naked and ill-fed. Government owes you much and can give you nothing. The patience and courage you have shown in the midst of this rocky wilderness are admirable; but they gain you no renown; no glory results to you from your endurance. It is my design to lead you into the most fertile plains of the world. Rich provinces and great cities will be in your power; there you will find honour, glory, and wealth. Soldiers of Italy, will you be wanting in courage or perseverance?

NETAJI SUBHASH CHANDRA BOSE

INTRODUCTION

Subhash Chandra was born on January 23rd 1897 in Cuttack as the ninth child among fourteen, of Janakinath Bose, an advocate, and Prabhavati Devi, a pious and God-fearing lady.

One of the veteran leaders of India's freedom movement, specially known for his forming an Indian National Army In 1943 to fight the British with the help of Japan. Reportedly killed In *an* air crash in 1945.

Awarded Bharat Ratna (posthumously In 1992).

EXCERPTS FROM AN ADDRESS TO AN ARTISTS' MEET AT CALCUTTA IN HIS YOUNG DAYS. THIS SPEECH SHOWS HIS PATRIOTIC SPIRIT SOUND LOGIC AND SOLID CHARACTER.

NEVER think that my vision is narrow or parochial. I do indeed believe in the "greatest good of the greatest number." but that good I do not equate to purely material. Economists say that all works are either productive or unproductive. But the question which of these are really productive gives rise to furious logomachines. I for one cannot look upon art and its kindred activities as unproductive nor despise philosophic contemplation or spiritual quest as futile and pointless. I may not be an artist myself, I know I am not—but for that it isn't I who am responsible, it is Nature or God if you will, Of course if you say that I am reaping in this birth what I sowed in my last then I go to the wall. Leaving it at that, the real reason, in a nutshell, why I did not shape into an artist is : I couldn't But this does not mean a layman is debarred even from enjoying art. And the amount of training necessary to a proper appreciation of an art isn't. I think, hard to acquire for a cultivated person.

Some of the artists who sigh regretfully have been wasting their days on music when, to put it in Shakespeare's language, "the time is out of joint." Flood our whole countryside, my friend, with songs and recapture for life the spontaneous joy we have forfeited. He who has no music in his composition, whose heart is dead to music, is unlikely to achieve anything big or great in life. Carlyle used to say that he who had no throb of music in his blood was capable of any misdeed. Whether this be true or not, I am persuaded that he who cannot respond to music can never scale heights of thought or action. We want that the experience of *ananda*—sheer causeless delight— should quicken every drop of our blood, because we only create in the fullness of *ananda*. And what is there that can outwell *ananda* like music?

But we must make the artistic and its kindred joys amenable to the poorest of the poor. High research in music will, of necessity, continue in small expert coteries, but simultaneously, music must be dispensed as a spiritual pabulum of the masses. Just as the high ideals of art are stultified through lack of adequate research, even so art must wilt when, sundered from the life-soil of the masses, it is made inaccessible to all and sundry. I think art joins up with life through folk-music and folk-dance. The Western civilization has hewed away this isthmus between the two continents of art and life, without substituting anything in its ,place. Our *jatra, kathakata kirtan*. etc. survive today almost as relics of the past One shudders to think of the poverty of life that must ensue if our artists and musicians fail to restore the connection between art and life. How fascinated

I had been by the beauty of the *gambhira* music of Maldah. In it music is happily blended with dance. I do not know of any other place in Bengal where such a happy union has been effected. But in Maldah it is sure to die away soon unless, first, new vitality is injected into it and in the second place, people in other parts of Bengal come forward to take it up. *Gambhira* in my opinion has little or no element of complexity or grandeur about it. Its salient features are spontaneity and simplicity. Our indigenous music and dance of the people still survive, I think, in Maldah alone. So those who would revive such folk-art may as well start work from there.

From the point of view of folk-music and folk-dance Burma is a marvellous country. Pure native dance and music is in full swing there and they cater for tens of thousands zigzagging deep into the heart of remote villages. After having mastered the different idioms of our Indian music one may as well study the Burmese. It may not be an evolved art, but its capacity of delighting the illiterate poor has somehow appealed to me. I am told that their dance too is very beautiful. Furthermore, its art is not confined to select coteries, because, I imagine, there is no caste system in Burma, (As a result art here has infiltrated everywhere.) And probably also because folk-music and folk-dance have always had a tremendous vogue in this country. So the common folk have gone to a deeper understanding of beauty than the Indian.

In fact I gave to my country my heart's deep adhesion and reverent "love not so much because I happened to be in politics, as because I had come to know things from my personal experience in life. Once I lived with Deshbandhu in jail for eight months— for two months in the same cell, for six in the adjacent one. I took refuge under his feet because I came to know him thus through a very close relationship.

Let me refer here to Shri Aurobindo. He is a *dhyani* (a contemplative) and, I feel, goes even deeper than Vivekananda, though I have a profound reverence for the latter. So I agree with many intellectuals who say that one may from time to time—and on occasion for a long spell—remain withdrawn in silent contemplation of perfect seclusion. But here there is a danger: the active side of a man might get atrophied if he remained cut off for too long from the tides of life and society. This need not indeed apply to a handful of authentic seekers of uncommon genius, but the common run, the majority, ought, I think, to take to action in a spirit of service as the main plank of their *sadhana*. For a variety of reasons our nation has been sliding pauselessly down to the zero line in the sphere of action ; so what we badly need today is a double dose of the activist serum, *rajas*.

I agree with majority of you who are artists that each of us must strive to develop his powers to their fullness. Real service is only achieved when we dedicate what is the best in our composition. Not till our inner being, our *swadharma*, has fulfilled itself, shall we have won through to our inalienable right, *adhikar*, to what I call real service. To put it in the language of Emerson, we must be moulded from within. This does not mean that we all have to tread the same path, though it is possible that the same ideal may inspire us all. The artist's *sadhana* is not the same as the activist's, no more than the contemplative's *sadhana* is the same as the savant's though I think, in the last analysis, the ideals of all are one. But in the practical field of self-realisation I wouldn't put a round peg in a square hole. One who was true to oneself could hardly be false to humanity. The nature of each must indicate the clue to the path that is his, the path that leads to his self-amelioration and self-expansion. If each of us could fulfil himself following his native capacity and temperament then a new sunrise would outbreak over the entire life of the nation. It is indeed possible that a man may have to lead, during a particular phase of his *sadhana* a life which looks on the surface like selfishness or ego-centrism. But while he is passing through that phase he must follow the dictates of his own conscience—not those of public opinion. The public shall judge till the results of the *sadhana* are published. Consequently, once you choose to tread the true path of self-unfoldment you may well ignore, at least momentarily, the public opinion.

RAJIV GANDHI

INTRODUCTION

Grandson of Jawaharlal Nehru, son of Mrs. Indira Gandhi, a commercial pilot turned politician, India's Prime Minister from 1984 to 1989; assassinated in 1991. A fiery planner of economic development. He was born in 1944.

AT THE UNITED NATIONS GENERAL ASSEMBLY. NEW YORK, JUNE 9, 1988

WE are approaching the close of the twentieth century. It has been the most bloodstained century in history. Fifty -eight million perished in two World Wars. Forty million more have died in other conflicts. In the last nine decades, the ravenous machines of war have devoured nearly one hundred million people. The appetite of these monstrous machines grows on what they feed. Nuclear war will not mean the death of a hundred million people. Or even a thousand million. It will mean the extinction of four thousand million: the end of life as we know it on our planet Earth. We come to the United Nations to seek your support. We seek your support to put a stop to this madness.

Humanity is at a crossroads. One road will take us like lemmings to our own suicide. That is the path indicated by doctrines of nuclear deterrence, deriving from traditional concepts of the balance of power. The other road will give us another chance. That is the path signposted by the doctrine of peaceful coexistence, deriving from the imperative values of nonviolence, tolerance and compassion.

In consequence of doctrines of deterrence, international relations have been gravely militarized. Astronomical sums are being invested in ways of dealing with death. Ever new means of destruction continue to be invented. The best of our scientific talent and the bulk of our technological resources are devoted to maintaining and upgrading this awesome ability to obliterate ourselves. A culture of armaments and threats and violence has become pervasive.

For a hundred years after the Congress of Vienna, Europe knew an uncertain peace based on a balance of power. When that balance was tilted - or more accurately, when that balance was perceived to have been tilted - Europe was plunged into an orgy of destruction, the like of which had never been known before and which spread to engulf much of the world. The unsettled disputes of the First World War led to the Second.

Humankind survived because, by today's standards, the power to destroy, which was then available was a limited power. We now have what we did not then have: the power to ensure the genocide of the human race. Technology has now rendered obsolete the calculations of war and peace on which were constructed the always dubious theories of the balance of power.

It is a dangerous delusion to believe that nuclear weapons have brought us peace. It is true that in the past four decades, parts of the world have experienced an absence of war. But a mere absence of war is not a durable peace. The balance of nuclear terror rests on the retention and augmentation of nuclear armories. There can be no ironclad guarantee against the use of weapons of mass destruction. They have been used in the past. They could be used in the future. And, in this nuclear age, the insane logic of mutually assured destruction will ensure that nothing survives, that none lives to tell the tale, that there is no one left to understand what went wrong and why. Peace which rests on the search for a parity of power is a precarious peace. If we can understand what went wrong with such attempts in the past, we may yet be able to escape the catastrophe presaged by doctrines of nuclear deterrence.

There is a further problem with deterrence. The doctrine is based on the assumption that international relations are frozen on a permanently hostile basis. Deterrence needs an enemy, even if one has to be invented. Nuclear deterrence is the ultimate expression of the philosophy of terrorism: holding humanity hostage to the presumed security needs of a few.

There are those who argue that since the consequences of nuclear war are widely known and well- understood, nuclear war just cannot happen. Neither experience nor logic can sustain such dangerous complacency. History is full, of miscalculations. Perceptions are often totally at variance with reality. A madman's fantasy could unleash the end. An accident could trigger a chain reaction, which inexorably leads to doom. Indeed, the advance of technology has so reduced the time for decisions that, once activated, computers programmed for Armageddon pre-empt human intervention and all hope of survival. There is, therefore, no comfort in the claim of the proponents of nuclear deterrence that everyone can be saved by ensuring that in the event of conflict, everyone will surely die.

The champions of nuclear deterrence argue that nuclear weapons have been invented and therefore, cannot be eliminated. We do not agree. We have an international convention eliminating biological weapons by prohibiting their use in war. We are working on similarly eliminating chemical weapons. There is no reason on principle why nuclear weapons too cannot be so eliminated. All it requires is the affirmation of certain basic moral values and the assertion of the required political will, underpinned by treaties and institutions, which insure against nuclear delinquency.

The past few years have seen the emergence of a new

danger: the extension of the nuclear arms race into outer space. The ambition of creating impenetrable defenses against nuclear weapons has merely escalated the arms race and complicated the process of disarmament. This has happened in spite of the grave doubts expressed by leading scientists about its very feasibility. Even the attempt to build a partial shield against nuclear missiles increases the risk of nuclear war. History shows that there is no shield that has not been penetrated by a superior weapon, nor any weapon for which a superior shield has not been found. Societies get caught in a multiple helix of escalation in chasing this chimera, expending vast resources for an illusory security while incurring the risk of certain extinction.

The new weapons being developed for ·defense against nuclear weapons are part of a much wider qualitative arms race. The development of the so-called "third generation nuclear weapons" has opened up ominous prospects of their being used for selective and discriminate military operations. There is nothing more dangerous than the illusion of limited nuclear war. It desensitizes inhibitions about the use of nuclear weapons. That could lead, in next to no time, to the outbreak of full—fledged nuclear war.

There are no technological solutions to the problems of world security. Security can only come from our asserting effective political control over this self-propelled technological arms race. We cannot accept the logic that a few nations have the right to pursue their security by threatening the survival of humankind. It is not only those who live by the nuclear sword who, by design or default, shall one day perish by it. All humanity will perish.

Nor is it acceptable that those who possess nuclear weapons are freed of all controls while those without nuclear weapons are policed against their production. History is full of such prejudices paraded as iron laws: that men are superior to women; that the white races are superior to the colored; that colonialism is a civilizing mission, that those who possess nuclear weapons are responsible powers and those who do not are not.

Alas,. nuclear weapons are not the only weapons of mass destruction. New knowledge is being generated in the life sciences. Military applications of these developments could rapidly undermine the existing convention against the military use of biological weapons. The ambit of our concern must extend to all means of mass annihilation.

New technologies have also dramatically expanded the scope and intensity of conventional warfare. The physical destruction, which can be carried out by full-scale conventional war, would be enormous, far exceeding anything known in the past. Even if humankind is spared the agony of a nuclear winter, civilization and civic life as we know it would be Irretrievably disrupted. The range, precision and lethality of conventional weapons is being vastly increased. Some of these weapons are moving from being 'smart' to becoming 'intelligent'. Such diabolical technologies generate their own pressures for early use, thus increasing the risk of the outbreak of war. Most of these technologies are at the command of the military blocs. This immensely increases their capacity for interference, intervention and coercive diplomacy.

Those of us who do not belong to the military blocs would much rather stay out of the race. We do not want to accumulate arms. We do not want to augment our capacity to kill. But the system, like a whirlpool, sucks us into its vortex. We are compelled to divert resources from development to defense to respond to the arsenals, which are constructed as a sideshow to great power rivalries. As the nature and sophistication of threat to our security increase, we are forced to incur huge expenditure on raising the threshold of our defences.

There is another danger that is even worse. Left to ourselves, we would not want to touch nuclear weapons. But when tactical considerations, in the passing play of great power rivalries, are allowed to take precedence over the imperative of nuclear non-proliferation, with what leeway are we left?

Even the mightiest military powers realize that they cannot continue the present arms race without inviting economic calamity. The continuing arms race has imposed a great burden on national economies and the global economy. It is no longer only the developing countries who are using disarmament to channel resources to development. Even the richest are beginning to realize that they cannot afford the current levels of the military burden they have imposed upon themselves. A genuine process of disarmament, leading to a substantial reduction in military expenditure, is bound to promote the prosperity of all nations of the globe. Disarmament accompanied by coexistence will open up opportunities for all countries, whatever their socio-economic systems, whatever their levels of development.

The technological revolutions of our century have created unparalleled wealth. They have endowed the fortunate with high levels of mass consumption and widespread social welfare. In fact, there is plenty for everyone, provided distribution is made more equitable. Yet, the possibility of fulfilling the basic needs of nutrition and shelter, education and health remains beyond the reach of vast millions of people in the developing world because resources which could give fulfillment in life are pre-empted for death.

The root causes of global insecurity reach far below the calculus of military parity. They are related to the instability spawned by widespread poverty, squalor, hunger, disease and illiteracy. They are connected to the degradation of the environment. They are enmeshed in the inequity and injustice of the present world order. The effort to promote security for all must be underpinned by the effort to promote opportunity for all the equitable access to achievement. Comprehensive global security must rest on a new, more just, more honourable world order.

When the General Assembly met here last in Special Session to consider questions of disarmament, the outlook was grim. The new cold war had been revived with full force. A new programme of nuclear armament had been set in motion. As a result, during the years that followed, fear and suspicion cast a long shadow over all disarmament negotiations. Humankind was approaching the precipice of nuclear disaster.

Today, there is a new hope for survival and for peace. There is a perceptible movement away from the precipice. Dialogue has been resumed. Trust is in the air.

How has this transformation occurred? We pay tribute to

the sagacity of the American and Soviet leaderships. They have seen the folly of nuclear escalation. They have started tracing the outlines of a pattern of disarmament. At the same time, we must recognise the role of countless enlightened men and women all over the world, citizens of the non-nuclear weapon States as much as of the nuclear weapon States. With courage, dedication and perseverance they kept the candle burning in the enveloping darkness. The Six-Nation Initiative voiced the hopes and aspirations of these many millions. At a time when relations between the two major nuclear weapon states dipped to their nadir, the Six Nations-Argentina, Greece, India, Mexico. Sweden and Tanzania refocused world attention on the imperative of nuclear disarmament. The appeal of May 1984, issued by Indira Gandhi, Olof Palme and their colleagues, struck a responsive chord. Negotiations stalled for years began inching forwards. The process begun in Geneva has led to Reykjavik, Washington and Moscow.

We have all welcomed the ratification of the INF Treaty concluded between General Secretary Gorbachev and President Reagan. It is an important step in the right direction. Its great value lies in its bold departure from nuclear arms limitation to nuclear disarmament. We hope there will be agreement soon to reduce strategic nuclear arsenals by 50 per cent. The process should be carried forward to the total elimination of nuclear weapons. Only then will we be able to look back and say that the INF Treaty was a truly historic beginning. India believes it is possible for the human race to survive the second millennium. India believes it is also possible to ensure peace, security and survival into the third millennium and beyond. The way lies through concerted action. We urge the international community to immediately undertake negotiations with a view to adopting a time -bound Action Plan to usher in a world order free of nuclear weapons and rooted in nonviolence.

We have submitted such an Action Plan to this Special Session on Disarmament of the United Nations General Assembly. Our Plan calls upon the international community to negotiate a binding commitment to general and complete disarmament. This commitment must be total. It must be without reservation.

The heart of our Action Plan is the elimination of all nuclear weapons, in three stages, over the next twenty-two years, beginning now. We put this Plan to the United Nations as a programme to be launched at once.

While nuclear disarmament constitutes the centerpiece of each stage of the Plan, this is buttressed by collateral and other measures to further the process of disarmament. We have made proposals for banning other weapons of mass destruction. We have suggested steps for precluding the development of new weapon systems based on emerging technologies. We have addressed ourselves to the task of reducing conventional arms and forces to the minimum levels required for defensive purposes. We have outlined ideas for the conduct of international relations in a world free of nuclear weapons.

The essential features of the Action Plan are:

First, there should be a binding commitment by all nations to eliminating nuclear weapons in stages, by the year 2010 at the latest.

Second, all nuclear weapon States must participate in the process of nuclear disarmament. All other countries must also be part of the process.

Third, to demonstrate good faith and build the required confidence, there must be tangible progress at each stage towards the common goal.

Fourth, changes are required in doctrines, policies and institutions to sustain a world free of nuclear weapons. Negotiations should be undertaken to establish a Comprehensive Global Security System under the aegis of the United Nations.

We propose simultaneous negotiations on a series of integrally related measures. But we do recognize the need for flexibility in the staging of some of these measures.

In Stage-I, the INF Treaty must be followed by a fifty per cent cut in Soviet and U.S. strategic arsenals. All production of nuclear weapons and weapons grade fissionable material must cease immediately. A moratorium on the testing of nuclear weapons must be undertaken with immediate effect to set the stage for negotiations on a Comprehensive Test Ban Treaty.

It is already widely accepted that a nuclear war cannot be won and must not be fought. Yet, the right is reserved to resort to nuclear war. This is incompatible with a binding commitment to the elimination of nuclear weapons. Therefore, we propose that all nuclear weapons be leached of legitimacy by negotiating an International convention which outlaws the threat or use of such weapons. Such a convention will reinforce the process of nuclear disarmament.

Corresponding to such a commitment by the nuclear weapon States, those nations, which are capable of crossing the nuclear weapons threshold, must solemnly undertake to restrain themselves. This must be accompanied by strict measures to end all covert and overt assistance to those seeking to acquire nuclear weapons.

We propose that negotiations must commence in the first stage itself for a new Treaty to replace the NPT, which expires in 1995. This new Treaty should give legal effect to the binding commitment of nuclear weapons States to eliminate all nuclear weapons by the year 2010 and of all the non-nuclear weapon States to not cross the nuclear weapons threshold.

International law already bans the use of biological weapons. Similar action must be taken to ban chemical and radiological weapons.

The international community has unanimously recognised outer space as the common heritage of mankind. We must expand international cooperation in the peaceful use of outer space. The essential prerequisite for this is that outer space be kept free of all weapons. Instead, there are plans of developing, testing and deploying a Space weapons system. The nuclear arms race cannot be ended and reversed without a moratorium on such activity. It should be followed by an agreement to forestall the militarisation of outer space. This is also an indispensable condition for attaining the goal of comprehensive global security based on a nonviolent world order free of nuclear weapons.

The very momentum of developments in military technology is dragging the arms race out of political control. The race cannot be restrained without restraining the development of such technology. We need a system, which fosters technological development but interdicts its application to military purposes. The arms control approach has focused on the quantitative growth of arsenals. The disarmament approach must devise arrangements for controlling the continuous qualitative upgradation of nuclear and conventional weapons. To achieve this purpose, the essential requirement is increased transparency in research and development in frontier technologies with potential military applications. This requires a systematic monitoring of such developments, an assessment of their implications for international security, and widespread dissemination of the information obtained. There is also need for greater international cooperation in research into new and emerging technologies for these technologies to open on new vistas of human achievement. Here, let us recall the vision of an open world voiced by one of the most remarkable scientists of our time, Niels Bohr. In his Open Letter to the United Nations on June 9 1950, thirty-eight years ago today, he said:

"The very fact that knowledge itself is a basis for civilization points directly to openness as the way to overcome the present crisis."

By the closing years of the century, there must be a single integrated multilateral verification system to ensure that no new nuclear weapons are produced anywhere in the world. Such a system would also help in verifying compliance with the collateral and other disarmament measures envisaged in the Action Plan. It would serve as an early warning system to guard against violations of solemn international treaties and conventions.

Beyond a point, nuclear disarmament itself would depend upon progress in the reduction of conventional armaments and forces. Therefore, a key task before the international community is to ensure security at lower levels of conventional defence. Reductions must, of course, begin in areas where the bulk of the world's conventional arms and forces are concentrated. However, other countries should also join the process without much delay. This requires a basic restructuring of armed forces to serve defensive purposes only. Our objective should be nothing less than a general reduction of conventional arms across the globe to levels dictated by minimum needs of defence. The process would require a substantial reduction in offensive military capabilities as well as confidence building measures to preclude surprise attacks. The United Nations needs to evolve by consensus a new strategic doctrine of non-provocative defence.

The Plan for radical and comprehensive disarmament must be pursued along with efforts to create a new system of comprehensive global security. The components of such a system must be mutually supportive. Participation in it must be universal.

The structure of such a system should be firmly based on non-violence. When we eliminate nuclear weapons and reduce conventional forces to minimum defensive levels, the establishment of a non-violent world order is the only way of not relapsing into the irrationalities of the past. It is the only way of precluding the recommencement of an armaments spiral. Non-violence in international relations cannot be considered an Utopian goal. It is the only available basis for civilised survival, for the maintenance of peace through peaceful coexistence, for a new, just, equitable and democratic world order. As

Mahatma Gandhi said in the aftermath of the first use of nuclear weapons:

"The moral to be legitimately drawn from the supreme tragedy of the bomb is that it will not be destroyed by counter bombs, even as, violence cannot be destroyed by counter-violence. Mankind has to get out of violence only through non-violence."

The new structure of international relations must be based on respect for various ideologies, on the right to pursue different socio-economic systems, and the celebration of diversity. Happily, this is already beginning to happen. Post-war bipolarity is giving way to a growing realisation of the need for coexistence. The high rhetoric of the system of military alliances is gradually yielding to the viewpoint of the Nonaligned Movement.

Nonalignment is founded on the desire of nations for freedom of action. It stands for national independence and self-reliance. Nonalignment is a refusal to be drawn into the barren rivalries and dangerous confrontations of others. It is an affirmation of the need for self-confident cooperation among all countries, irrespective of differences in social and economic systems. Nonalignment is synonymous with peaceful coexistence. As Jawaharlal Nehru said:

'The alternative to co-existence is co-destruction."

Therefore, the new structure of international relations to sustain a world beyond nuclear weapons will have to be based on the principles of coexistence, the non-use of force, non-intervention in the internal affairs of other countries, and the right of every state to pursue its own path of development. These principles are enshrined in the Chapter of the United Nations, but they have been frequently violated. We must apply our minds to bringing about the institutional changes required to ensure their observance. The strengthening of the United Nations system is essential for comprehensive global security. We must resurrect the original vision of the United Nations. We must bring the United Nations Organisation in line with the requirements of the New World order.

The battle for peace, disarmament and development must be waged both within this Assembly and outside by the peoples of the world. This battle should be waged in cooperation with scientists, strategic thinkers and leader of peace movements who have repeatedly demonstrated their commitment to those ideals. We, therefore, seek their cooperation in securing the commitment of all nations and all peoples to the goal of a non-violent world order free of nuclear weapons.

The ultimate power to bring about change rests with the people. It is not the power of weapons or economic strength, which will determine the shape of the world beyond nuclear weapons. 'Mat will be determined in the minds and the hearts of thinking men and women around the world. For, as the Dhammapada of the Buddha teaches us:

"Our life if shaped by our mind; we become what we think. Suffering follows an evil thought as the wheels of a cart follow the oxen that draw It. Joy follows a pure thought like a shadow that never leaves. For hatred can never put an end to hatred; Love alone can. This is the unalterable law."

RAJENDRA PRASAD

INTRODUCTION

Rajendra Prasad was born in Zeradei, in the Siwan district of Bihar. Dr. Rajendra Prasad was the first President of India. He was a great freedom fighter, and the architect of the Indian Constitution, having served as President of the Constituent Assembly that drafted the Constitution of the Republic from 1948 to 1950. He had also served as a Cabinet Minister briefly in the first Government of Independent India. He was a very important leader of the Indian Independence Movement.

ADDRESS TO PARLIAMENT, MAY 13. 1957.

Maintaining the Tempo of Development

YOU and the Members of the legislatures of the States, chosen by an electorate of nearly two hundred million voters of our country, in accord with our Constitutional procedures, have called me once again to the high office of the President of the Republic. I am deeply conscious of the honour and I am grateful for the confidence which you have reposed in me. It shall be my endeavour to continue to deserve the trust and the affection of which I have been so long the happy recipient.

It gives me great pleasure to welcome you, as Members of

the Second Parliament in the history of our Republic. Some of you have been members of one or other of the Houses of Parliament, or come to Parliament with rich experience in your state legislatures. There are others among you who have been elected to Parliament for the first time. All of you will find, in your life and duties as Members of Parliament, both in the legislature and your constituencies, immense and varied opportunities; and fields of constructive work in the service of our country and people. I wish you all good fortune and a very successful tenure of Parliamentary life.

We are in the second year of our Second Five Year Plan. There has been some inevitable slowing down in the first year of the Plan, resulting partly from the reorganization of the States. This imposes a greater strain and calls for added effort both by the Government and the people during the remaining period of that Plan. My Government are fully conscious of this.

The economic situation, more particularly in relation to the Plan, confronts us with factors which, while they do not warrant grave apprehensions, are matters of serious concern and they are engaging he attention of my Ministers. The deficit in the Central and State budgets and the strain on our foreign exchange resources occasioned by the requirements of the Plan and of industrial development generally as well as by external factors, call for determined and planned efforts. They call for both conservation and expansion of our resources by effecting real economies, by planned restrictions on certain imports, by expansion of export trade and by increasing national self-sufficiency both in the fields of industry and agriculture. They will call for savings to be utilized for production and the abandonment of unproductive and anti-social habits of hoarding and speculation. These can only be effectively achieved by efforts and vigilance not only on the part of the Government but by the people as well.

It would be the easier, but not the gainful or constructive way, to bridge the gaps to which I have referred, by halting development. This will, however, provide no real or long-term remedy. Our endeavour has to be to mobilise and conserve resources for greater productivity and for maintaining and improving development. My Government are fully aware of the problem and of the effort required. They are equally concerned that our temporary difficulties should not lead us in the direction of retarding progress and development but that the difficulties should be overcome, where necessary, by reconsideration and revision of methods and by planned mobilisation of resources and not by either the abandonment or slowing down of the progress towards our objectives.

Public opinion plays a large and important conclusive part in the success and such endeavour. The determination and fevour of our people, their readiness to accept discipline, to respond to the call for efforts and their resolve not to be led into anti-social behaviour, such as by hoarding or wasteful spending, alone will help the country to pass successfully through the present crucial period of our Second Five Year Plan.

Members of Parliament, the country looks to you a great deal for that sustained and special effort in support of the policies and endeavours which my Government will initiate in this behalf, which will help us to surmount difficulties and to achieve success.

While food production has increased, and the increases have been maintained except for the results of natural calamities, more especially in certain parts of Bihar and the eastern districts of Uttar Pradesh, we have a considerable way to go before our country becomes fully self-sufficient in food. There are signs of slight abatement in the rising trend of food prices and my Government have taken several measures to bring about this trend. Intensive efforts have increased food production and improved crop prospects. Except in the case of some of the coarse grains adversely affected by climatic conditions, the crop yields and estimates not only do not indicate a shortfall but have recorded appreciable increases.

My Government have also entered into arrangements for necessary imports of foodgrains and for building up reserve, which will prevent price increases and bridge the gaps that still remain. A large storage construction programme has been undertaken. The behaviour of the public is a large and often determining factor in preventing rise in food prices which is often caused by the apprehension of shortages resulting in the resort to hoarding as well as to the tendency to panic. The food situation, thanks to the increased production and the steps taken by my Government does not warrant any lack of public confidence in regard to supplies. My Government propose to keep Parliament informed of the position in regard to food and the estimates of supply and requirements. It may be hoped that a knowledge of the true facts will help to allay needless apprehensions and prevent artificial shortages and higher prices.

My Government are happy to state that their decision to lay stress on food production and agriculture generally in the Community Project plans has yielded handsome results. The Community Development and the National Extension Service programmes have made great strides. Higher targets in agriculture, health and sanitation have been achieved. The National Sample Survey shows that, at the end of the First Five Year Plan, the crop yields in the Community Development Projects and National Extension Service Blocks areas were approximately 25 per cent higher than for the country as a whole. The Community Projects and National Extension Blocks now cover 2,22,000 villages.

State undertakings continue to make notable progress and new targets have been reached in almost every enterprise. There has also been expansion in the private sector. Khadi and Village industries will receive a further impetus with the setting up of the Khadi and Village Industries Commission as a statutory body. Among the major new projects that will soon be inaugurated is the Neyveli Lignite Project where the first mine-cut will be made this month. My Government attach importance to the building up of a plant for the manufacture of heavy machinery and steps are being taken to this end.

To reduce the pressure on our resources of foreign exchange, my Government are making efforts to obtain deferred payment arrangements for major projects. Long term credits for certain projects are being negotiated.

Consequent on the reorganisation of the States, Advisory Committees have been set up for the Union Territories and Territorial Councils have been established in Himachal Pradesh, Manipur and Tripura. A Corporation for Delhi will be soon established. A new Union Territory of the Lacadives, Minicoy and Amindivi Islands has come into existence and the Five Year Plan for the Andamans Islands at a total cost of Rs. 592.50 lakhs will include the development of communication between the islands and the mainland.

Shipyard construction and the building of ships of modern design have made great progress at Vishakhapatnam and plans for a second shipyard are now in hand.

My Government have initiated measures to relieve housing shortages and promote housing standards, slum clearance and Plantation Housing Schemes and housing for low income groups and subsidised industrial housing. An urgent requirement of Delhi and the other big cities of India is the clearance of slum areas, and this problem is receiving the consideration of the Central and State Governments and the Corporations concerned.

Two Ordinances have been promulgated since the last session of Parliament. Bills dealing with these Ordinances will be placed before Parliament. These are :

(i) The Life Insurance Corporation (Amendment) Ordinance, 1957.

(ii) The Industrial Disputes (Amendment) Ordinance, 1957.

My Government will also submit to Parliament a number of other Bills during the current session.

An interim statement of revenue and expenditure for 1957-58 was presented to parliament during its last session and votes on account authorising expenditure for a part of the year were passed. That statement of revenue and expenditure will be presented again to Parliament in this session with such changes as are considered necessary, and Parliament will be asked to approve funds for the whole year.

Our relations with foreign countries continue to be friendly. Since I addressed Parliament last, we have had the pleasure of receiving as the guests of the Republic, Mr. Jozef Cyrankiewlcz, Prime Minister of Poland, Dr. Heinrich Von Brentano, Foreign Minister of the Federal German Republic and Mr. Oscaldo Sainte Marie, Foreign Minister of Chile.

My Prime Minister will attend the meeting of Commonwealth Prime Ministers in London at the end of June. During his absence abroad, he will take the opportunity of visiting Syria, Denmark, Finland, Norway, Sweden, the Netherlands, Egypt and Sudan.

While the situation in the Middle East continues to be unsatisfactory and charged with tension, it is a matter of gratification that the Suez Canal has been re-opened for navigation. My Government welcome the Declaration made by the Government of Egypt, prior to the opening of the Canal, which reaffirms the Convention of 1888 and the determination of Egypt to continue to abide by the principles of the Charter of the United Nations and of International Law. The Declaration provides for the reference of disputes arising from interpretations of the Convention and its application as well as certain other matters to the World Court and also to abide by its decisions. The main provisions in the Declaration are, in the view of my Government, reasonable and adequate to safeguard the legitimate interests of the world community, if they are worked in a spirit of co-apportion and mutual understanding by all concerned. A notable feature of the Declaration is that, while it is made by the Government of Egypt, that Government has declared that it has the status of an International Instrument and this has been registered with the United Nations. My Government feel that this Declaration and its status as an International Instrument is a notable contribution to the lowering of tensions in that area and will provide a solution of the difficulties that followed the nationalisation of the Suez Canal.

Dr. Gunnar Jarring, a former President of the Security Council, visited Pakistan and India in pursuance of a Resolution passed by the Security Council on the 21st of February this year at the end of the debate on Kashmir. Dr. Jarring visited India twice and conferred with my Prime Minister. He has submitted a report to the Security Council.

The sub-committee of the Disarmament Commission has been sitting in London for some time, but no agreement appears to have been reached on any aspect of Disarmament, including the suspension of explosions of nuclear and thermo-nuclear weapons. The proposals of my Government in regard to Disarmament were once again referred by the General Assembly of the United Nations at the last session, along with all other proposals, to the Disarmament Commission.

Meanwhile the United States, the Soviet Union, and now the United Kingdom continue their experiments to explode these weapons of mass destruction. World opinion is increasingly concerned about the harmful effect of radiation which has been increasingly and more frequently felt in various parts of the world. The demand for the suspension of these explosions is widespread and continues to the impressed upon the nuclear powers, but hitherto without success.

My Government do not consider that the compromise proposals suggested from diverse quarters for the so-called limitation of these explosions or for their registration will ever rid the world of their harmful effects, or open the way to the abandonment of these weapons of mass destruction. On the other hand, such regularisation of these tests tends to make thermo-nuclear war legitimate and as having the sanction of the world community. Reports of experiments with more and more deadly weapons of war continue to be received. It is, however, a matter of some gratification that the volume of world opinion against the continuance of experiments has reached a higher level than ever before. My Prime Minister in a statement before the Lok Sabha in April 1954 put forward for consideration the proposal for a "Standstill Agreement" to suspend these explosions. These proposals have since gained much support and the movement of world opinion in favour of it has gathered momentum. My Government will continue to exert their influence with other nations and in the counsels of the world to bring about the abandonment of these test explosions and the prohibition of nuclear and thermo-nuclear weapons.

We meet here today one hundred years after the great rising which began in Meerut and spread over considerable parts of India. That was the first major challenge to foreign rule and threw up notable figures, famous in India's history. The uprising was cruelly suppressed, but the spirit of freedom and the desire to be free from foreign domination continued and found expression on many subsequent occasions. Ultimately it led to a great national movement which followed peaceful methods and succeeded in achieving the independence of India. Quite many people gave their lives or otherwise suffered so that India may be free.

India has been independent for nearly ten years now and during this period Parliament has laboured for the well-being and advancement of this country and her people and for peace and co-operation in the world. These labours have produced substantial results which we see all round us in the country. The progress we have made during these years in our own land has produced in our people hope and self-reliance. This is a substantial foundation on which we can build for the future.

Abroad, my Government have striven strenuously to help solve existing tensions in the world and to serve the cause of peace. The country has also accepted heavy responsibilities in the pursuit of this policy, in regard to maintaining the independence of its approach as well as in making contributions to the maintenance of peace, as in Korea, Indo-China and now in the Middle-East.

The tasks that confront us both at home and abroad are not only considerable but at times appear overwhelming. But these tasks have to be faced, difficulties surmounted and objectives achieved if the fruits of independence are to be ensured to our people and if we are to help the world to stop spreading the continual stress and horror of impending catastrophe.

My Government will continue their strenuous endeavors in all these directions, to the best of their capacity, conscious of the confidence reposed in them by the country and fortified by the conviction that despite clouds of war, and even despair, the desire for survival and progress is inherent in humanity. Our capacities and resources are limited and our voice in the world may be but small. But neither our national interests nor our history and traditions, nor our convictions chart any other course for us. Happily for us, this is the common aim and the firm desire of all our people.

Members of Parliament, I wish you success in your labours.

ADDRESS AT THE STATE BANQUET GIVEN IN HONOUR OF PRESIDENT DWIGHT D. EISENHOWER OF U.S.A., NEW DELHI, DECEMBER 10. 1959.

Indo-U.S. Friendship

MAY I on behalf of the people and the Government of India extend to you a hearty welcome to our country? Our Prime Minister had the privilege of visiting your great country, Mr. President, two years after India achieved independence and then again in 1956. Through all these years it has been the hope of the people of India that the President of the United States of America would be able to visit and honour us with his presence and see for himself the high regard in which the people of India hold the American people. It is for the first time in history that a President of the United States of America is visiting our ancient land and we are indeed happy that you have been able to come.

It has been our pleasure and privilege to have you, Mr. President, amidst us for a little over 24 hours and I may assure you that within this short time you have been able to create an impression the impact of which is going to be of a far-reaching character in cementing the bonds of friendship that exist between your country and mine.

Between the United States and India friendly and cordial relations existed even before India gained her independence. No Indian can forget that in the days of our struggle for freedom we received from your country and your people a full measure of sympathy and support.

We have, Mr. President, much in common in our aims and ideals. Like yours ours is a democratic country, a Federation and a Republic. Our two Republics have a common faith in democratic institutions and the democratic way of life and are dedicated to the cause of peace and freedom. We admire the many qualities which have made your country great, and more especially, the humanity and dynamism of your people and the great principles to which the feathers of the American revolution gave utterance. We wish to learn from you and to enlist your co-operation and sympathy in the great task we have undertaken in our own country.

Our struggle for freedom was based on the principles of peace and non-violence and behind us is the centuries old tradition of peaceful living. We believe in the message of peace and freedom, in the right of every man and woman to peace and happiness in life. In international affairs, we have endeavoured to follow these principles. In the United Nations and in other international forums, whenever freedom has been menaced or justice threatened, we have raised our voice in the defense of these sacred principles, principles which are enshrined in the consciousness of our nation as they are in the hearts of the American people. We believe that the interest of mankind lies in not resorting to war and bloodshed to settle differences. Indeed, today, when distance between country and country has almost been eliminated, security could only lie in a warless world.

We are happy that you, Mr. President, whose humanity and whose distinguished and devoted service to the cause of peace have won for you a unique place among the statesmen of the world, and the leaders of other great and powerful nations have been meeting and will be meeting soon in an endeavour to end the cold war and to achieve world co-operation. So that the tremendous advances in science and technology could be directed towards the economic and social progress of the people all over the world. For us, as indeed for all others, it is imperative that world peace should be assured; that there should he no more wars, great or small. It is gratifying, therefore, to discern indications that the great nations and their statesmen are applying their minds and bending their energies in the direction of discovering means and creating conditions for lessening tension and, in due course, eliminating war. You, Mr. President, are making your own invaluable contribution to it and will be happy consummation when we could all sing in joy that "peace hath her victories no less glorious than war."

We in India are engaged in an economic revolution of vast dimensions. This is a stupendous task which because of our arrested growth, demands that we catch up more rapidly with the advanced nations in an effort to raise the standard of living of our people. We value the co-operation and assistance we have received from the American people. We greatly appreciate the friendship and goodwill which your great country has always extended to us. These have strengthened the invisible yet unbreakable bonds of understanding between your people and ours.

I thank you again, Mr. President, for having found the time to come to our country. I earnestly hope that you will see glimpses of the changing face of India. I feel confident that your visit will enrich further the deep friendship between our two countries. May I ask you to take back with you a message of affection, friendship and goodwill from the people of India to the people of the United States of America?

S. RADHAKRISHNAN

INTRODUCTION

Dr. S. Radha Krishnan was born in 1888. India's Scholar, philosopher, writer and statesman, Free India's first Vice-President (1952-63) and second President after Rajendra Prasad (1962-67). Was earlier Professor at Oxford and Chairman of UNESCO.

Bharat Ratna 1964 Templeton Award 1975. Author of *Hindu View of life, Indian Philosophy* and *Bhagavat Gita.*

ON THE TWENTIETH ANNIVERSARY CELEBRATIONS OF UNITED NATIONS, JUNE 26, 1965

THOUGH the achievements of the United Nations in these twenty years have been impressive, its failures have been considerable. The most notable of them all has been in regard to disarmament. The first atom bomb was detonated by the United States of America on July 16, 1945, near Alamagardo, New Mexico. On August 6, 1945, an atom bomb was dropped on Hiroshima. The Soviet Union announced Its first atomic blast on September 23, 1949. The United States exploded the first hydrogen bomb on November 1, 1952. On August 12, 1953, the Soviet Union touched off its first hydrogen bomb explosion. On May 15, 1957, Britain conducted its first hydrogen bomb test in the Pacific region. On February 13, 1960, France exploded an atomic device in the Sahara desert. On October 16, 1964, the Peoples Republic of China exploded its first atomic device. They have now had the second explosion also.

We all know that if the nuclear arms race is not arrested and reversed the prospects of mankind are very grim. Some nuclear power in anger or excitement, by some miscalculation or misunderstanding, may set the world ablaze and the resulting ruin will find no distinction between the victor and the vanquished, between the Capitalist and the Communist, the Arab and the Jew.

We have to protect humanity against war. Peace is not the absence of war. It is the presence of fellow feeling and of respect for man as man regardless of his race or nation, class or creed. It is the disarmament of minds that is called for. The future is not all bleak. An old Arab proverb says, "Do not grieve that rose trees have thorns, rather rejoice that thorny bushes bear roses". The present climate of fear, suspicion, intolerance and misunderstanding has to be changed. On October 10, 1963, a treaty banning nuclear tests, except beneath earth's surface, came into effect: it was signed by the United States Of America, by the Soviet Union, by Britain and more than 100 other countries. France and China are not parties to this treaty, though they may be expected to change their minds. Scientific collaboration and cooperation in space research are increasing. We have to strengthen the United Nations, so that it can insulate dangerous situations of conflict or potential war and bring them within the sphere of peaceful settlement. We can do so only by adhering to the principles and purposes of the Charter.

A few years ago, Jawaharlal Nehru asked us to emphasize the opportunities for understanding and cooperation and not merely those of misunderstanding and conflict. So this year Is designated the Year of International Cooperation.

The path of peace is, however, thorny and difficult and the world body has passed through many crises. Even today it is faced with disagreements among member States in, regard to the authorization and financing of peacekeeping operations which are intended to maintain and restore international peace and security.

SWAMI VIVEKANANDA

INTRODUCTION

Swami Vivekananda was born Narendranath Dutta, son of a well known lawyer of Calcutta, Biswanath Dutta, and a very intelligent and pious lady, Bhuvaneshwari Devi, in the year 1863.

He established Shri Ramakrishan Mission to carry on the propagation of his ideas.

Swamiji left his body at an young age of 39 on the 4th of July 1902.

EXCERPTS FROM HIS FAMOUS UTTARPARA, 1898.

Voice of God

WHEN I was arrested and hurried to the Lal Bazar hajat, I was shaken in faith for a while, for I could not look into the heart of His intention. Therefore I faltered for a moment and cried out in my heart to Him, "What is this that has happened to me? I believed that I had a mission to work for the people of my country and until that work was done, I should have Thy protection. Why then am I here and on such a charge?" A day passed and a second day and third, when a voice came to me from within, "wait and see". Then I grew calm and waited. I was taken from Lal Bazar to Alipore and was placed for one month in a solitary cell apart from men. There I waited day and night for the voice of God within me, to know what He had to say to me, to learn what I had to do. In this seclusion the earliest realisation, the first lesson came to me. I remembered then that a month or more before my arrest, a call had come to me to put aside all activity, to go into seclusion and to look into myself, so that I might enter into closer communion with Him. I was weak and could not accept the call. My work was very dear to me and in the pride of my heart I thought that unless I was there, it would suffer or even fail and cease; therefore I would not leave it. It seemed to me that He spoke to me again and said, "The bonds you had not strength to break, I have broken for you, because it is not my will nor was it ever my intention that that should continue. I have had another thing for you to do and it is for that I have brought you here, to teach you what you could not learn for yourself and to train you for my work." Then he placed the Gita in my hands. His strength entered into me and I was not only to understand intellectually but to realise what Sri Krishna demanded for Arjuna and what He demands of those who aspire to do his work.

He made me realise the central truth of the Hindu religion. He turned the hearts of my jailors to me and they spoke to the Englishman in charge of the jail, "He is suffering in his confinement ; let him at least walk outside his cell for half an hour in the morning and in the evening." So it was arranged, and it was while I was walking that His strength again entered into me. I looked at the jail that secluded me from men and it was no longer by its high walls that I was imprisoned; no, it was Vasudeva who surrounded me. I walked under the branches of the tree in front of my cell but it was not the tree, I knew it was Vasudeva, it was Sri Krishna whom I saw standing there and holding over me his shade. I looked at the bars of my cell, the very grating that did duty for a door and again I saw Vasudeva. It was Narayana who was guarding and standing sentry over me. Or I lay on the coarse blankets that were given me for a couch and felt the arms of Sri Krishna around me, the arms of my Friend and Lover. This was the first use of the deeper vision He gave me. I looked at the prisoners in the jail, the thieves, the murderers, swindlers, and as I looked at them I saw Vasudeva, it was Narayana whom I found in these darkened souls and misused bodies. Amongst these thieves and dacoits there were many who put me to shame by their sympathy, their kindness, the humanity triumphant over such adverse circumstances. One I saw among them especially, who seemed to me a saint, a peasant of my nation who did not know how to read and write, an alleged dacoit sentenced to ten years' rigorous imprisonment, one of those whom we look down upon in our Pharasaical pride of class as *chhotalok*. Once more He spoke to me and said, "Behold the people among whom I have sent you to do a little of my work. This is the nature of the nation I am raising up and the reason why I raise them."

When the case opened in the lower court and we were brought before the magistrate I was followed by the same insight. He said to me, "When you were cast into jail, did not your heart fail and did you not cry out to me, where is Thy protection? Look now at the Magistrate, look now at the Prosecuting Counsel." I looked and it was not the Magistrate whom I saw, it was Vasudeva, it was Narayana who was sitting there on the bench. I looked at the Prosecuting counsel and it was not the Counsel for the prosecution that I saw; it was Sri Krishna who sat there, it was my Lover and Friend who sat there and smiled. "Now do you fear?" He said, "I am in all men and I overrule their actions and their words. My protection is still with you and you shall not fear. This case which is brought against you, leave it in my hand. It is not for you. It was not for the trial that I brought you here but for something else. The case itself is only a means for my work and nothing more." Afterwards when the trial opened in the Sessions Courts, I began to write many instructions for my Counsel as to what was false in the evidence against me and on what points the witnesses might be cross-examined. Then something happened which I had not expected. The arrangements which had been made for my defence were suddenly changed and another Counsel stood there to defend me. He came unexpectedly—a friend of mine, but I did not know he was coming. You have all heard the name of the man who put away from him all other thoughts and abandoned all his practice, who sat up half the night day after day for months and broke his health to save me,—Sriyut Chittaranjan Das. When I saw him, I was satisfied, bit I still thought it necessary to write instructions. Then all that was put from me and I had the message from within, "This is the man who will save you from the snares put around your feet. Put aside those papers. It is not you who will instruct him. I will instruct him." From that time I did not of myself speak a word to my Counsel about the case or give a single instruction, and if ever I was asked a question I always found that my answer did not help the case. I had left it to him and he took it entirely into his hands, with what result you know. I knew all along what He meant for me, for I heard it again and again, always I listened to the voice within; "I am guiding, therefore fear not. Turn to your own work for which I have brought you to jail and when you come out, remember never to fear, never to hesitate. Remember that it is I who am doing this, not you nor any other. Therefore whatever clouds may come, whatever dangers and sufferings, whatever difficulties, whatever impossibilities, there is nothing impossible, nothing difficult. I am in the nation and its uprising and I am Vasudeva, I am Narayana, and what I will, shall be, not what others will. What I choose to bring about, no human power can say."

Meanwhile he had brought me out of solitude and placed me among those who had been accused along with me. You have spoken much today of my self-sacrifice and devotion to my country. I have heard that kind of speech ever since I came out of jail, but I hear it with embarrassment, with something of pain. For I know my weakness, I am a prey to my own faults and backslidings. I was not blind to them before and when they all rose up against me in seclusion, I felt them utterly. I knew then that I the man was a mass of weakness, a faulty and imperfect instrument, strong only when a higher strength entered into me. Then I found myself among these young men and in many of them I discovered a mighty courage, a power of self-effacement in comparison with which I was simply nothing. I saw one or two who were not only superior to me in force and character—very many were that—but in the promise of that intellectual ability on which I prided myself, He said to me, 'This is the young generation, the new and mighty nation that is arising at my command. They are greater than yourself. What have you to fear? If you stood aside or slept, the work would still be done. If you were cast aside tomorrow, here are the young men who will take up your work and do it more mightily than you have ever done. You have only got some strength from me to speak a word to this nation which will help to raise it." This was the next thing He told me.

Then a thing happened suddenly and in a moment I was hurried away to the seclusion of a solitary cell. What happened to me during that period I am not impelled to say, but only this that day after day, He showed me His wonders and made me realise the utter truth of the Hindu religion. I had had many doubts before. I was brought up in England amongst foreign ideas and an atmosphere entirely foreign. About many things in Hinduism I had once been inclined to believe that they were imaginations, that there was much of dream in it, much that was delusion and Maya. But now day after day I realised in the mind, I realised in the heart, I realised in the body the truths of the Hindu religion they became living experiences to me, and things were opened to me which no material science could explain. When I first approached Him, it was not entirely in the spirit of the Bhakta, it was not entirely in the spirit of the Jnani. I came to Him long ago in Baroda some years before the Swadeshi began and I was drawn info the public field.

When I approached God at that time, I hardly had a living faith in Him. The agnostic was in me, the atheist was in me, that sceptic was in me, and I was not absolutely sure that there was a God at all. I did not feel His presence. Yet something drew me to the truth of the Vedas, the truth of the Gita, the truth of the Hindu religion. I felt there must be a mighty truth somewhere in this Yoga, a mighty truth in this religion based on the Vedanta. So when I turned to the Yoga and resolved to practice it and find out if my idea was right, I did it in this spirit and with this prayer to Him, "If thou art, then Thou knowest my heart, Thou knowest that I do not ask for Mukti. I do not ask for anything which others ask for. I ask only for strength to uplift this nation, I ask only to be allowed to live and work for this people whom I love and to whom I pray that I may devote my life." I strove long for the realisation of Yoga and at last to some extent I had it, but in what I most desired I was not satisfied. Then in the seclusion of the jail, of the solitary cell I asked for it again. I said, "Give me Thy Adesh. I do not know what work to do or how to do it. Give me a message." In the communion of Yoga two messages came. The first message said, "I have given you a work and it is to help to uplift this nation. Before long the time will come when you will have to go out of jail; for it is not my will that this time either you should be convicted or that you should pass the time, as others have to do, in suffering for their country. I have called you to work, and that is the Adesh for which you have asked. I give you the Adesh to go forth and do my work." the second message came and it said, "Something has been shown to you in this year of seclusion, something about which you had your doubts and it is the truth of the Hindu religion. It is this religion that I am raising up before the world, it is this that I have perfected and developed through the Rishis, saints and Avatars and now it is going forth to do my work among the nations. I am raising up this nation to send forth my word. This is the Sanatana Dharma, this is the eternal religion which you did not really know before, but which I have now revealed to you. The agnostic and the sceptic in you have been answered, for I have given you proofs within and without you, physical and subjective, which have satisfied you. When you go forth, speak to your nation always this word, that it is for the Sanatana Dharma that they arise, it is for the world and not for themselves that they arise. I am giving them freedom for the service of the world. When therefore it is said that India shall rise, it is the Sanatana Dharma that shall rise. When it is said that India shall be great, it is the Sanatana Dharma that shall be great. When it is said that India shall expand and extend herself, it is the Sanatana Dharma that shall expand and extend itself over the world. It is for the Dharma and by the Dharma that India exists. To magnify the religion means to magnify the country. I have shown you that I am everywhere and in all men and in all things, that I am in this movement and I am not only working in those who are striving for the country but I am working also in those who oppose them and stand in their path. I am working in everybody and whatever men may think or do they can do nothing but help on my purpose. They also are doing my work, they are not my enemies but my instruments. In all your actions you are moving forward without knowing which way you move. You mean to do one thing and you do another. You aim at a result and your efforts subserve one that is different or contrary. It is Shakti that has gone forth and entered into the people. Since long ago I have been preparing this uprising and now the time has come and it is I who will lead it to its fulfilment."

WINSTON CHURCHILL

INTRODUCTION

The Right Honourable Sir Winston Leonard Spencer Churchill (1874-1965), the son of Lord Randolph Churchill and an American mother, was educated at Harrow and Sandhurst. After a brief but eventful career in the army, he became a Conservative Member of Parliament in 1900. He held many high posts in Liberal and Conservative governments during the first three decades of the century. At the outbreak of the Second World War, he was appointed First Lord of the Admiralty - a post which he had earlier held from 1911 to 1915. In May, 1940, he became Prime Minister and Minister of Defence and remained in office until 1945.

"IRON CURTAIN"
MARCH 5, 1946

THE United States stands at this time at the pinnacle of world power. It is a solemn moment for the American democracy. For with this primacy in power is also joined an awe-inspiring accountability to the future. As you look around you, you must feel not only the sense of duty done, but also you must feel anxiety lest you fall below the level of achievement. Opportunity is here now, clear and shining, for both our countries. To reject it or ignore it or fritter it away will bring upon us all the long reproaches of the aftertime.

It is necessary that constancy of mind, persistency of purpose, and the grand simplicity of decision shall rule and guide the conduct of the English-speaking peoples in peace as they did in war. We must, and I believe we shall, prove ourselves equal to this severe requirement.

I have a strong admiration and regard for the valiant Russian people and for my wartime comrade, Marshal Stalin. There is deep sympathy and goodwill in Britain — and I doubt not here also — toward the peoples of all the Russias and a resolve to persevere through many differences and rebuffs in establishing lasting friendships.

It is my duty, however, to place before you certain facts about the present position in Europe.

Warsaw, Berlin, Prague, Vienna, Budapest, Belgrade, Bucharest and Sofia; all these famous cities and the populations around them lie in what I must call the Soviet sphere, and all are subject, in one form or another, not only to Soviet influence but to a very high and in some cases increasing measure of control from Moscow.

The safety of the world, ladies and gentlemen, requires a unity in Europe, from which no nation should be permanently outcast. It is from the quarrels of the strong parent races in Europe that the world wars we have witnessed, or which occurred in former times, have sprung.

Twice the United States has had to send several millions of its young men across the Atlantic to fight the wars. But now we all can find any nation, wherever it may dwell, between dusk and dawn. Surely we should work with conscious purpose for a grand pacification of Europe within the structure of the United Nations and in accordance with our Charter.

In a great number of countries, far from the Russian frontiers and throughout the world, Communist fifth columns are established and work in complete unity and absolute obedience to the directions they receive from the Communist center. Except in the British Commonwealth and in the United

States where Communism is in its infancy, the Communist parties or fifth columns constitute a growing challenge and peril to Christian civilization.

The outlook is also anxious in the Far East and especially in Manchuria. The agreement which was made at Yalta, to which I was a party, was extremely favorable to Soviet Russia, but it was made at a time when no one could say that the German war might not extend all through the summer and autumn of 1945 and when the Japanese war was expected by the best judges to last for a further eighteen months from the end of the German war.

I repulse the idea that a new war is inevitable — still more that it is imminent. It is because I am sure that our fortunes are still in our own hands and that we hold the power to save the future, that I feel the duty to speak out now that I have the occasion and the opportunity to do so.

I do not believe that Soviet Russia desires war. What they desire is the fruits of war and the indefinite expansion of their power and doctrines.

But what we have to consider here today while time remains, is the permanent prevention of war and the establishment of conditions of freedom and democracy as rapidly as possible in all countries. Our difficulties and dangers will not be removed by closing our eyes to them. They will not be removed by mere waiting to see what happens; nor will they be removed by a policy of appeasement.

What is needed is a settlement, and the longer this is delayed, the more difficult it will be and the greater our dangers will become.

From what I have seen of our Russian friends and allies during the war, I am convinced that there is nothing they admire so much as strength, and there is nothing for which they have less respect than for weakness, especially military weakness.

For that reason the old doctrine of a balance of power is unsound. We cannot afford, if we can help it, to work on narrow margins, offering temptations to a trial of strength.

Last time I saw it all coming and I cried aloud to my own fellow countrymen and to the world, but no one paid any attention. Up till the year 1933 or even 1935, Germany might have been saved from the awful fate which has overtaken her and we might all have been spared the miseries Hitler let loose upon mankind.

There never was a war in history easier to prevent by timely action than the one which has just desolated such great areas of the globe. It could have been prevented, in my belief, without the firing of a single shot, and Germany might be powerful, prosperous and honored today; but no one would listen and one by one we were all sucked into the awful whirlpool.

We must not let it happen again. This can only be achieved by reaching now, in 1946, a good understanding on all points with Russia under the general authority of the United Nations Organization and by the maintenance of that good understanding through many peaceful years, by the whole strength of the English-speaking world and all its connections.

If the population of the English-speaking Commonwealth be added to that of the United States, with all that such cooperation implies in the air, on the sea, all over the globe, and in science and in industry, and in moral force, there will be no quivering, precarious balance of power to offer its temptation to ambition or adventure. On the contrary there will be an overwhelming assurance of security.

If we adhere faithfully to the Charter of the United Nations and walk forward in sedate and sober strength, seeking no one's land or treasure, seeking to lay no arbitrary control upon the thoughts of men, if all British moral and material forces and convictions are joined with your own in fraternal association, the high roads of the future will be clear, not only for us but for all, not only for our time but for a century to come.

"BLOOD, TOIL, TEARS AND SWEAT"

MAY 13, 1940

FIRST SPEECH AS PRIME MINISTER TO THE HOUSE OF COMMONS

I beg to move,

THAT this House welcomes the formation of a Government representing the united and inflexible resolve of the nation to prosecute the war with Germany to a victorious conclusion.

On Friday evening last I received His Majesty's commission to form a new Administration. It as the evident wish and will of Parliament and the nation that this should be conceived on the broadest possible basis and that it should include all parties, both those who supported the late Government and also the parties of the Opposition. I have completed the most important part of this task. A War Cabinet has been formed of five Members, representing, with the Opposition Liberals, the unity of the nation. The three party Leaders have agreed to serve, either in the War Cabinet or in high executive office. The three Fighting Services have been filled. It was necessary that this should be done in one single day, on account of the extreme urgency and rigour of events. A number of other positions, key positions, were filled yesterday, and I am submitting a further list to His Majesty to-night. I hope to complete the appointment of the principal Ministers during to-morrow. the appointment of the other Ministers usually takes a little longer, but I trust that, when Parliament meets again, this part of my task will be completed, and that the administration will be complete in all respects.

I considered it in the public interest to suggest that the House should be summoned to meet today. Mr. Speaker agreed, and took the necessary steps, in accordance with the powers conferred upon him by the Resolution of the House. At the end of the proceedings today, the Adjournment of the House will be proposed until Tuesday, 21st May, with, of course, provision for earlier meeting, if need be. The business to be considered during that week will be notified to Members at the earliest opportunity. I now invite the House, by the Motion which stands in my name, to record its approval of the steps taken and to declare its confidence in the new Government.

To form an Administration of this scale and complexity is a serious undertaking in itself, but it must be remembered that we are in the preliminary stage of one of the greatest battles in history, that we are in action at many other points in Norway and in Holland, that we have to be prepared in the Mediterranean, that the air battle is continuous and that many preparations, such as have been indicated by my hon. Friend below the Gangway, have to be made here at home. In this crisis I hope I may be pardoned if I do not address the House at any length today. I hope that any of my friends and colleagues, or former colleagues, who are affected by the political reconstruction, will make allowance, all allowance, for any lack of ceremony with which it has been necessary to act. I would say to the House, as I said to those who have joined this government: "I have nothing to offer but blood, toil, tears and sweat."

We have before us an ordeal of the most grievous kind. We have before us many, many long months of struggle and of suffering. You ask, what is our policy? I can say: It is to wage war, by sea, land and air, with all our might and with all the strength that God can give us; to wage war against a monstrous tyranny, never surpassed in the dark, lamentable catalogue of human crime. That is our policy. You ask, what is our aim? I can answer in one word: It is victory, victory at all costs, victory in spite of all terror, victory, however long and hard the road may be; for without victory, there is no survival. Let that be realised; no survival for the British Empire, no survival for all that the British Empire has stood for, no survival for the urge and impulse of the ages, that mankind will move forward towards its goal. But I take up my task with buoyancy and hope. I feel sure that our cause will not be suffered to fail among men. At this time I feel entitled to claim the aid of all, and I say, "come then, let us go forward together with our united strength."

"THEIR FINEST HOUR"
JUNE 18, 1940

I SPOKE the other day of the colossal military disaster which occurred when the French High Command failed to withdraw the northern Armies from Belgium at the moment when they knew that the French front was decisively broken at Sedan and on the Meuse. This delay entailed the loss of fifteen or sixteen French divisions and threw out of action for the critical period the whole of the British Expeditionary Force. Our Army and 120,000 French troops were indeed rescued by the British Navy from Dunkirk but only with the loss of their cannon, vehicles and modern equipment. This loss inevitably took some weeks to repair, and in the first two of those weeks the battle in France has been lost. When we consider the heroic resistance made by the French Army against heavy odds in this battle, the enormous losses inflicted upon the enemy and the evident exhaustion of the enemy, it may well be the thought that these 25 divisions of the best-trained and best-equipped troops might have turned the scale. However, General Weygand had to fight without them. Only three British divisions or their equivalent were able to stand in the line with their French comrades. They have suffered severely, but they have fought well. We sent every man we could to France as fast as we could re-equip and transport their formations.

I am not reciting these facts for the purpose of

recrimination. That I judge to be utterly futile and even harmful. We cannot afford it. I recite them in order to explain why it was we did not have, as we could have had, between twelve and fourteen British divisions fighting in the line in this great battle instead of only three. Now I put all this aside. I put it on the shelf, from which the historians, when they have time, will select their documents to tell their stories. We have to think of the future and not of the past. This also applies in a small way to our own affairs at home. There are many who would hold an inquest in the House of Commons on the conduct of the Governments—and of Parliaments, for they are in it, too—during the years which led up to this catastrophe. They seek to indict those who were responsible for the guidance of our affairs. This also would be a foolish and pernicious process. There are too many in it. Let each man search his conscience and search his speeches. I frequently search mine.

Of this I am quite sure, that if we open a quarrel between the past and the present, we shall find that we have lost the future. Therefore, I cannot accept the drawing of any distinctions between members of the present Government. It was formed at a moment of crisis in order to unite all the Parties and all sections of opinion. It has received the almost unanimous support of both Houses of Parliament. Its members are going to stand together, and, subject to the authority of the House of Commons, we are going to govern the country and fight the war. It is absolutely necessary at a time like this that every Minister who tries each day to do his duty shall be respected; and their subordinates must know that their chiefs are not threatened men, men who are here today and gone tomorrow, but that their directions must be punctually and faithfully obeyed. Without this concentrated power we cannot face what lies before us. I should not think it would be very advantageous for the House to prolong this debate this afternoon under conditions of public stress. Many facts are not clear that will be clear in a short time. We are to have a secret session on Thursday, and I should think that would be a better opportunity for the many earnest expressions of opinion which members will desire to make and for the House to discuss vital matters without having everything read the next morning by our dangerous foes.

The disastrous military events which have happened during the past fortnight have not come to me with any sense of surprise. Indeed, I indicated a fortnight ago as clearly as I could to the House that the worst possibilities were open; and I made it perfectly clear then that whatever happened in France would make no difference to the resolve of Britain and the British Empire to fight on, if necessary for years, if necessary alone.

During the last few days we have successfully brought off the great majority of the troops we had on the line of communication in France; and seven-eighths of the troops we have sent to France since the beginning of the war—that is to say, about 350,000 out of 400,000 men—are safely back in this country. Others are still fighting with the French, and fighting with considerable success in their local encounters against the enemy. We have also brought back a great mass of stores, rifles and munitions of all kinds which had been accumulated in France during the last nine months.

We have, therefore, in this Island today a very large and powerful military force. This force comprises all our best-trained and our finest troops, including scores of thousands of those who have already measured their quality against the Germans and found themselves at no disadvantage. We have under arms at the present time in this Island over a million and a quarter men. Behind these we have the Local Defense Volunteers, numbering half a million, only a portion of whom, however, are yet armed with rifles or other firearms. We have incorporated into our Defense Forces every man for whom we have a weapon. We expect very large additions to our weapons in the near future, and in preparation for this we intend forthwith to call up, drill and train further large numbers. Those who are not called up, or else are employed during the vast business of munitions production in all its branches—and their ramifications are innumerable—will serve their country best by remaining at their ordinary work until they receive their summons. We have also over here Dominions armies. The Canadians had actually landed in France, but have now been safely withdrawn, much disappointed, but in perfect order, with all their artillery and equipment. And these very high-class forces from the Dominions will now take part in the defense of the Mother Country.

Lest the account which I have given of these large forces should raise the question: Why did they not take part in the great battle in France? I must make it clear that, apart from the divisions training and organizing at home, only twelve divisions were equipped to fight upon a scale which justified their being sent abroad. And this was fully up to the number which the French had been led to expect would be available in France at the ninth month of the war. The rest of our forces at home have a fighting value for home defense which will, of course, steadily increase every week that passes. Thus, the invasion of Great Britain would at this time require the transportation across the sea of hostile armies on a very large scale, and after they had been so transported they would have to be continually maintained with all the masses of munitions and supplies which are required for continuous battle—as continuous battle it will surely be.

Here is where we come to the Navy—and after all, we have a Navy. Some people seem to forget that we have a Navy. We must remind them. For the last thirty years I have been concerned in discussions about the possibilities of oversea invasion, and I took the responsibility on behalf of the Admiralty, at the beginning of the last war, of allowing all regular troops to be sent out of the country. That was a very serious step to take, because our Territorials had only just been called up and were quite untrained. Therefore, this Island was for several months particularly denuded of fighting troops. The Admiralty had confidence at that time in their ability to prevent a mass invasion even though at that time the Germans had a magnificent battle fleet in the proportion of 10 to 16, even though they were capable of fighting a general engagement every day and any day, whereas now they have only a couple of heavy ships worth speaking of—the Scharnhorst and the Gneisenau. We are also told that the Italian Navy is to come out and gain sea superiority in these waters. If they seriously intend it, I shall only say that we shall be delighted to offer Signor Mussolini a free and safeguarded passage through the Strait of Gibraltar in order that he may play the part to which he aspires. There is a general curiosity in the British Fleet to find out whether the Italians are up to the level they were at in the last war or whether they have fallen off at all.

Therefore, it seems to me that as far as sea-borne invasion on a great scale is concerned, we are far more capable of meeting it today than we were at many periods in the last war and during the early months of this war, before our other troops were trained, and while the B.E.F. had proceeded abroad. Now, the Navy have never pretended to be able to prevent raids by bodies of 5,000 or 10,000 men flung suddenly across and thrown ashore at several points on the coast some dark night or foggy morning. The efficacy of sea power, especially under modern conditions, depends upon the invading force being of large size; It has to be of large size, in view of our military strength, to be of any use. If it is of large size, then the Navy have something they can find and meet and, as it were, bite on. Now, we must remember that even five divisions, however lightly equipped, would require 200 to 250 ships, and with modern air reconnaissance and photography it would not be easy to collect such an armada, marshal it, and conduct it across the sea without any powerful naval forces to escort it; and there would be very great possibilities, to put it mildly, that this armada would be intercepted long before it reached the coast, and all the men drowned in the sea or, at the worst blown to pieces with their equipment while they were trying to land. We also have a great system of minefields, recently strongly reinforced, through which we alone know the channels. If the enemy tries to sweep passages through these minefields, it will be the task of the Navy to destroy the mine-sweepers and any other forces employed to protect them. There should be no difficulty in this, owing to our great superiority at sea.

Those are the regular, well-tested, well-proved arguments on which we have relied during many years in peace and war. But the question is whether there are any new methods by which those solid assurances can be circumvented. Odd as it may seem, some attention has been given to this by the Admiralty, whose prime duty and responsibility is to destroy any large sea-borne expedition before it reaches, or at the moment when it reaches, these shores. It would not be a good thing for me to go into details of this. It might suggest ideas to other people which they have not thought of, and they would not be likely to give us any of their ideas in exchange. All I will say is that untiring vigilance and mind-searching must be devoted to the subject, because the enemy is crafty and cunning and full of novel treacheries and stratagems. The House may be assured that the utmost ingenuity is being displayed and imagination is being evoked from large numbers of competent officers, well-trained in tactics and thoroughly up to date, to measure and counterwork novel possibilities. Untiring vigilance and untiring searching of the mind is being, and must be, devoted to the subject, because, remember, the enemy is crafty and there is no dirty trick he will not do.

Some people will ask why, then, was it that the British Navy was not able to prevent the movement of a large army from Germany into Norway across the Skagerrak? But the conditions in the Channel and in the North Sea are in no way like those which prevail in the Skagerrak. In the Skagerrak, because of the distance, we could give no air support to our surface ships, and consequently, lying as we did close to the enemy's main air power, we were compelled to use only our submarines. We could not enforce the decisive blockade or interruption which is possible from surface vessels. Our submarines took a heavy toll but could not, by themselves, prevent the invasion of Norway. In the Channel and in the North Sea, on the other hand, our superior naval surface forces, aided by our submarines, will operate with close and effective air assistance.

This brings me, naturally, to the great question of invasion from the air, and of the impending struggle between the British and German Air Forces. It seems quite clear that no invasion on a scale beyond the capacity of our land forces to crush speedily is likely to take place from the air until our Air Force has been definitely overpowered. In the meantime, there may be raids by parachute troops and attempted descents of airborne soldiers. We should be able to give those gentry a warm reception both in the air and on the ground, if they reach it in any condition to continue the dispute. But the great question is: Can we break Hitler's air weapon? Now, of course, it is a very great pity that we have not got an Air Force at least equal to that of the most powerful enemy within striking distance of these shores. But we have a very powerful Air Force which has proved itself far superior in quality, both in men and in many types of machine, to what we have met so far in the numerous and fierce air battles which have been fought with the Germans. In France, where we were at a considerable disadvantage and lost many machines on the ground when they were standing round the aerodromes, we were accustomed to inflict in the air losses of as much as two and two-and-a-half to one. In the fighting over Dunkirk, which was a sort of no-man's-land, we undoubtedly beat the German Air Force, and gained the mastery of the local air, inflicting here a loss of three or four to one day after day. Anyone who looks at the photographs which were published a week or so ago of the re-embarkation, showing the masses of troops assembled on the beach and forming an ideal target for hours at a time, must realize that this re-embarkation would not have been possible unless the enemy had resigned all hope of recovering air superiority at that time and at that place.

In the defense of this Island the advantages to the defenders will be much greater than they were in the fighting around Dunkirk. We hope to improve on the rate of three or four to one which was realized at Dunkirk; and in addition all our injured machines and their crews which get down safely—and, surprisingly, a very great many injured machines and men do get down safely in modern air fighting—all of these will fall, in an attack upon these Islands, on friendly soil and live to fight another day; whereas all the injured enemy machines and their complements will be total losses as far as the war is concerned.

During the great battle in France, we gave very powerful and continuous aid to the French Army, both by fighters and bombers; but in spite of every kind of pressure we never would allow the entire metropolitan fighter strength of the Air Force to be consumed. This decision was painful, but it was also right, because the fortunes of the battle in France could not have been decisively affected even if we had thrown in our entire fighter force. That battle was lost by the unfortunate strategical opening, by the extraordinary and unforseen power of the armored columns, and by the great preponderance of the German Army in numbers. Our fighter Air Force might easily have been exhausted as a mere accident in that great struggle, and then we should have found ourselves at the present time in a very serious plight. But as it is, I am happy to inform the House that our fighter strength is stronger at the present time relatively to the Germans, who have suffered terrible losses, than it has ever been; and consequently we believe ourselves possessed of the capacity to continue the war in the air under better conditions than we have ever experienced before. I look forward confidently to the exploits of our fighter pilots—these splendid men, this brilliant youth—who will have the glory of saving their native land, their island home, and all they love, from the most deadly of all attacks.

There remains, of course, the danger of bombing attacks, which will certainly be made very soon upon us by the bomber forces of the enemy. It is true that the German bomber force is superior in numbers to ours; but we have a very large bomber force also, which we shall use to strike at military targets in Germany without intermission. I do not at all underrate the severity of the ordeal which lies before us; but I believe our countrymen will show themselves capable of standing up to it, like the brave men of Barcelona, and will be able to stand up to it, and carry on in spite of it, at least as well as any other people in the world. Much will depend upon this; every man and every woman will have the chance to show the finest qualities of their race, and render the highest service to their cause. For all of us, at this time, whatever our sphere, our station, our occupation or our duties, it will be a help to remember the famous lines:

He nothing common did or mean, Upon that memorable scene.

I have thought it right upon this occasion to give the House and the country some indication of the solid, practical grounds upon which we base our inflexible resolve to continue the war. There are a good many people who say, 'Never mind. Win or lose, sink or swim, better die than submit to tyranny—and such a tyranny.' And I do not dissociate myself from them. But I can assure them that our professional advisers of the three Services unitedly advise that we should carry on the war, and that there are good and reasonable hopes of final victory. We have fully informed and consulted all the self-governing Dominions, these great communities far beyond the oceans who have been built up on our laws and on our civilization, and who are absolutely free to choose their course, but are absolutely devoted to the ancient Motherland, and who feel themselves inspired by the same emotions which lead me to stake our all upon duty and honor. We have fully consulted them, and I have received from their Prime Ministers, Mr. Mackenzie King of Canada, Mr. Menzies of Australia, Mr. Fraser of New Zealand, and General Smuts of South Africa—that wonderful man, with his immense profound mind, and his eye watching from a distance the whole panorama of European affairs—I have received from all these eminent men, who all have Governments behind them elected on wide franchises, who are all there because they represent the will of their people, messages couched in the most moving terms in which they endorse our decision to fight on, and declare themselves ready to share our fortunes and to persevere to the end. That is what we are going to do.

We may now ask ourselves: In what way has our position worsened since the beginning of the war? It has worsened by the fact that the Germans have conquered a large part of the coast line of Western Europe, and many small countries have been overrun by them. This aggravates the possibilities of air attack and adds to our naval preoccupations. It in no way diminishes, but on the contrary definitely increases, the power of our long-distance blockade. Similarly, the entrance of Italy into the war increases the power of our long-distance blockade. We have stopped the worst leak by that. We do not know whether military resistance will come to an end in France or not, but should it do so, then of course the Germans will be able to concentrate their forces, both military and industrial, upon us. But for the reasons I have given to the House these will not be found so easy, to apply. If invasion has become more imminent, as no doubt it has, we, being relieved from the task of maintaining a large army in France, have far larger and more efficient forces to meet it.

If Hitler can bring under his despotic control the industries of the countries he has conquered, this will add greatly to his already vast armament output. On the other hand, this will not happen immediately, and we are now assured of immense, continuous and increasing support in supplies and munitions of all kinds from the United States; and especially of aeroplanes and pilots from the Dominions and across the oceans coming from regions which are beyond the reach of enemy bombers.

I do not see how any of these factors can operate to our detriment on balance before the winter comes; and the winter will impose a strain upon the Nazi regime, with almost all Europe writhing and starving under its cruel heel, which, for all their ruthlessness, will run them very hard. We must not forget that from the moment when we declared war on the 3rd September it was always possible for Germany to turn all her Air Force upon this country, together with any other devices of invasion she might conceive, and that France could have done little or nothing to prevent her doing so. We have, therefore, lived under this danger, in principle and in a slightly modified form, during all these months. In the meanwhile, however, we have enormously improved our methods of defense, and we have learned what we had no right to assume at the beginning, namely, that the individual aircraft and the individual British pilot have a sure and definite superiority. Therefore, in casting up this dread balance sheet and contemplating our dangers with a disillusioned eye, I see great reason for intense vigilance and exertion, but none whatever for panic or despair.

During the first four years of the last war the Allies experienced nothing but disaster and disappointment. That was our constant fear: one blow after another, terrible losses, frightful dangers. Everything miscarried. And yet at the end of those four years the morale of the Allies was higher than that of the Germans, who had moved from one aggressive triumph to another, and who stood everywhere triumphant invaders of the lands into which they had broken. During that war we repeatedly asked ourselves the question: 'How are we going to win?' And no one was able ever to answer it with much precision, until at the end, quite suddenly, quite unexpectedly, our terrible foe collapsed before us, and we were so glutted with victory that in our folly we threw it away.

We do not yet know what will happen in France or whether the French resistance will be prolonged, both in France and in the French Empire overseas. The French Government will be throwing away great opportunities and casting adrift their future if they do not continue the war in accordance with their treaty obligations, from which we have not felt able to release them. The House will have read the historic declaration in which, at the desire of many Frenchmen—and of our own hearts—we have proclaimed our willingness at the darkest hour in French history to conclude a union of common citizenship in this struggle. However matters may go in France or with the French Government, or other French Governments, we in this Island and in the British Empire will never lose our sense of comradeship with the French people. If we are now called upon to endure what they have been suffering, we shall emulate their courage, and if final victory rewards our toils they shall share the gains, aye, and freedom shall be restored to all. We abate nothing of our just demands; not one jot or tittle do we recede. Czechs, Poles, Norwegians, Dutch, Belgians have joined their causes to our own. All these shall be restored.

What General Weygand called the Battle of France is over. I expect that the Battle of Britain is about to begin. Upon this battle depends the survival of Christian civilization. Upon it depends our own British life, and the long continuity of our institutions and our Empire. The whole fury and might of the enemy must very soon be turned on us.

Hitler knows that he will have to break us in this Island or lose the war. If we can stand up to him, all Europe may be free and the life of the world may move forward into broad, sunlit uplands. But if we fail, then the whole world, including the United States, including all that we have known and cared for, will sink into the abyss of a new Dark Age made more sinister, and perhaps more protracted, by the lights of perverted science.

Let us therefore brace ourselves to our duties, and so bear ourselves that if the British Empire and its Commonwealth last for a thousand years, men will still say, 'This was their finest hour.'